IN BLACKBERRY TIME

Study of Sid Chaplin
reading Dodds "history of
Spennymoor.

Cornish. 60

IN BLACKBERRY TIME

Sid Chaplin

EDITED BY MICHAEL & RENE CHAPLIN

BLOODAXE BOOKS

ISBN: 1 85224 031 8 hardback
      1 85224 032 6 paperback

First published 1987 by
Bloodaxe Books Ltd,
P.O. Box 1SN,
Newcastle upon Tyne NE99 1SN.

Bloodaxe Books Ltd acknowledges
the financial assistance of Northern Arts.

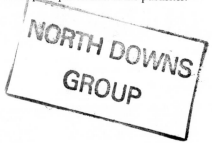

Typesetting by Bryan Williamson, Manchester.

Printed in Great Britain by
Bell & Bain Limited, Glasgow, Scotland.

Acknowledgements

Acknowledgements are due to the editors of the following publications in which some of these stories and articles first appeared: *Daily Express, Guardian, The Journal* (Newcastle), *Penguin New Writing, Queen Magazine* and *Stand*; and also to the BBC for 'The Man Who Nearly Walked to London' (Home Service) and 'Seven Years in a Smithy' (BBC Schools), and to Frank Graham for 'Black River', first published in *A Tree with Rosy Apples* (1972).

For material used in the accompanying notes and commentary, acknowledgements are due to Frank Graham for excerpts from 'Walking the Bounds' and 'The Ring of Burnished Steel'; to Edward Arnold Ltd for excerpts from an interview with Sid Chaplin in *The British Working-Class Novel in the 20th Century* (ed. Jeremy Hawthorn, Stratford upon Avon Studies, 2nd series, 1984); to the Department of Sociology, the University of Durham, for excerpts from 'Durham Mining Villages', a talk given by Sid Chaplin published in *Working Papers in Sociology* (1972); and to Fircroft College, Birmingham, for excerpts from 'Fircroft Years' published in the *Fircroft Magazine* (1984).

The frontispiece portrait of Sid Chaplin is by Norman Cornish, and thanks for photographs are due to Mike Golding (page 10), Beamish North of England Open Air Museum (30), Joe Ging and the Joicey Museum, Tyne & Wear Museums (61), Les Palmer (182-83) and *Coal* Magazine (37, 158 & 231); and to Frank Manders and Newcastle City Library for the 'Chaplin Country' map on page 22.

For kindly agreeing to check the manuscript for technical details, thanks are due to Tom Dobbin; and also, for help with other details, to Joe Chaplin.

Contents

Sid Chaplin

1916 Born in Shildon, Co. Durham, on 20 September.
1930 Left school and went to work in a bakery.
1931 Began his life-long involvement with the coal industry when he was taken on at Dean and Chapter Colliery, Ferryhill.
1932 Became an apprentice blacksmith.
1939 Won a scholarship to Fircroft College for Working Men, Birmingham, to study economics. Switched to literature, but was forced to return to the pit on outbreak of war. Began to write in earnest.
1941 Married Rene Rutherford on New Year's Day.
Poem 'A Widow Wept' published in *Penguin New Writing*.
1942 Daughter Gillian born.
1944 Son Christopher born.
1950 Moved to London on being offered job as reporter on *Coal* magazine.
1951 Son Michael born.
1957 Offered new job by National Coal Board and moved to Newcastle.
1965 Visited Soviet Union as first of many books is published behind the Iron Curtain.
1972 Takes early retirement from the NCB to concentrate on writing.
1975 Undergoes heart bypass surgery at Shotley Bridge Hospital.
1977 Awarded OBE for services to the arts in the North-East.
1986 Died at Grasmere in Cumbria on 10 January.

Foreword

When Sid Chaplin had been awarded the OBE, but was unforthcoming about it, my wife said to him, 'Tell us, then, Sid, who performed the investiture?'

'It was Prince Charles.'

'And what did he say to you?'

'He'd obviously been well briefed. He said "This is for services to the arts in the North-East. You're a writer. And you were a pitman. You were born on Tyneside..." No, I wasn't, I told him. I was born in Durham. In fact, if I'd been born any farther south I'd have been a Yorkshireman.' A measured pause, while I detected in his look across the room at me just the shadow of a ghost of a twinkle as he waited for my wife to give him the feed.

'And what did he say to that?'

'He said, "Well, Mr Chaplin, you'd have been none the worse for that".'

Yes, though he set some of his finest work on Tyneside, West Durham was the country of his heart, as any number of pieces in this commemorative collection of his work bear out. To listen while Sid talked to a group of aspirant writers about the oral roots of his storytelling was to be fascinated by home-spun warmth, the patent sincerity of the man and his total lack of pretentiousness. Yet that only hinted at the craft he brought to the written word: the virtuoso narrative impersonation of *The Day of the Sardine*, the richly laden prose of *The Mines of Alabaster*, the spring and dazzle of *The Big Room*.

He and I first met in February 1961, on the occasion of a live broadcast from the old Dickinson Road studios of the BBC in Manchester of a television programme called *Points North*. In this one John Morgan and Brian Redhead examined the phenomenon of so much writing talent having broken through in the north of England in only a few years. Taking part besides Sid and myself were John Braine, Len Doherty, David Storey and Keith Waterhouse. Most of us were meeting for the first time. Sid was already the senior figure, the veteran. We all acknowledged his example. *The Leaping Lad* had shown us all that it was possible to write without meretriciousness from the inside of working-class life; Braine's *Room at the Top*, eleven years later, had given encouraging signs that it was possible to earn some money while doing it.

Michael Chaplin draws attention (somewhat ruefully) to the period of intense creativity in his father's life in the decade from the late 1950s, and I have never had any doubt that the emergence on to the scene of so many younger writers had more than a little to do with the reinvigoration of his talent. Here was a climate made for creative work, and Sid used it to the full.

Michael's reference to the creative task with which Sid struggled in the late 1970s allows me to mention what I might not have done otherwise. When I became aware of the cycle of depression Sid had become victim of after the major surgery that nearly killed him, I took the great liberty of reversing our usual roles and writing to him with some encouragement and advice. What I suggested he do, and what a number of people were waiting for, was remarkably close to what he was indeed attempting: a big novel about a people caught in the industrial decline of several decades. It was, with the perspective his particular experience and his accumulated wisdom could have thrown on it, a theme no other English author was so uniquely equipped to explore.

It was not to be. But we have the rich body of work he did achieve, and to the novels and stories I've already mentioned, and the thickness and depth of the rendered world of one of my special favourites *The Watchers and the Watched*, we can now add the gems of this present collection so skilfully presented with a linking commentary by his son. Among them are *Tom Patrick*, superb in its craftsmanship yet free of all tired literary contrivance, and the haunting resonance behind the comedy of *A Weekend in Arcady*; both pieces I had to wait for their creator's death to read, both of which I know will live with me and grow in my mind, as all good stories do.

Sid Chaplin possessed the quality I have over the years come to prize above all others in a writer. When it is combined with skills like his it is unsurpassable. It is the quality of tenderness. I mean neither glycerine sentimentality nor calculated tear-jerking, but an instinctive reverence for the rhythms of life, for all living things, and for 'the holiness of the heart's affections'. It comes through his every line.

I knew him for 25 years and I can think of no greater privilege in my life than that of having been counted his friend.

STAN BARSTOW

Introduction

When I was a lad, growing up in Newcastle, my father embarked on the most creative period of his life. In little over six years, he wrote and published four novels: *The Big Room*, *The Day of the Sardine*, *The Watchers and the Watched* and *Sam in the Morning*. He also turned out a stream of short stories – his first love as a writer – and a prodigious amount of journalism. For three years he wrote a weekly column for the *Guardian* and polished off countless articles and book reviews for the national and local press. During the same period in the early 60s, he helped to found the first regional arts association in the country and became an accomplished public speaker and broadcaster. All this on top of a demanding job with the National Coal Board.

It's not surprising that I didn't see all that much of him.

He would come in from work, eat his tea, have a shave and then retire to the front room to 'do a bit typing'. This normally took him from about seven o'clock till eleven, sometimes into the early hours. He worked intensively, accompanied usually by jazz on the radio, the station not *quite* properly tuned. I would be sent in on the way to bed with a cup of tea for him: there he sat at the big desk, in the middle of a ferocious fog of cigarette smoke, quite distracted, but coming round for a moment to smile and murmur, 'Night, son.'

It was the same at weekends: he stuck to a regimen that to this novice spare-time writer is quite awesome in its scale and commitment. For the boy though, the drawbacks were obvious. While my pals went off for outings and picnics, I skulked at home on my own, savagely kicking a ball against the backyard wall or slicing the tops off thistles 'down the burn' with a stick.

But sometimes, late on a Sunday, Dad would emerge from the fog and shout through the house, 'Fancy a trip to the coast?' Half an hour later, we'd be walking the long sands at Whitley Bay; the oblique rays of the dying sun catching the surf, the flashing light from the white tower of St Mary's beginning to twinkle and the snap of a dozen little terriers echoing back from the cliff. I never ran and gambolled in the sea myself; my routine was to follow an unwavering course along the tide-line, a few paces behind Mam and Dad, head down, my eyes fixed on the glistening sand.

For Whitley Bay wasn't just a place with a golden beach; to me, it was a place of magic and mystery. You see, on these long perambulations of the strand, I never failed to find treasure: usually lots of pennies and ha'pennies, but sometimes, joy of joys, a bob or a florin or even a whole half-crown. It wasn't just the money, you understand, that made me linger in the gathering dusk; it was the strange half-glimpse of other people's lives that really fascinated. What kind of people had dropped the money? Was it breathless little boys who ran in the surf and cried all the way home in the bus when they discovered their loss? Was it the bare-legged fat women who screeched when the North Sea tickled their toes? Or was it a kindly old millionaire who smiled as he picked the coins from the pocket of his frock coat and flung them to the four winds? I never did fathom the mystery at the time. That's just as well, I suppose, but I do know that as I trudged to the bus-stand, trouser pockets brimming, I went home with a glow. That, and the huge chocolate-flaked cornet that I always got at the Venetian ice cream parlour by the Spanish City, made up for a lot: the lack of a car, the family outings we didn't have, the sorely-missed company of a father who had another life.

Years later, not so very long ago, when I was past 30 and my own bairns were long past the dandling stage, I learned at last that there was no mystery at all behind the treasure in the sand. The coins had of course all been dropped by my father, whose reward had been the ever changing expression of anticipation, joy and wonder on his son's face. But when I heard the truth of his game, I was at first touched – and then saddened. I well remember looking at my father and seeing the reflection of my feelings in his face. We were grateful for the memory of this little bond between father and son. But both of us felt that something had gone, the mystery had been swept away and with it, a little bit of the magic of my childhood.

I mention that story here not so much to indicate that Sid Chaplin had the gift to tune his own feelings to the wavelength of a child, though that is true, but because it seems to me that in many ways it's the kind of incident that could have been turned into a Chaplin story. It has many of the essential ingredients: a sense of place; a touch of humour; a relationship between father and son that is rich in subtlety; most of all, a gnawing sense of loss, mingled inextricably with the flavour of the sweetness of life.

There's something else too – it's a piece of life experienced by perfectly ordinary people. It's real.

The first, and possibly the most important, discovery my father made as a writer was that literature might be made out of such material. Of course it's taken for granted now that fine novels or stories can be made out of the lives of ordinary, working-class people. But 50 years ago, this was a fairly novel idea; there'd been relatively few books written in which the common people appeared other than as bit-players.

More to the point, it was rarer still for the author of such books to have actually *lived* the life he or she had recorded, rather than merely observed it. So, in later life, Sid Chaplin came to rejoice at the luck which during the mid-30s brought him under the joint influence of D.H. Lawrence and a little Scots blacksmith called Alex Wylie (celebrated in this volume in *Seven Years in a Smithy*). Between them they convinced the young Chaplin that the lives of those around him were fascinating, just as interesting as those of dukes and kings and people who agonised in the drawing rooms of Bloomsbury. And so it came to pass that the young pitman began to write, with a special, distinctive voice: the voice of the insider, a man who, unlike Lawrence or Orwell, knew what it was like to work the thin seam in the cold and the wet, knew what it was like to carry more than one good friend out of the pit.

Central to the man's working methods was the notebook, which went wherever he went, from the 1930s until the day he died, spoiling the shape of many a good jacket in the process. There are dozens and dozens of notebooks – some of them sitting on a shelf above me as I write – and in them the intrepid genealogist can work out the pedigree of many a story: from notes of incidents in his life or those of his friends and family, bits of overheard conversation, items of arcane information, and lots of good jokes. As he said himself in an introduction to one volume of stories: 'All the people and all the happenings and virtually everything in these stories, except for one thing, came to me out of my own experience.

Any person who cares to watch, and listen, can draw on rich experience. The exception I mentioned is the pattern each story takes, particularly the way in which a story ends. Very few stories end in real life. The writer as detective must discover the true beginning and deduce, sense, the right ending. Every ending is only provisional.'

In selecting the material for this book and searching for a theme to unify it, the editors eventually stumbled on their own pattern. If the author's own experience formed the raw material for much of his own work, why not use a selection of the very best of his unpublished output – stories, poems and essays – to tell the story of his life?

And so this final volume of Sid Chaplin's is a kind of biography, using, for the most part, his own words. But it is far from being a mere record of one man's life; it has a significance way beyond that.

The reason, you see, why Sid Chaplin was driven so hard by the urge to record was that he had such a wealth of experience to set down; his writing life became a race against time. Fate had put him in a place and at a time when a whole way of life – and all the attitudes that went with it – were dying. He was born when the great northern coalfield was at its height and he died when it was on its last legs. A major part of his work is concerned with how people lived this mining life – with its own traditions, customs and particular outlook – and of how they reacted to its going. Anybody who wants to know what it was like has no need of statistics or history books. It's all there, in *A Leaping Lad* and *The Thin Seam* and, we hope, in this book too: 'The dust and darkness, the laming and the maiming, the bitter waters and blood and sweat that mingles with comradeship on the coalface.' Sid Chaplin found, and fixed forever, what otherwise might have been forgotten.

Later in life, the writer struck a similar seam when he moved to Newcastle. There he observed the painful process of disintegration at work in the old working-class districts of Elswick, Scotswood and Byker and described it with passion, and a fine anger, in *The Day of the Sardine* and *The Watchers and the Watched*. But there was hope too – not a sloppy, easy sort of optimism, but a conviction deep within the man that people could, against all the odds, hang on to their dignity, their compassion, their humanity. He was convinced too that the writer had a part to play in this. While rejecting agit-prop, he believed passionately that his stories, novels, poems and plays had a moral purpose; 'a message in a bottle' he called it. The message related to the central concern of his life, as a writer and as a man: the education of the human heart. That too is the purpose of this, his final book.

MICHAEL CHAPLIN

Miner's Prayer

When into darkness Ah descend
Strength with courage wilt Thou blend?
When Ah sweat in tunnels low,
Let Thy sweet peace with me go;
When Ah break the virgin coal,
Wilt Thou break this selfish soul?
If crucified by coal, Ah pass,
Grant Thy blessing on our lass;
Lead my bairns intae Thy light,
Let them dae the thing that's right.

[1941]

CHAPLIN COUNTRY

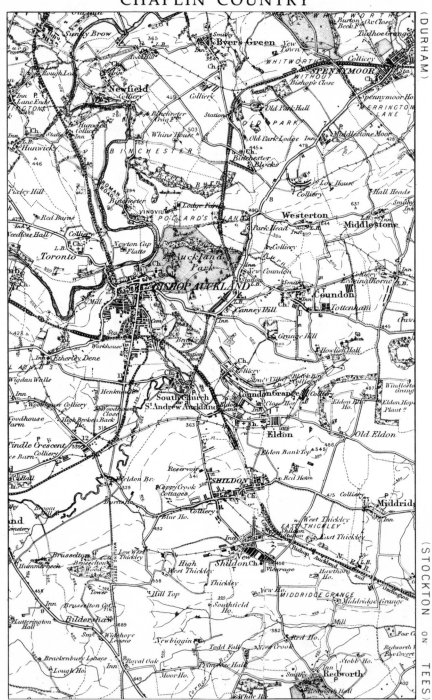

Surveyed in 1856-57
Revised in 1903

First Memory

My first conscious memory is of being jogged on my father's shoulders along the high road which bypasses Byers Green, and hearing the wind moaning in the telephone wires, as counterpoint to the comfortable conversation of my parents far below; then all of a sudden we came over the tops and it was as if the Milky Way had dropped down, and was spread out on the darkling ground as far as the eye could see; not only the blazing fire-holes of all the pits, but also the coke-ovens which went with them, arranged in ruby-red geometrical patterns which were each absolutely constant – excepting that every now and then one of the ruby lights would explode when a coke-oven was discharged as a white-hot worm, intensely white in the darkness and so lighting up the night that one could see the columns of steam rise up as the almost molten coke was quenched or cooled.

This was my first encounter with part of Durham's vast empire of coke and coal. Needless to say it left an indelible impression on my mind.

My second encounter was with Westerton Colliery at close quarters, again in the darkness. In the far distance was the tall winding-house, almost like a pele tower, with its long narrow windows illuminating from within not only the building itself but also the lower part of the timber sheer-legs – leaving cables and pulley wheels and the cables upon which the cages were suspended in complete darkness; while the blazing coal braziers suspended from every convenient point above the waggon sidings lent an element of mystery.

But most awesome of all to me were the long rows of old-fashioned beehive coke-ovens which probably dated back to the foundation of the pit in about 1840, and which closely flanked the public highway, so near in fact that it was more prudent to cross to the other side of the road when any one of the brick-built kilns was on the point of discharging its contents. This was a job which was so far from being automated

23

that every individual operation had to be carried out by a brawny gang of coke-burners; some demolishing the brick-stopping, while yet others pulled out the semi-molten mass of coke with long handled iron rakes. I seem to remember that most of these men wore sacks draped over their heads like cowls; and that a water-hose played continually upon them as they worked. I remember the glow reflected on their streaming faces as, each stripped to the waist, they toiled away. Yet again not the slightest element of fear was involved, only a wonderful feeling of security and comfort.

It was as if the pit, the coke-ovens and every one of those toiling coke-burners, even the fiery pit-rucks which seemed to be always on the point of erupting were, after all, simply an extension of the street in which we lived. The fact that a public right of way was maintained through every pit-yard we knew helped to maintain a feeling of belonging; and it is this feeling which still sweeps over me today, whenever I hear the song of the telephone wires. Only now it has been transferred to whatever landscape in which I happen to find myself. From that moment onwards I became, I suppose, a noticing child.

[c. 1984]

Sid Chaplin was born on 20 September 1916, not at Westerton, but at 23 Bolckow Street, Shildon, Co. Durham. Running parallel to Bolckow was another row of relatively spacious colliery houses called Vaughan Street. Thus were commemorated two ironmasters who'd played a not inconsiderable role in forging the great coalfield of Durham. Only a few yards from the house was an outpost of their empire, Shildon Lodge Colliery, or Datton; and between them ran the railway line that carried the pit's top-quality coking coal away along George Stephenson's historic route to the B & V blast furnaces at Middlesbrough. As a toddler the young Chaplin was woken each morning by the "tankies" on the line, by the characteristic whuff-whuff of Timothy Hackworth's horizontal winding engine, by the crashing of the cages bringing the coal tubs to bank. It was almost as a matter of course that Sid Chaplin followed his forefathers down the shafts, and that he rode them, sometimes as pitman, sometimes as observer, for the rest of his life. Coal was in his blood.

The house in Bolckow Street was where Isaiah and Elsie Chaplin began their married life, before they embarked on the seemingly endless wanderings in search of settled employment that took them from Shildon to Westerton, from Westerton to Byers Green, from Byers Green to Newfield. The house actually belonged to Elsie's parents. The Charltons had once been Weardale leadminers and before that, so the story goes, border reivers in the wilds of Northumberland, their only possessions being a hardy nag and a sword. But the time came when they eventually drifted down from the hills and sold themselves to the mineowners as waggoners. In the mid-19th century the family began to prosper: Sid Chaplin's great-grandfather, George Frederic Agna Charlton, became Chief Engineer at Datton and moved into the house in Bolckow Street (known locally as Leathercap Row after the skullcaps worn by the "gaffers" who settled there). Here he lived, and painfully died, after a girder which was being lowered down the shaft slipped from its sling and fell on him, breaking every bone in his body. His son, Elsie's father, rose to be an enginewright too and lived to dismantle Datton, watching the water slowly flood the shaft.

Ike's family had been immigrants as well, part of that great tide of people (about 150,000 of them, it's reckoned) from Wales, Lancashire and Yorkshire who'd been lured to Durham in the 19th century by the prospect of work. The Chaplins actually came from Norfolk, where Great-Grandfather Chaplin had begun his working life, at the age of eight, scaring the birds in the fields. Later, he'd heard of work which was better-paid and started to walk north in search of it, not stopping until he reached the first pit, which happened to be two hundred miles away, in Shildon. His job was to fire and work the furnaces at the bottom of the shaft; by drawing air through the pit and sending it up to the surface, these contraptions provided a basic form of ventilation. Eventually Great-Grandad retired and went back to his first calling; he bought a piece of land and a couple of cows and set up a successful milk round. But there was to be no escape for his sons or for his grandsons, among them the young electrician Ike. They all followed him into the pit.

The Chaplins and the Charltons were part of a booming industry that by the time of the First World War employed 166,000 people in Durham alone. It was a mighty enterprise, an Eldorado that enriched Newcastle and London. Precious little of this wealth was lavished on places like Shildon, or Newfield, or Binchester Blocks. But then they did have glories of their own, of the kind gold sovereigns could never buy.

Shildon Lodge Colliery

Sid Chaplin grew up with the sights, sounds and smells of Shildon Lodge, or Datton, as it was called; he was born in a house 30 yards from the pit yard. His grandfather and great-grandfather were "leathercaps" (men of responsibility) at the pit.

27

Hame

Sight of the crested peewit crying
God alone knows what or why.

Sight of the green smoke-flecked valley,
With the mist-tinged mountains beyond the moors.

Sight of you, my own love,
And the light in your eyes for me.

[1943]

Westerton banner.

Larks Sang on Banner Day

Born in 1916, just three years after the British coal industry achieved its peak bulk output, I grew up in time to see the first convulsive death-throes of Durham as a great coal exporting coalfield. Not that I ever saw it that way.

To me all seemed largely pits and pit villages, set against which hills, fields and river – together with clouds continually scudding eastwards – constituted little more than a perpetual scenic backdrop. At every journey's end was a pit, and pits were all important, particularly your own. Shildon, Westerton, Byers Green, Newfield and Dean & Chapter (in all of which my father worked in turn) were in turn the be-all and end-all of life. Those men who didn't have a nickname were known by their job at the pit; and how they did it established their rank in the community. The pit regulated not only all the men's comings and goings but the life and being of every soul in the village, whether man, woman or child. And the pit was an entity, loved as well as hated. I still recall how shattered my grandfather was when they closed Shildon Lodge. But normally the pit was the real core of the village. That piston-beat of the winder which went on at Thornley to the end was symbolical of the heart of every Durham tribe. Even when at school we lads were conscious that the real education was for pit-work.

Individual though my first pit may have been with its tall winding house so like a borderer's pele tower, it was the lodge banner – its virtual embodiment – that left the most lasting mark upon me. At another time and place I crystallised just how seminal this first glimpse of identity proved to be for a child not yet five years of age:

Black was the first pit I knew; its heapstead and pulleys and the muck around, black as an old sow's back. By day she swallowed up clean laughing lads and men, only to disgorge them black and bone weary in the evening. But larks sang the day they hoisted the banner and to my childish mind it was the loveliest sight in all Creation when, with a sharp flap, the picture billowed and sailed away.

Oddly enough, after my first meeting with a banner I took little notice of the many other banners that came my way. This may have been due to the sheer size and glorious colouring of that first banner – more than 50 years later I walked straight up to it at an exhibition in Durham's DLI Museum, even though the leading (named) side was not exhibited. It wasn't the picture so much (The Good Samaritan) as the memory of the colours, still miraculously preserved, if somewhat faded, which led me homing straight to it. This was the Westerton banner. The others I hardly noticed (not in detail, anyway), and I can only suppose that, boy-like, I was more attracted to the bands. No banner is complete without a brass or silver band. But now that I think of it, the banner was there all the time, essential if now no more than commonplace.

And so too were the pits. Pits were everywhere then. Although our own was hidden we continually heard the clash of its screens, and the clank of its tankie engine. Over the brow of the hill was Byers Green, to which it was joined underground.

On a clear day you could see – and hear – a whole ring of pits, all the way from Bishop Auckland to Brancepeth and beyond... the pits of the Wear Valley. In the early morning you could hear the staccato beat of their winding exhaust pipes, the whir of their ventilation fans and the sharp shouts of the lads driving their ponies and loaded stone tubs along the long low ridges of the faraway pit heaps – many a plume of smoke too, as coal trains snaked down the colliery lines to the LNER.

Slowly I entered my wider heritage. At six I found the immense sands, the pounding sea, at Seaton Carew, and saw by Tees the night sky light up and the yellow smoke billowing – though no one told me then that the blast-furnaces were fed with coking coal from home. At ten I stayed with an aunt along a narrow passageway in Old Elvet in Durham. Three things I remember: turning from the cathedral's reflection in the river and seeing the high pinnacles in all their solidity shiver then settle again; slim-boats turning like water-spiders below Prebend's Bridge while spray revealed that it wasn't glass but a flow that went thunderously over the weir; and my aunt saying with a raised finger: 'When that clock strikes eight again a man will have been hanged.'

Years later I spent my last shilling going up the great tower and walked six miles home haunted by men shuffling round the prison yard. The erratic jackdaws, the levitating gulls, the crystal air had cried out insult. We were glad to escape and scamper down a winding street to see the bands and banners march out again. What a day! We had heard Wee Ellen Wilkinson and R.C. Attlee speak – flaming youth and calm cool maturity both bearing out the truth of St Paul's dictum that all things are possible through faith. Naturally, Wee Ellen was our pin-up while the little Captain seemed something of an oddity. Who would have guessed then that in little more than a decade this dry little man would head the greatest reforming government in British history!

In the full neaptide of Durham coal probably more than 300 banners paraded. Little more than 30 years ago there were 200. I arrived at my first Big Meeting about 50 years ago on the eight o'clock train from Ferryhill to find the first banners away. The last banner marched past the County Hotel at noon: I should know as I marched behind it.

Admittedly, the crowds are thinner and the intervals between banners grow progressively longer (what a pity, one often thinks, that the mechanised face teams operating machines which shear through the coal, cutting and loading 10 tonnes a minute, can't be invited complete with their own bannerettes, to march behind the various home banners); but then the Gala, which long ago began as a demonstration, has now evolved into a family gathering. Many like myself who have left the coal return again and again to meet old marrers and thousands who now work in the deep pits of South Yorkshire and the Midlands, wouldn't miss the great reunion for worlds. And the bright idea of augmenting the banners of the working collieries by the "fostering" of historical lodge banners carried by volunteers, and also inviting along lodges (together with their bands and banners) from Northumberland, Yorkshire and South Wales, must still further engender the larger family spirit, while at the same time reviving to a degree the great drawing power of thousands of pitmen and their wives and families marching peacefully for their ideals and aspirations. All the more so now that we are confronted again with a 1930s kind of situation, together with the need for painful rethinking *and* rebuilding.

Nearly 80 years ago my old friend Joseph Stubbs came to his first Big Meeting with his Da, who lifted the eight-year-old laddie on his shoulders. 'Now sing out the names on the banners, my lad!' And a few minutes later when young Joe yelled out, 'Here's Black Prince, Tow Law, Da!' the two fell in behind. The father, just then painfully learning to read, depended on his son to find his old workmates, who had moved on to the other pit. Incidentally, this was one occasion when a coalminers' lodge was played in by a leadminers' band – Rookhope lads, they had left home at four a.m. that Saturday and wouldn't get back till five the following morning – 25 hours on their feet and all for five bob a man!

In the old days every lodge struck its own union medal which the wives stitched into their husband's jacket lapels, so that every man marched under his own banner wearing the lodge medal, rank after rank with the sun glinting on the bronze. It was different in the 30s when I first went along to hear Jimmy Maxton and Wee Ellen Wilkinson; all too often the best blue Sunday suits of men marching four abreast were shiny with age. But how those 24-inch bottoms flapped!

Then it was understood that everybody *marched* in – the dancing under the banners was kept for the march out. And the marchers of the morning came in marching four deep with great precision – yet without a hint of militarism. The bonniest sight I ever saw was from the topmost room of the Castle. There, far below, the smooth glissade of water swept between the piers of Framwellgate Bridge, while counterwise on the road above, pent within the narrow walls went the other great flow of people. The banners came close and gay, all aglow in scarlet, gold and royal blue, each preceded by rank after rank of shining brass.

Mind you, the job of banner-carrier is no sinecure. Even in a slight breeze the great embroided silken squares billow and pull like sails. Caught by a high wind in the narrow funnel of Silver Street, they pitch and toss like ships in a storm. The stout poles transformed into live things with an impulse to lift off vertically can make bairns of brawny six-footers, wrestle as they will. Banners before now have been rent asunder.

As works of art the banners may be negligible. To me they are the most beautiful creations in all the world, and have been ever since the day when my Uncle Edward lifted me on to his shoulder to see Westerton's unfurled and played away. Although I was only four, the glory of that day is still with me. Their massed effect is of course terrific, either in swaying motion or spread out in proud array on the race course; but for mining folk they represent more than a mere spectacle. Here trysts were made and kept and later husbands met their wives and bonny bairns for a picnic in their shade, while veterans re-fought old battles with recalcitrant managers, or shifted (in retrospect) enough coal to keep every family on the field warm for the rest of their lives. The banners are at once the roof-tree of the mining family and the standards of the regiments of coal.

From some flutter a length of crêpe in token that one who marched last year will march no more. And there are other invisible battle honours. The banners commemorate generations of miners who rode down into the depths on a rope as heavy with men and boys as the vine with fruit; men who lost their grip and fell, or were crushed in the vine-press of the stratum, or were blasted to oblivion in the searing flame of firedamp.

Seven Jarrow pitmen were transported to Botany Bay and another was gibbeted higher than Haman over Jarrow Slake to crush the spirit of the rest, but they rose again and again. The first leader of the Durham miners to win them recognition had slept when a child in a hedge, just one victim of the mass evictions which were a commonplace of the early strikes. It is a triumph that the Durham miner of today, after three centuries of deep-mining, has pushed out the frontiers of the coalfield almost five miles underseas, to break production records. But his finest achievement is the sense of family and kinship he has built up and maintained with irrepressible gaiety and wit.

And it's the unrepentant mixture of fun and seriousness, of reunion and celebration, which makes the Big Meeting the event in the calendar it is. If the speeches are dull (and dull they can be) there are arguments in plenty to be had with the volatile young rebels whose purpose it is to resurrect Kropotkin or bring old Trotsky back. With more than the usual quota of razor-sharp minds among the passing multitude they often get as good as they give. Beer flows in cataracts and churches and chapels set all their good ladies working to provide their traditional ham and pease-pudding teas, unless you prefer to eat your hot dog walking.

The showfolk are hard at it, on one of the biggest days of their year, and those as gets tired of paying for a whirl can find a lass and dance to the music of folk groups, or the jazz and pop sections of the resting brass. There is jousting in boats on the river. And away up in the cathedral the great doors are thrown open and selected bands process in solemn procession. The moment is most solemn. There is a rustle as the vast congregation rises with one accord. St Cuthbert's folk have come to pay their respects again.

[1975]

Sid Chaplin enjoying a Big Meeting in the early 50s. The crêpe on the banner indicates a fatality in the pit in the previous year.

The boy himself (*right*), with his brother Jack.

The boy himself...

Yes, you were podgy, definitely, and pale underneath the freckles. Oh and your hair was fine and silky. Sign of premature baldness, as if that would worry you. You were shy and reticent. Nobody knew of the world within. People remarked that you read a lot, that you would be wearing spectacles before long, that it was bad manners to read at the table. Your father tanned you for this. Because you were quiet you were bullied. You never played football. But you liked to run and jump and swim like any normal boy. In a small way you were sensitive. You shuddered at the sight of crawling parasites in matted hair, at obnoxious human smells, at cruelty or harshness. You were a bit of a snob. Your Da was an electrician. You wondered and were curious. Why do wheels go round, fish swim, plants grow, birds fly? Where do babies come from? How did everything start? You remained in ignorance of sex; in that you were an exception. You never took part in the clumsy experiments in corners of the schoolyard, or scrawled on the lavatory walls. But you stole the juice from pineapple tins, by boring a hole with the point of Ma's scissors. You stole quite a lot...

[From *Topography of Childhood*, unpublished essay, written about 1938]

At the age of five, during the long miners' lock-out of 1921, this rather lonely boy found a friend, a very great friend. But Paddy Summersgill wasn't a boy; he was a big, brawny coal hewer who worked at Westerton Colliery alongside Ike Chaplin. Paddy had won coal all his life, apart from a spell in another dark, wet and dangerous place – the trenches of the Western Front. But for all his size and strength, Paddy was a gentle man with a priceless gift – the ability to talk to a youngster on equal terms, as adult to adult, or child to child. He taught Sid Chaplin the difference between a kestrel and a sparrowhawk, a rabbit and a hare; how to slide down a pit-heap on a shovel; and much besides. Tom Patrick *was written as a memorial.*

Tom Patrick

One morning the cat led me out of the house into bright tingling sunshine. What's he about, I wondered. For once he didn't run, but high-stepped it down the yard, looking upwards and about him as he went. Even behind him I could see his whiskers twitch. Instead of streaking over the gate the quicker to be in Grandma Richardson's and at his milk he paused and reached up the wall with his two front paws. There he stretched, benignly looking at me. He almost smiled – and even a child knows how rare is even the intimation of shared delight in a cat. Then, lowering himself, he went up and over the gate in a bound. Lifting the sneck I followed.

Grandma Richardson who wasn't really my grandma at all, but a grandma to everybody, put down his saucerful and Big Tom lapped. Straightening up, she announced: 'Well, here we are and it's spring again!'

'Spring?' I pondered, down on the proddy mat. In and out went the little red scoop of Big Tom's tongue.

'When all the flowers grow,' she said, as if that explained everything. But what use was that to one as green and unformed as me? I'd enough to do sorting out the puzzle of my own new-found identity.

A big man with rosy cheeks and a brown moustache rattled the sneck and walked in with the sunshine. 'Now Nelly; now canny bairn: by jox but Ah've got a thirst on me the morn!'

'Mind it would be summat different if tha' hadn't, Tom Pat!' she retorted. 'Tha' knows there's plenty o' watter i' the tap . . .' Nevertheless, all smiles, she brought out the grey hen and with the George V coronation mug she reserved for me a pint pot for the man. 'Tack care of the bairn first!' The milky ginger beer gurgled and frothed to a top as she poured. I smiled at the spectacle.

'And what's thy name, canny bairn?'

'That's out of the ordinary,' he gravely informed me, unlike the majority of people, who looked startled, or burst out 'Any

41

relation?' 'In fact, that's extra-ordinary!' I looked down at Big Tom. He had drunk every drop of his milk. When I looked up again the man had finished his ginger beer.

'You've got the same name as our cat, Mister,' I said. '*And* you drink as fast as well.'

For the first time a grown man slapped his knee and laughed out loud, not at but with me. 'There's thy character in a nut-shell,' triumphed Grandma Richardson.

'All the same, Ah'll have another.'

'The Lord help thi canny wife and bairns if iver thou tacks to drink, Tom Pat Gill,' she said, refilling his pot.

'The one that's on the way'll be the finish, Nellie.'

'There'll be more, Tom Pat; thou'll have a houseful.'

Standing up, he announced, 'One's enough for me: one wife, one bairn and one quart o' beer a day is enough for any man. Moderation in all things – that's my motto!'

'Off. with ye!' she threatened, and with a grin he backed out into the yard. I followed him. Stopping short, he looked down at me, 'Noo, what's thoo after?'

For answer I took his hand.

'Tha's got thisel' a bairn before time!' mocked Grandma Richardson. I returned in triumph an hour later with stories of being swung on a gate, plump partridges clapping up from our very feet, and the perfect interior silkiness of a hedge-spar-row's nest. But what couldn't be told was the first glimpse of the smokey blue depths of the wood, the way his laughter rippled like the stream his name and nature had been endowed with, the interest in and affection for me his whole being exuded, as indeed it did for all the good things of life around him.

Our relationship brought about a friendship between Tom Pat and his wife and my parents. But he remained my particu-lar friend. The trust between us was as inevitable as the blossom in the spring. It grew out of Grandma Richardson's obvious affection for him. Great shapeless mound of rectitude and comfort that she was, she was also the first woman I ever saw quicken to the life in a man. Time and time again I saw her become lovely in the presence of Tom Pat. Whenever I see the willow in the spring take on its splendid green-gold array I think of Grandma Richardson unfolding in the sunshine of Tom Patrick.

Tom Pat was quick and strong. A master of quoits, he ran

fleetly and was a mighty hitter with a bat. But what endeared him most to me was the level he offered in friendship. Quick to sense a mood, he was never patronising and knew the value of silence. When he made a pocket handkerchief rabbit hop from wrist to elbow, then bound over his shoulder, it was as much to entertain himself as me. Weaving a rattle of rushes, a whip or stripping away the delicate green skin to make a rose or lover's knot from the white pith, he was deep in his own delight and you were free to join in or not as you wished. Even when in the heat of the noon he made a little cap to preserve me from sunstroke it would be handed over so that I could put it on myself.

On the bad days it was sufficient for us to be together. A look was a conversation, and monosyllables spoke volumes. So to him belongs every spring wood in which I walk with its rife onion flowers, dusky red soldier's buttons and bluebells smelling of pleasantly doughy new bread. It may be hard for others to understand, but every good friendship since then and for evermore has the pungency of wild mint plucked by the water's edge.

That April Fool's Day all the pits shut down, and in the beginning this helped to cement our friendship. The lockout lasted three months. Since my father worked at the pit which lay over the hill to the west and Tom Pat at another which lay a mile eastwards out of view, I never saw the pulley wheels stop their interminable spinning and the winding engines fall silent, as if the giant slaves working inside the fortress-like winding-towers had at last toppled over with burst lungs and cracked hearts.

But I did miss the caller on his courses and, with the slog of boots on the pavement outside when the foreshift came home, the pit pungency which is a compound of sweat of man and smell of pony on coaldust-impregnated work duds. I missed too my father's whistle as he wheeled out his bicycle in the morning, missed the calm of a woman-ruled household. Above all, the time came when I began to miss Tom Pat's cheerful hail over the yard gate, calling me out to a walk, 'Anybody seen the young 'un?'

'Ah tell you what, we dinnat see ower much of Tom Pat these days,' said my father one morning, and my heart gave a leap.

'Her and her flamin' fire!' said my mother. 'She'll dae without nowt!'

'We'll toddle away up and see them this afternoon,' said my father. There was no holding me back when we set forth. 'Well, look who's turned up!' said Tom Pat, black as out of the pit when he opened the door.

Bessy Gill's house shone. You could see your face looking back at you out of the high shine of the tall press – unlike my grandmother's it didn't have mirrors on the doors, with white swans gravely swimming on them, and there was never a flyspot on the big picture of Tom Pat's father with a beard so long that could see only the bottom two buttons of his velveteen waistcoat. No matter where you sat the glow of the fire was reflected – how the blackleaded kitchen range resisted melting away is impossible of explanation! The only cool place in the kitchen was under the table, and looking out from there the fire roared away like an inferno. 'Thou should 'a' been colliery boilerman, Bessie!' charged my father.

I have never known anyone more prodigal of fuel. The great golden crust went almost up to the beginning of the chimney and the long flames curling away on each side relentlessly played upon the boiler and oven. How was I to know that I was looking at the enemy which had come between myself and Tom Pat? Day after day he was driven to gleaning on the peaks and low rambling ridges of Westerton pitheap to feed this insatiable creature. There was no satisfying it.

But what a spread! Unlike my mother, who made once do, Bessie baked thrice weekly – twice for crusty bread and fresh teacakes and once for fancy. Her fairy cakes melted away in your mouth and her tarts were so crisp and light that it was only necessary to bite and let the pastry melt and merge with delicious jam or lemon curd.

'How do you manage – how!' demanded my mother in mingled delight and exasperation. Tom Pat was having his bath in the scullery.

'Ah sent him down to his mother's this morning,' returned Bessie significantly, then lowered her voice. 'Me being the way I am, they always tip up. Rub it in about me mornin' sickness, I tell him; and it always works. Then while he went for coals I walked through the woods to Bishop Auckland and enjoyed myself in Lingfords.'

'You must have spent a fortune, really!' cried my mother.

'Ah went in with ten bob an' came out with one and thrippence in me purse,' she replied. 'As long as Ah've a bit money to start with, me charms'll look after the rest.' With a flicker of her long eyelashes: 'It's my charm that makes me such a manager.'

And what a manager of managers she was! Every Sunday without fail during the long three months of the strike she would send up a helping of her rice pudding for my father. My father was always ready for it, and Tom Patrick would silently watch. But one day a touch of the old merriment came to the surface.

'Ah'm sure it does me heart good just to watch ye, Ike,' he said.

'Naebody can touch your lass's rice pudding,' said my father. 'Naebody!'

'Aye, trust Bessie for the finishing touch and the fal-de-rals,' rejoined Tom Pat gaily, but when I next looked his face was clouded. The enforced idleness which had put fat around the middle of all the other men had worn him down to a spare, tired leanness. The bone shone through his face.

'It's the heap-riddin' that gets you down, lad,' said my father. 'How about tryin' the cut?'

'She winnit hear on it,' said Tom Patrick. 'Says the pollis'll be down like a ton of bricks one of these days.' Against his will he allowed my father to persuade him to go.

'Let's go and see the men working,' said my mother. We looked over the bridge into the cool leafy canyon with its gleaming rails, now transformed into a mine with the lid off. The place swarmed with men. Naked to the waist and precariously balanced on the slopes they swung their picks at the narrow seam of coal, fixed like the lead of a pencil in the yellow strata. There was no need to shovel. Down it tumbled to pile up in the drainage channels, while the marrers of the pickman above (no miner ever works alone if he can help it) joined forces to fill the sacks, or each with his burden toiled up the steep side of the cutting. Only the more fortunate who lived down the line were able to push their bicycles along and deliver almost at the coalhouse door. The place was a welter of picks and shovels and bicycles – and men who sang or jested as they worked. But there was no sign of my father or Tom Patrick. 'Where can they be?' asked my mother, screwing up her eyes.

Then all was changed as the fields on each side erupted

policemen who seemed nine feet tall in their helmets, swinging truncheons as they charged. Women screamed. Bairns started crying. Bicycles were abandoned and black coal spilled on the grass. Men dodged like coursed hares. Two forces entirely separate from those in the fields drove the men before them like sheep. One miner clambered up an almost perpendicular face of rock to where an Inspector, immaculate in white gloves and with his stick tucked back under his arm, impassively watched the mêlée below. When the miner reached the top he found first a pair of highly polished shoes, then, as his eyes travelled upwards, an officer resplendent and godlike. His mouth dropped open. The officer pointed with his stick, and the man went back down. This was the worst thing I saw. Then we hurried away home.

And there we waited. We waited for hours. 'They'll be gaoled for certain,' my mother wailed.

'Have a bit of pie,' suggested Bessie, 'while I put some coals on the fire.' In fact my father and Tom Patrick had been nowhere near the cutting. They had gone instead to the pitheap, and after seeing the police march by, decided to wait it out.

'Ah told you to stick to the heap,' said Bessie.

And this was what he did. One day we went to see him. The great round barrows burned slowly with a smell like hell's judgement, and far up one smoking flank a small figure toiled with pick, shovel and small-meshed riddle. Tom Pat slid down to join us. We sat on the grass and talked. Down below lay the quiet pit with its spidery headgear and twin winding-houses towering like empty castles. In full view was the gantry leading up to the cages. 'Ah never thought the day would come when I'd pray to get back down there,' said Tom Patrick.

The lockout ended and Tom Pat had his wish. Down the shaft he went, and one day he never came back. Alive as ever, I came again over the brow of the hill with my parents. The pit lay before me and in my state of innocence death, having no meaning as yet, could hold no dominion. Like our own familiar Tom Cat, the pit stretched lazily out over the place whence my friend would never return. The two fireholes glowing like eyes in the night, it stretched itself out and seemed ready at any moment to purr. Never did it occur to me that there was any connection between the going away of my friend and the stretching out in the night of the great, black, beautiful creature.

That had to wait upon my own experience of what might come of the careless flick of a paw, the implacable press of her immense belly.

The day after the funeral I accompanied mother on a visit to the bereaved wife, who greeted us at the door with be-floured arms and beaming face.

'Don't tell me you're bakin', lass!'

An unrepentant Bessie led us into a house which itself could have done service as an oven. 'Ah just took it into me head to bake a spice loaf for me mother,' she said. 'And then before Ah knew it Ah'd mixed enough pastry for a couple of pies and a baker's dozen griddle scones. The living have to be fed, you know. And it seemed such a waste – all that lovely fire.'

'Ah'm sure Ah don't know how you stand it – Ah'm sure you could fry an egg on that fender,' complained my mother.

'Here, take the bairn, and Ah'll bake you a nice bacon and onion pie for your tea.' Bessie thrust the baby into mother's arms. My mother, I noticed, made no complaint. And such a spread she made for us. It was the last of her great feasts, and she did it in style, proudly presiding over the teapot and queening it over us with face still flushed, and creamy arms yet pink from the heat.

After tea Bessie made preparations to leave with us, wishing to take the spice loaf to her mother. First mother washed in the cupboard under the stairs while Bessie changed and dressed the baby, then mother took the baby while Bessie completed her toilet.

'Do you like my soap, Elsie?' she enquired from the recess.

'Oh, but it's lovely. Ah do look forward to coming here for the soap!' I can hear them talking now. So long ago, and they were, after all, little more than girls.

Low and mysterious came Bessie's laugh; and even before she spoke I saw my mother turn sharply and look at the vague glow of womanhood out there in the shadows. 'Always look after your skin, Elsie,' she admonished. 'It's your face they look for first – a soft skin they like to touch...'

We left her with the child at the bottom of the street. 'Now did you ever hear the likes of that!' my mother demanded of me and then of a lark trilling high, in that order. 'Bessie's soap smells nice,' I firmly replied. We trudged along. To our left the pit lifted her standards high, and on our right the golden fields gently sloped to Binchester, a good two miles away.

'Ah wish it wasn't so far,' said my mother with a sigh.

And who should come spanking along but red-faced Butcher Wilkinson perched high up on the seat of his bright red van! The high wheels spun, the cabriolet-like box rocked on its springs, and the butcher, majestic below his bowler, shouted 'Whoa!'

'How about a lift?' he shouted, but already we were running to overtake him.

'Ye don't know what a welcome sight you are!' panted my. mother as he helped her from the step to the seat. 'Oops a daisy does it!' he said. 'Now how about the nipper? Should we put him in the van to keep the beef and mutton company!' It was all God bless you, as far as I was concerned. I was already waiting at the other side, quite unafraid of the champ and twitch of the horse. A hand was extended and in a trice, planted on the right of the butcher, I had been given command of the whip.

Then away we bowled while I, admiring the smooth rolling motion of the bay mare's hindquarters, wondered just what might happen if I dared touch them with the tip of the whip. The countryside was wide and open around us and blue smoke lifted perpendicularly from the chimneys of solitary farmhouses snuggled in the folds of little hills. A magpie flagged low over the railway field. Rooks cawed. In the September light all things were bright and clear. But I had no eyes for this. With the metal-bound wheels singing and the whip held high I rode along in triumph.

'– And him only buried yesterday,' my mother was saying. 'There she was, flour up to her elbows when we landed. "You can't bake for the dead, and that's a fact, Elsie," she told me; as sure as I'm sitting here.'

'It's a bonny funny carry-on – but then she always was a bit peecoolyar...'

'Peecoolyar isn't the word for it,' said my mother, unconsciously miming Butcher Wilkinson. 'You should have seen the carry-on when she got ready to go out – clear soap, two lots of water to wash with, the face cream, the scent!'

'She always did look like a woman that took care of herself,' ruminated the butcher. 'And she never did settle. Always ready to joke on.' My mother looked at him. 'Here, give us the whip, young 'un!' he demanded. That he didn't use it made me doubly resentful.

'It's sad,' he murmured at last.

'She'll pick, you watch!' said my mother.

'Oh, she'll pick – you need have no fears of that,' said the butcher robustly. And now he flicked the horse. Her ears went up. 'Hey, lass!' he said in an injured tone, and flicked her again. The mare's head went up and she stretched herself, licking us along to the brow at a fine pace. 'Whoa!' he cried, pulling. 'Now there's your lift home for ye!' he laughed. Picking me up he lowered me to the ground. At the other side he was one-handing my mother down. 'All the same, it's a sad case,' he said. Glancing down at me he said, 'Ye'd better come round and take hold of the lad.'

My eyes were fixed on bushes heavy with fruit. 'What's these black things, Mr Wilkinson?'

'What's them! What's them!' he demanded. 'Did you hear that, Elsie? Canny bairn, your education's been badly neglected. Tell him what the black things are, Elsie!'

'Why, they're blackberries,' she told me.

'Are they nice to eat?' Both adults looked down and laughed at me.

'You just try one,' said Butcher Wilkinson, watching as I picked and hesitantly took one to my mouth. 'Go on, pop it in,' he said. The berry was soft and yet firm between my fingers. 'Between your teeth,' encouraged the butcher, and oh, the smile that spread over his face as I tasted my first blackberry, the juice spurting out, taking its tart faintly acid sweetness to a million instantly alert and rejoicing taste-buds. 'Was I right?' he demanded, but already my hand had darted to select another. 'Now you've started something,' said my mother. Laughing, Butcher Wilkinson whipped away.

We picked and picked until our teeth, our lips and fingers were stained and stung with the sweet pain of the insidious little thorns. There was no driving me home that evening. If I'd had my way we should have feasted on blackberries for evermore. So the pride and vain glory of the whip and the high seat, and the taste of all those fine ripe blackberries that hung heavy on the branch, quite jostled out of mind and memory the passing of Tom Patrick. Only tenuously was his living presence linked up in my mind with the words of Grandma Richardson: 'Such a beautiful skin. All those years in the pit and there wasn't a mark on him.'

And yet again the iron-bound wheels of the years carried

me back to the churchyard where his gravestone leans, and a Tom Patrick Gill aged 23, fatally injured at Binchester Colliery. No more than a boy, he almost certainly went out as unblemished as on the day he was born. I am old now, but I can still hear his laugh. Surely this is a miracle. Tom Patrick is gone and the pit which overlaid him is obliterated, but still he walks beside me. 'Noo mind the bluebells, gan canny over the bonny flowers. Here, under the hawthorns where it's damp and cool, you're always sure to find them growing,' he says to the child I was then, and am no longer: that wild innocent creature who had still to taste his first blackberry. And to this day the sight of the cuckoo pints, each erect and sturdy, each guarding the life within it, has never yet failed to drive a pang like a nail through my heart.

[1982]

Pay Day

Twenty lads, so hearty, went down the pit
Today.
Twenty lads, once hearty, will never again draw
Pay.

[*c.* 1942]

During the 1920s, families like the Chaplins and the Summersgills had to struggle to survive: there were two very long stoppages, falling wages, a poor standard of living. Many people only got by with help from their families or the Board of Guardians, though the latter was often in the form of loans which had to be paid back. Ike Chaplin often recalled how it had taken him nearly ten years to repay the few pounds he'd been given so that his family could eat during the long winter of 1926.

Even when their fathers were in work, pitmen's children only had margarine to spread on the home-made bread – and a disgusting commodity it was too, 60 years ago. Yet once upon a time, not so very long before, the pitmen of the North had been among the aristocracy of labour, enjoying a comfortable standard of living. It wasn't until after the First World War, when the coalowners sought to combat falling demand for coal, and the difficulties of working dwindling seams, by lowering wages, that mining folk began to feel the pinch.

Naturally men like Ike were acutely aware of how they had come down in the world: when he was a lad, in the early years of the century, there was butter on the table and new boots under it; and, from time to time, outings and little holidays. The following story, The Outing, an embellished account of one such treat that passed into family legend, conveys a sense of this Edwardian comfort. It was in 1907 that Grandfather Chaplin took his large brood to Signor Pepi's New Hippodrome Theatre in Darlington; the music-hall star that caused the walk-out in real life was Florrie Forde.

The Outing

'I'll never forget that day as long as I live,' said my father.

'Which day?' I asked.

'The day your Grandpa took your Grandma and all the family to the theatre,' he said.

The word theatre touched off a memory. Grandma was always saying that the pictures and the stage were of the world, worldly; traps set for the unwary by Satan. She told me so one day when I asked her for threepence to go to the pictures. And she also added that she'd only stepped inside a theatre once, and once was enough for her. I pretended to accept this statement, since it was useless to argue with Grandma. But at the same time I was wondering if I could manage to wheedle threepence out of mother. But Grandma was as sharp as a needle. I suppose a boy's mind was an open book to her after bringing up seven of them. She put her head to one side and said, 'Well, are ye still going?'

'Not after what you've just told me, Grandma,' I said.

'But you'll be pestering your mother for threepence in ten minute's time, likely! Ah'll give ye sixpence if ye promise not to go to the pictures.' That was cunning.

'Ah promise, Grandma,' I said before she'd time to get her breath or change her mind. She smiled. She was like a good chess-player, always two moves ahead.

'What will ye do wi' the sixpence?' she demanded. I was at a loss for a moment, then said, 'Ah'll walk to Bishopton and buy some bullets at the stall in the market and look round the shops, 'specially the second-hand book shop and perhaps buy a book.'

'Good enough,' she snapped approvingly. 'Here's your sixpence.' So I walked to Bishopton and went to the pictures there. I didn't dare risk going to the little tin-shanty of a cinema at Gomorrah. She would have known I was there long before the show was over. I wasn't sure, for that matter, that I was safe at Bishopton, and for a week or two afterwards my conscience gave me a bad time whenever I was in her company.

Remembering this I said to my father, 'Grandma once told me that she was never inside a theatre but once.'

My father nodded. That was the time, he said. And this is how it came about. I remember the night when it all started. All the family had gone out, excepting Pa, who was getting ready to go; and Annie, whose turn it was to clean out the shop. Your Uncle Tom had been the first to leave. He was courting. Frank, Fred and Phillip had departed for the Junior Bible Class, together with Lizzie and Betty. I had some homework to do and was sitting at the little table (which belonged to me by unwritten rule) trying to make a start with it. I was eleven. I had another two years to go before I left school. I hated school. It was only a month or two after this that I ran away and tried to join the Army as a bugler-boy. But that's another tale. Ma was knitting, or, at least, trying to knit in between Pa's frantic calls for his studs, his collar, a new boot-lace, and finally at long last, the clothes-brush. This last to brush round his bowler. He was very particular about his bowler. I can see him now, putting the bowler on, having a last look at himself in the mirror, giving the bowler a last rakish tip, a final touch for his tie, then making for the door, the proper picture of a gentleman.

Just as he reached the door Ma said, 'Where to tonight, Joe?'

He gave her a sharp look; he didn't like anybody to ask him questions like that.

Ma said, 'Just so that Ah'll know when to have your supper ready, Joe?'

'Oh!' he said. 'Well, I'll be late tonight. Going with the Swan glee-party. To Marley. Bit of a concert.'

'That's a long way to walk,' she said.

'No walking tonight,' said Pa gaily. 'I've got the loan of your Lizzie's brake. Ta-ta, Meg lass.' And away he went.

After the storm, peace at last, and I settled down to my homework. But Ma was in a talkative mood. I'd hardly started the first sum when she sighed and said, 'Jim, Ah wish your Pa was like other men.'

'What d'ye mean, Ma?'

'Other men stop indoors between tea and supper. They sit in front of the fire and read a book and smoke a pipe.'

'Joe Todd's Pa helps him with his homework,' I said.

'Your Pa would if he ever stayed in. But he's never at home. There's always something on; somewhere to go; something to do.'

'Perhaps it's with being cooped up in the shop all day,' I suggested. 'Mr Todd's out with his butcher-cart all day and it's a change for him to stay in nights.'

She nodded. 'Perhaps there's something in what you say, boy. But Ah wish he'd be content to sit in front of the fire and smoke his pipe just once in a while. And then, perhaps it's too much to ask of him. Your Pa's got too active a nature.'

'Well, then Ma,' I said. 'He should take you out with him. And us too. Mr Todd takes his family on trips!'

That touched your Grandma the wrong way. She stopped knitting and said, 'Mr Todd can afford to do a lot of things that we can't. Jim, don't think Ah'm grumbling about your father. Ye've got the best father in the world, and don't forget it!'

'Yes, Ma,' I said, and managed to make a start with my sums.

I may be wrong, but I think the idea of our little outing to Darlton came from that conversation. Something I said must have planted the idea in her head. But anyway, the next Saturday there was such a commotion in the old house as never was. Your Grandma must have been out of bed at five o'clock, for when we came downstairs at eight the fireplace had been black-leaded, the fire-irons polished, the mats shaken and the floors washed. And all our best clothes were laid ready in neat piles. We stared in amazement.

'What's up, Ma?' asked Tom. He was over twenty, the oldest and earning big money at the pit, so he had the right to ask questions.

'Your Pa's taking us all to Darlton for the day. The brake's calling for us at ten, so ye'll all have to look sharp.'

'But Ma, Ah don't want to go to Darlton,' said Tom. We all knew why. He was courting Peggy Hopkinson and this meant he wouldn't be able to see her.

'Nonsense!' said Ma. 'Your Pa said you all had to be ready by ten. And *all* includes you, Tom.'

'But Ma –' protested Tom.

'That's enough!' snapped Ma. 'Ah'm not having any lip!'

And Tom had to be content with that.

When Pa came downstairs at nine we were all ready to go. At least, we thought we were. But after he'd finished his breakfast he lined us all up and gave us a thorough inspection. When his examination was completed most of us were in disgrace. I had to get washed again, Phillip also. As a matter of fact he said that Phillip hadn't washed his neck for a couple of months and to make sure took the soap and flannel himself and rubbed so hard that Phillip was wondering which would wear through first, flannel or skin.

He also discovered a missing button on Fred's jacket, and a knotted bootlace. He was ordered to get a new bootlace and stitch a new button on himself. Then he started with the girls. He didn't like the way they'd done their hair; and he discovered a hole so small in one of Annie's stockings that you'd need a microscope to see it. Then he sat back and watched us all dashing about. The only one who passed the inspection was Tom, and he sat in a corner sulking.

'What's the matter with him?' asked Pa.

'He doesn't want to go,' said Ma.

The contented smile left Pa's face. 'He doesn't want to go!' he said incredulously. 'He doesn't want to go! Why?'

Now Tom was in a fix. You see, his courting was unofficial at the time, although I fancy Ma knew all about it. There wasn't much she didn't know. So Tom blurted out the first thing that came into his mind. He said, 'Ah'm too old to be goin' to Darlton with a lot of kids.'

'Ah yes,' said Pa softly. 'I apologise, Tom lad. A big fellow like you shouldn't be going on a family outing. You're past that stage. It was thoughtless of me; most thoughtless. Well, my lad, you've solved me a problem. If you don't want to go, by all means stay at home.'

Tom brightened up a bit at this. His face lit up like a condemned man's when he gets a reprieve. But Pa soon wiped the smile away.

'Yes lad, you've solved my problem,' he said. 'I was wondering what to do about the shop while we were away. But since you don't want to go, *you* can look after the shop.' He looked sharply at Tom. 'I must say,' he said in a hurt tone of voice, 'you don't know what to do to please the modern generation. A man doesn't know what to do to please his own children!'

By some miracle we were all ready to Pa's satisfaction when the brake arrived. But before we departed he gave us all our instructions. 'There'll be no fratching or fighting among you, mind, while we're away. I don't intend to be shown up by any of you in Darlton. You'll not be to tell twice to get off the brake and walk up the banks. And when we get to Darlton there'll be no running away on your own and perhaps getting lost. You'll all walk in two's behind me and your Ma, with Ralph and Jack bringing up the rear to see that nobody strays.' He stood a moment and gave us a keen looking over. Then he said, 'You've all got your hankies?'

'Yes, Pa,' we chorused. But he made us all bring them out for him to see, just to make sure. Then we went out to the brake. It was a boat-shaped affair with seats inside, open to the four winds of heaven and drawn by two horses. He saw us all into our seats, then got up beside the driver. The driver said, 'Ready?' and raised his whip. 'I'll tell you when,' said Pa, and like the good general he was he turned round to make sure his regiment was in order. Then we were off at a gallop through the streets of Little Gomorrah, the clop-clop-clop of the horses' hooves and the crack of the whip bringing everybody to the door to see us in all our glory; your Grandpa sticking his chest out and your Grandma sitting amongst us all as proud as punch. We waved goodbye to Tom who was standing at the shop door, but he went in without waving back. He'd arranged to meet Peggy after tea and I suppose he was studying how to let her know.

That was one of the red-letter days of my life, even though there was to be a disappointment in store for us. We toured all the big shops and went up in a lift for the first time. Our party had to split into three to do it. Then we had lunch in a big café with waiters rushing about at Pa's behest. The way they bowed and scraped you'd have thought he was a Duke with his retinue. Well, if he wasn't a Duke he certainly had his retinue, for there were eleven of us, and we kept three waiters busy bringing in the food. Each waiter was rewarded with a tip. I have an idea Pa gave them each a threepenny bit (for he used to collect them in a special pocket) because I saw one of them standing behind a screen looking at a threepenny bit as if he couldn't believe his eyes.

After we had been marshalled in correct order we left the café, and I might say we caused quite a stir, for Pa told us to

57

lift our feet well, and we did. I was marching behind Ma and Pa, and I overheard this snatch of conversation.

'Where to next, Joe.'

'To the Palace Theatre, Meg.' Ma stopped dead and caught hold of Pa's arm and we pulled up to in ragged formation.

'Joe Castle,' said Ma. 'You're not taking me and those canny bairns into any den of vice and iniquity!' For answer Pa pulled a bunch of tickets out of his pocket and waved them under her nose.

'Oh,' she wailed. 'The waste of it, the terrible waste of it all! Ye've bought those tickets and ye know that it's against me principles to go to the theatre!'

'Rules, regulations and principles are made to be broken,' said Pa. 'Furthermore,' he added, 'it's just a simple little musical comedy which won't do you or the bairns an ounce of harm. So come along!'

For once Ma was defeated. She was against the theatre; but she was also against wilful waste, and I suppose it was really the thought of those tickets being wasted which persuaded her to go. That's the worst of having strict principles; there always comes a time when they get into competition with each other.

Pa had booked seats in the front circle. It was the Palace, and to us it seemed a Palace indeed. Our feet seemed to sink in the thick carpets; the ceiling seemed as high as the sky and we gazed in amazement at the steady, unwinking electric lights. We were tired after the long journey and the shopping tour, and we quickly found ease for our tired bodies in the comfortable seats. Of course, Phillip and I soon discovered how easy it was to tip the empty seats in front of us by stretching out our feet and giving them a push, but that game was soon stopped. Then a girl came round with apples and oranges and sweets on a tray, and we all got an apple or an orange and Ma a packet of boiled sweets.

Then Lizzie's eye caught the pictures painted in the big panels around the walls. 'Are them angels on there, Ma?' she asked. Ma hadn't had the opportunity to look at them until then. She took out her spectacles and looked at them a long time. I could see her lips tightening.

'They seem to be half-naked women to me,' she snapped. 'Don't look at them Lizzie.'

Pa stroked his moustache. 'That's art,' he said.

'Ah don't care what they are!' said Ma. 'They're disgraceful and all of ye keep your eyes in front!' And since poor Lizzie was sitting next to Ma she had to keep her eyes pinned in front, but you can be sure we all had a good look, and they kept us entertained until the orchestra came out and started to play the overture. The lights went out and the curtains opened.

All I remember of the story is that it was about a beautiful girl who ran away from her home in the country. She went to London and became an actress. Soon she was famous, and young men with top-hats and canes used to wait outside the stage-door just to get a glimpse of her when she came out after the show to get into her cab. Among these, was a young man, poor but honest, whom she scorned. But he still kept on loving her. He was always popping on the stage to sing a song about still loving her. Then there was a Sir Somebody who also wanted to marry her. But he was a bit of a fool and she just led him on. She was a born breaker of hearts. I can't tell you any more because at this point the leading lady came on with a row of girls, all in short skirts, and started to kick their legs. Everybody was laughing, including Pa. But in the middle of all Ma gathered up her bags and stood up and said, 'Disgraceful! Ah'm not staying here a minute longer!' Pa was very agitated at this.

'Sit down, Meg!' he whispered urgently.

'If you think Ah'm going to sit here while these bairns have their minds poisoned you're mistaken,' she said. 'You can stay here if you like, Joe Castle, but Ah'm going out and Ah'm taking the bairns with me!'

'Be quiet, Meg! Sit down! Everybody's watching,' said Pa. It was funny. Pa was whispering, but Ma didn't bother to lower her voice. The sweat was standing on Pa's brow. But Ma pushed her way out. 'Follow me, bairns!' she ordered. We didn't want to go, but we had to. And away we trooped, leaving poor Pa all on his own. The actors were doing their best on the stage but nobody had an eye for them. Our retreat from the Palace stole the show.

It was the end of the outing for us. Ma marched us down to the Haymarket and sent Ralph into the Golden Lion in search of the driver. He came out protesting violently, but one look at Ma's stern face was enough to silence him. Lizzie said, 'But what about Pa?' as we drove away.

'He'll find his way home as best as he can,' said Ma. 'And

girl, Ah've told ye before not to speak until you're spoken to.' At this the three girls burst into tears. It was a mercy that Gomorrah was in darkness when we arrived. All the way home our driver had vented his spite on the horses and they had lost all spirit by the time we drew up in front of the shop. Silently and sullenly we dismounted from the brake. If anybody had seen us they'd have thought we were a funeral party just come back from burying Pa.

It's an ill wind that blows nobody any good and Tom was able to meet his Peggy after all. Ma wasn't in the best of tempers and he was lucky to escape her wrath. We couldn't do anything right for her, and we were all glad to get to bed.

But I couldn't sleep. I tossed and turned long after the others had fallen asleep. It must have been about eleven when I decided I was thirsty and crept downstairs for a drink. The kitchen door was ajar and I peeped through. I was glad to see Pa at home, sitting eating his supper with his stockinged feet stretched gratefully under the table. And Ma was there too, sitting beside the fire in her rocky-chair. Just as I looked she dropped her knitting and leaned forward, 'And what happened after that?' she said. Pa speared a pickled onion and looked long and lovingly at it.

'Ah, now,' he said. 'Let me see ... oh, after that she left the stage –'

'About time too!' said Ma.

'– and went to live in a cottage in the country. And the poor but honest young man followed her there. It was a beautiful scene. There she was in a beautiful garden with a lot of flowers and a real fountain. Cutting herself a bunch of roses. Then this young chap came and stood at the gate and she looked up and saw him and held out her arms and he just jumped over and gave her a kiss. And that was the end.'

'Ah can just imagine it,' said Ma dreamily. Then she picked up her knitting. 'Though why they should spoil it by bringing in all those disgraceful girls showing their limbs I don't know!'

'You're a funny old girl, Meg,' said Pa. 'Suppose I give *you* a pickled onion kiss?'

Somehow, I wasn't thirsty any more. The stairs creaked a lot as I made my way back to bed, but nobody seemed to hear.

[1942]

The music-hall star who caused the
walk-out in real life – Florrie Forde.

A very large number of Sid Chaplin's stories have a pedigree like that one. It began life as a piece of real experience and then became a "good story", being honed down in the telling around the kitchen table. For in the Durham coalfield until very recently there flourished a vigorous oral society, in which the talents of the preacher, the ranter, the political orator and the storyteller were exalted:

I can remember one old bearded preacher opening the Bible, and without looking at it, saying 'My next text for today is from the Gospel of John, chapter one, verse one: In the beginning was the Word, and the Word was with God, and the Word was God.' And then he preached a sermon without a note. I thought, how marvellous! But the thing that stuck in the mind was 'In the beginning was the Word' and that there was something holy about the word!

Not just in the chapel, but also in the union lodge meeting, at the street corner, in the club or the kitchen, Sid Chaplin learned the 'point and the pith, the power and the sanctity of the word'. In the beginning, he wanted to be a raconteur himself, but soon discovered that he was hopeless at it:

I found out that I always missed the point of any story I was telling. Part of the reason I'm a writer is that you can be more sure of getting the story right in writing it down, whereas a raconteur, you know, it just drops off his lips. I haven't got the performer's ability; it's got to be born in you. It's the greatest art, oral storytelling, no doubt about it.

In view of the reverence he had for the old raconteurs, it's not surprising that many of Sid Chaplin's stories take the form of one person telling a tale to another (often a father to son). This is the case with The Night of the News, *which although not a family story, is clearly based on some small boy's real adventure at the turn of the century.*

The Night of the News

It's so easy to forget dates, said my father. I can't remember the exact year: for the life of me I can't remember it. It was about the turn of the century. But it's all so small and vague now, as if you were looking down the diminishing years through the wrong end of a telescope, and you can't distinguish the faded names of the besieged cities, if you can call them cities, and the big generals that led the besieged and the besiegers; and you forget how important it all was, and you only remember the songs they sung as they marched away. And sometimes the name of a man you know who marched away with them and never returned; or stray bits of arguments about strategy and tactics; and the Kaiser, for instance saying that the new century wouldn't start until 1901; there was a great deal of arguing about that, and I remember also how indignant everybody was when he sent that telegram to the President saying how pleased he was that they were doing so well. But all very vague and mixed up.

My Uncle Jim was in that lot you know. I can remember him coming into our house before he enlisted and leaving his bag with Ma till he came back. I was named after Uncle Jim. He was a tinker, wandering around the countryside until he joined the Army, a lean restless rake of a man with a taste for trouble. But he always clung to Ma and she clung to him because he was her youngest brother. Wherever he was he would write to her, even when he was doing a spell in gaol. But then he joined the Army to get out of some scrape or other and they sent him out there. Out of the frying-pan into the fire, for he had a rough time of it in every sense of the saying. But that's how history narrows down. All that the news meant to Ma was that Uncle Jim, harum-scarum, happy-go-lucky Jim was safe. And that's how I remember everything that happened on the night of the news when everything else is so vague. Because the news was linked with Uncle Jim everything is crystal clear and fresh as if it happened yesterday.

It was a spring evening. I think it must have been in May. But anyway, it was spring. I remember the hawthorns decked with blossom, so much of it that you had to look twice to see the fresh green of the leaves, so much of it that you could lie in bed with the window open a little and smell the scent of the blossom, that faintly unpleasant scent of the dead; as if the wind had wafted a memorial to them all the way from Africa.

I was sleeping in the same bed with Frank, Fred and Phillip, lying between Fred and Phillip. Phillip's leg was heavy across my chest with a nervous twitch going through it all the time, and Fred was lying with his face buried in the pillow, snoring like an old engine with one arm flung over my face. It was this that awakened me, a feeling that I was bound and being strangled. I was in a cold sweat and it took me several minutes to realise where I was and rid myself of the entanglements. Then I lay, listening. All was quiet in the house but through the window there came a mixture of sounds. First and foremost, the jangling of the church bell. More subdued and in tune, the sound of a band. Then a mixed hum, as of a crowd of folk, some talking, others singing and shouting. Something unusual was undoubtedly happening, and I decided to investigate. There was a moon flooding the room with light, and I can remember looking at Frank as I went to the window. He was half in, half out of the bed, one hand and one foot resting on the floor. In spite of that he seemed perfectly comfortable balanced there on the edge of the bed. He was smiling in his sleep and the moonlight caught his fair hair so that it seemed to be made of fine strands of silver. I eased the window up a little and looked out. A row of star-like lights twinkled and moved unevenly where I knew the pit-heap gantry to be: the afternoon shift of repairers coming out. I knew from this that it was turned eleven o'clock. By leaning right out I could see the furnace at the steelworks outlined in a sort of smoky radiance as it was recharged. Although the church bells were still having their way most of the noise seemed to be coming from the streets around the works. As I watched I saw flames shoot into the sky from a dozen points; as if bedlam had broken loose and lunatics were lighting bonfires and dancing round them. There was one in the market-place, and dark linked figures danced around the fire there.

I decided to pull on my clothes and go out to get to the bottom of the mystery. It was a mad thing to do, to sneak out of the house at this time, but I was sure there was something unusual going on. For those were the days when people were early to bed. Generally Little Gomorrah was as quiet as the tomb every night at ten, that is, apart from men coming home from work or pub. I waited until I was safely out of the house before I put my boots on. I pulled them on in a hurry, just fastening the laces into big granny-knots. I made for the market-place first of all. People were standing at open doors asking each other what was the matter. You could see the bronze reflection of fires in the cup of the sky.

As I passed the Rectory I saw a tall figure hurry in front of me. It was the Rector, Mr Alloway, I knew immediately. There was no mistaking that tall, stiff-legged form, the drain-pipe trousers, flying tails and high silk hat; and the big muffler streaming over his shoulder like a banner as he hurried along. Perhaps he thought the church was on fire, I thought, though in that case, who was ringing the bell? The church (we called it the Roman church) stood at the head of the market-place. It was a very old, ivy covered church with a flat roof, but in a bad state of repair, and later they pulled it down and built the fine new ugly church that stands there now in its place. I scented some excitement and followed him, stepping when he did, to view the blazing fire and dancing figures in the centre of the market-place. He didn't look very long at them but said something short and sharp under his breath as he hurried on his way again. The churchyard gates were wide open, light flooded out from the open door of the church itself. Mr Alloway increased his pace and I had to run to keep him in sight. I heard his high squeaky voice as he entered the porch.

'Who gave you men authority to ring the bell?' he demanded. Then I saw two men standing behind the still swinging rope, the shadow of it crossing and recrossing their faces. Their faces were familiar, but I didn't know their names, I think they were steelworkers. They stood there like a couple of sheepish boys. The bigger of the two was the spokesman; he had a chest like a barrel, and sidewhiskers and great tufts of hair springing from his nostrils like ferns' forms from a cavern. 'Well, sir,' he said, 'The door was open; and we thought it was only proper to ring t' bell, wi' the news comin' so late, that it was a way of letting 'em know.' His companion nodded uneasily. 'We knew it'd be all right wi' ye, Mr Alloway.'

'You knew nothing of the sort,' said Mr Alloway. 'You've no right at all to break into my church and ring the bell without my permission.'

'But a night like this –' protested the big man.

'I've no time to argue with you; no time at all,' said the Rector coldly. 'Now will you kindly remove yourselves so that I can lock the door?' For a moment it seemed possible that he might himself be removed; I saw their lips tighten and their fists clench. Then Mr Alloway continued, 'Or shall I go for the police?' That did it. They walked out without another word.

The Rector turned out the gas and locked the door. I was still standing outside the porch and as he turned to leave his eye caught mine. 'Boy,' he said. 'You should be in bed at this time of the night.'

I made my escape. It was easy to see that he was in no mood for argument. The two men were standing at the gate. 'Good evening,' said Mr Alloway pleasantly, perhaps feeling in a better mood now that he'd got his own way. Or maybe he didn't recognise them, his mind already anticipating the pleasant warmth of his study and the great books he would read far into the night. The men didn't answer. One of them spat viciously as he walked away.

'Miserable old b –,' he said. It was the little man, of course.

'What's it all about, Mister?' I asked. He stared at me. 'Don't ye know? The news came through on the telegraph at half-ten. Mafeking's been relieved. They've fought their way through to our lads at last!'

So that was it. Mafeking relieved at long last! That meant Uncle Jim was safe. Not that Uncle Jim meant much to me; I'd only seen him a bare half-dozen times before he left his tinker's bag with Ma and left to fight for the Queen. But he was Ma's youngest brother, and I knew that she'd worried about him. A worry all the deeper because it was silent. So I was glad for her. My cap went up into the air and I gave an hurrah for Uncle Jim and Baden-Powell and Ma. As my cap came down and I caught it, the big man said, 'Can ye climb, laddy?'

'What for, Mister?' I asked.

'Think ye could climb up t' church wall and ring t' bell?'

'Ah don't know,' I said uneasily. 'What if Mr Alloway comes back.'

'He's not capable of climbin' up after ye,' he grinned. That grin put us on a level. And it occurred to me that this news meant the ending of Ma's worries; that was enough reason to ring a bell and make a joyous sound. He put his hand in his pocket, 'Here's a shilling if ye'll do it,' he said. 'No,' I said. 'Ah don't want a shilling for it.' But he pressed it on me, and when I still refused, dropped it into my pocket.

A minute later I was climbing the wall with the shilling in my pocket for ballast. It was easy enough. The old church was clothed in ivy, with creepers as thick as my wrist. I was soon on the flat roof, making my way to the belfry. Within ten minutes of the Rector leaving us the bell was ringing again. And by the time I'd changed hands twice he was back again, in a rare old fury this time, thinking, I suppose, that they'd broken into the church. Quite a crowd had gathered to see the fun, for the smaller of my two conspirators had rushed over to the bonfire to tell the people there. He scattered them with his stick and marched into the churchyard. I would have given my shilling willingly to have seen his face when he found the door locked as he had left it. But I did the next best thing; I let the rope idle for a moment and heard him banging the door with his stick and shouting, 'Open up! Open up, you scoundrels. I'll have the law on you for this!' Then I started ringing again. The poor man must have thought he was going mad until the laughter and upturned faces of the crowd gave him a clue.

The next thing I knew he was standing beside the church-yard gate, waving his stick and trying to shout against the bell. The Rector was a scholar and a dreamer but they tell me he used some words that night which some of the eavesdrop-ping pitmen and steel-workers had never heard before. Then he went in search of Big Feet. And I decided that my fellow-conspirators had had their shillingsworth and retired from the belfry forthwith.

I had more sense than reveal myself to the crowd. When I had made my descent I kept to the shadows and went out by the wicket-gate at the east end of the churchyard. I should have liked being there when the Rector returned with Big Feet – torn from a warm bed – but it was too risky. I heard later that Big Feet, who was no respecter of persons, had said some hard words to the Rector; and that Mr Alloway had retaliated in the same measure.

The celebrations continued into the early hours of the following morning, but I didn't stay to see and hear all. I was sorry for this afterwards, for it was a night of nights by all accounts. Down by the Puddlers Arms they were hoisting a barrel of tar onto the bonfires when Ralph Anderson the blacksmith came out to see the fun. By then the barrel was blazing.

'By lad, yon's a good blaze! What's that they've got on top of her, there? Tar barrel, isn't it? Aye, it's good stuff for a blaze!' he said – not knowing that it was his barrel, stolen from his shop-yard. At three o'clock, when the dancing in the streets was finished, for there's a limit to everything, the remnants of the makeshift band, euphonium, cornet and big drum, emigrated unsteadily to Sharon Hill, Nathan Bradley's big house on the outskirts of the town.

They expected a gratuity for their playing, of course, and they must have been pretty drunk, for anyone in his true senses knew that Nathan would never part with a penny if he could help it. They got the contents of a chamber pot for their trouble, and that was the damp ending of the daftest, maddest night that Little Gomorrah ever knew.

But long before this I went home, bursting with the news for Ma. I took off my clothes and tiptoed upstairs. But everyone was sound asleep, and how they had slept through it I shall never know. I tapped at the bedroom door. 'Ma,' I whispered, 'are ye awake?' I had to repeat this several times before I finally heard the sound of a striking match.

'Who's that?'

'It's me, Jim.'

'What ever on earth's the matter? Come in, boy.'

She was resting on her hand, half raised in the bed, with the blankets tumbled around her and the dark braids of her hair framing her face. You remember her eyes, how beautiful and wise they were in age. But it was not until that night that I realised how beautiful Ma really was. Not because she had classical features, or that she had taken care of her skin, but because she had always loved deeply and strongly. She was looking at me when I opened the door as she had probably looked at me when I was a small child. For there was something disturbingly familiar about her look, and I realised afterwards that to a mother her boy is always the small child who once clung to her, however old he may be. And the moonlight enhanced her beauty. I couldn't speak, so sudden was the revelation.

'What is it, Jim? Have ye been dreamin'?'

'No, Ma,' I managed to say, 'Ah wanted to tell ye the news.'

'News! At this time of night!'

'Mafeking's been relieved, Ma! Uncle Jim's safe!' Her hand clutched my wrist and drew me to her. 'You've been dreamin', boy. How could ye know; ye've been dreamin',' she whispered. You could see her setting herself against it, setting her mind against anything so wonderful, against her Jim being safe. It wasn't Mafeking she saw, but Jim. It throbbed in the beat of pulse and the light of her eyes, but she steeled herself against acceptance. No wishful thinking for Ma.

'You've been dreamin', boy; that's it, isn't it, now?' Her voice was very soothing. but the question couldn't be avoided.

'Ah'm not dreamin', Ma. It's true!'

'How could ye know, boy, and asleep in bed!'

I was in a quandary. I didn't want to lie, but at the same time I didn't want her to know that I'd been out of the house. Somehow the proper words came unbidden to my lips.

'Ah – Ah heard the men say, Ma,' I stammered.

'Men? Which men?'

'The men down in the street.'

'What did they say?'

'That Mafeking's been relieved. And Ma, Ah didn't dream it. Ah heard the people shouting. And when Ah looked out of the window there were bonfires burning in the streets. One down by the steelworks and another in the market-place. And there's others. And the church bell ringin', too. Although I didn't realise it this was well said. Without knowing it I had walked a tightrope suspended between truth and falsehood.

'Come here, Jim, boy,' she said. I moved cautiously forward and she drew me down to her and kissed me on the brow. It was not often that Ma kissed us. We were a reticent family. Then she said, 'Bless ye for coming and telling me, boy. Now go back to bed and get some sleep.'

I turned to the door – 'Jim,' she said, 'What made ye waken me to tell me about it?'

'Why, Ma –' I began, then stopped for want of words. She smiled.

'It doesn't matter, boy. Ah think Ah know why.'

I returned to my bed – or rather – our bed. On my way I heard her getting out of bed. I remember the low murmur of her voice lulling me to sleep. At first I was puzzled. Pa had not stirred from his sleep during our conversation. Perhaps she had wakened him after I had left. But I could not catch his familiar voice. And, anyway, if she had wakened him he would have been out in a minute. After a while I understood. Ma was giving thanks.

The next morning our neighbours were in early with the news. For although we knew of the relief of Mafeking, there was still a great deal to tell. Of how, Miss Rainbird, our post-mistress, had gone to bed and had been aroused by the incessant tapping of the telegraph machine, and how she had taken the message and ran into the street with it, and how the news had spread like wildfire; and the bonfires and the dancing and the street parties – and the bell-ringing. Especially the bell-ringing. I was the unknown hero of Mafeking night. All Gomorrah was talking about it and wondering who it was that had defied the Rector and climbed to the belfry. 'Whoever he was, he must have had a nerve, climbing up that ivy,' said Pa. 'I pity him if ever old Alloway ever gets his hands on him.'

We were all sitting around the table, listening to the talk, having finished breakfasting. Ma was clearing the table. As she leaned over to pick up my plate and mug her sharp eyes found something that clung to my jacket. She picked it off, and only barely glanced at it before she threw it into the fire. My heart stood still as she looked at it. There's no mistaking the hairy twig broken from ivy. She watched it burn away before she spoke.

'Well, whoever he was, he was a brave lad,' she said slowly, still looking into the fire. 'If Ah'd been out there last night Ah'd have felt like climbing up myself to ring the bell. It was a seemly thing to do; it was an occasion for bell-ringing. And if ever the Rector does find out who the lad is Ah hope Ah'm there to stand between him and the lad!'

Pa looked at her curiously. 'Why, Meg, lass, whatever in the world makes you say that!'

'Because he climbed up to that belfry and risked his neck and rang that bell for me, since Ah wasn't there to do it,' said Ma. 'That's why. And if Ah thought it was one of my lads that did it Ah'd be the proudest woman in Little Gomorrah!'

She never looked at me as she said this; but it was as good a way as any of telling me that my secret – and hers – was safe.

[*c*. 1948]

During his childhood, Sid Chaplin lived in a succession of villages in the valleys of South-West Durham: Middlestone Moor, Byers Green, Binchester Blocks, Newfield, Eldon Lane, Ferryhill. Of all of them, he was happiest in Newfield, which straddles a hillside above a lazy loop of the Wear and looks due west to the distant moors and hills of the Pennines. Here he learnt to swim and how to jarp Easter eggs; he played with penkers, and shutty ring with glass alleys, and sometimes the men joined in games of tipcat. There were many such exotically-named games: hitchy-dabber, duckstones, mount-a-kitty, buttony, Jack-shine-the-Maggie . . . But of all the childhood pastimes, the one that the boy loved best was played with a ring of round, well-burnished iron, about three feet six inches in diameter, along with the hook used to propel it. The booler:

You could race it down the street and back again, or ten laps round the circuit – down Stonebank Terrace and along past the Co-op, then, with a simulated roar of Bluebird engines, up past the wooden houses and in a tight curve round to level going again. High speeds were attained, and it was often quite impossible to brake by snatching your booler quite clear of the ground, or by stamping hard inside the ring. I still shudderingly recall the general panic when our road was blocked by a haycart led by two shire horses that reared and showed their teeth, and the lead man sat down with his booler hooked and the rest of us piled on top of him.

Gradually though, as the 20s wore on, the outside world began to seep into the intimacy of village life. Ike was the first in the village to get hold of a crystal set; one night he tickled the cats' whiskers of the crystal and the family heard a very distant choir singing an old English carol on Radio 2LO, the forerunner of the BBC. Talking pictures arrived at the ramshackle picture house at Willington. And then one day a butcher from West Cornforth called Jackie Ormston bought an old biplane and began to practise his loops and passes on sunny Sundays, waving at the children below.

Out of all these elements Sid Chaplin constructed The Great Aeroplane Race, *a tale of growing up:*

The booler still encircles my heart. Often in the spring I wish I could trot along with the hook in my hand and the ring of steel running companionably and melodiously by my side. But I should have to be a boy again; and that cannot be!

The Great Aeroplane Race

One bright morning – and a great one it was too, one of the best I ever remember – I left our house and says to the lads outside: 'Howay, men, let's get crackin'. Today's the day we race the aeroplanes!' Mind you, for all my bounce I wasn't so sure I'd get away with it.

'What aeroplanes?' asks Bobbie Claxton.

'Charlie Parker's Ma told mine all about it,' I said. 'They're holdin' it at Mount Slowly and they call it a Flyin' Circus. They're goin' to have a big race. We'll wait for them here and race them back to the field.'

'Well, Ah'm game for a try, if nobody else is,' said Small John McCann, but our kidder – that's my younger brother – said nothing. It takes concentration to lace up an invisible machine-gun with ammunition, and he was now too busy firing quick bursts at Chloe Robson's cat over the road to be bothered much with us. I looked at Bobbie. 'Well, Ah think it's crazy!' he retorted. Which should have burst my bubble there and then, only I was ready and waiting. 'Nobody's forcin' you to go, Bobbie,' I replied. Although I was grinning, I wanted him all the same. Bobbie not only knew every inch of the road but was also the real boss of our gang, and if he came the rest would follow. 'Only you're the best we have with a booler – the bestest and the fastest!' I said regretfully.

'Garn – go on, butter me up some, I like it,' he says, but all the same I could see he was pleased. 'Never mind, a good run never did anybody any harm. But we'll have to have Charlie to pace me. Anybody know where he is?'

'Swillin' the backyard for his Ma, last Ah heard,' says our kidder.

'Go fetch him, Chris,' said Bobbie, and off I went – the long way round. Nobody with any sense went through Alice Parker's kitchen if they could help it. Although she'd give the last bite in her house to a starving beggar she was also so mad house-proud that she met you with a hand-brush and shovel and mucked after you all the way into the house and out again, her boody-teeth going fifty to the dozen all the time.

So down the fronts and up the unpaved backs I went, and when I arrived Charlie hadn't even started. Seated on an upturned bucket he was sketching in a used-up school-book, his pencil so busy you could hardly see it. It was so good it could have hopped right off the page. 'Hey that's great, Charlie,' I says. 'Ah wouldn't mind havin' a pouch myself. Useful for marbles – or the family jewels.'

'Not if you were a kangaroo, you wouldn't,' he answered – and I wondered what he was on about; till he drew in a little baby 'un looking out. And that was Charlie; the best drawer I ever knew, the stickler, the man who never turned back. With Charlie everything had to be right, or he tore it up. There he sat in the middle of the yard that morning and drew lions and tigers, and a giraffe that spread over two whole pages, and he never flagged; while I went and got another bucket and swilled the yard around him. I even had to ask him to lift his feet when I got to where he was sitting.

Anyway, eventually we joined the others. By now the village was coming to life. Women went by with cans for milk warm from the cow; a brewer's dray toiled uphill with its Clevelands shaking fetlocks like Zulu anklets every time they lifted their hooves, and, yawning and leather-aproned, Cass Mason the glee-eyed cobbler came out and took down the shutters of his shop-window. Finally, along comes young Willy Watson. He was wearing a pistol and riding a mustang.

'Hiya, fellas, how about ridin' posse with me?' he asks; and before anybody could stop him our kidder had gone and told him all about the race with the aeroplanes. 'That's a great idea,' says Willy. 'Can Ah go and get my booler?'

'Sorry, kid, you haven't got the handicap,' says John McCann, and Willy goes white as white.

'Mebbe my handicap's better than you think!'

'Nick off, Willy, this is right out of your class,' said Bobbie Claxton.

'You nick off yourself!' says Willy, and Bobbie saw red.

'Go on, beat it!' he said. 'You little dull-alley.'

'Dull-alley?' said Willy. 'Mebbe you're the biggest dull-alley around here.' But he was too good a runner for Bobbie to catch. Then, just as luck would have it, a whole bunch of pitmen came clattering down the street – big coal-hewers, putters with leather back aprons and drivers cracking their whips – and they quickly scented fun. 'What's on, lads, eh? Off for a sprint? We're bettin' on little Willy!'

But one shouted, 'Fifteen to one against Claxton's big daft lads!'; and that was worst of all.

'Who'd take them clots on,' shouted Willy. 'Fancy – they're goin' to race aeroplanes in the sky with kids' boolers!'

'Never in the world, hinny,' said the men. 'They must be havin' you on!'

'Not a chance,' said Willy, who although little had a piercing voice. 'Ah might be a farmer's son but Ah'm not so green as Ah'm cabbage-lookin'!' At which the men roared – it was the way he said it, you see. Never had we been laughed at so hard – I'm not kidding, they were rolling about – and briefly the fate of the great aeroplane race hung in the balance. It was Claxton who saved the day. 'Come on, lads,' he cried, clicking the hook into his booler. 'We'll meet at the top of the hill!'

Then we were off – and at the first touch of my hook on the booler, I remembered the tinker: I just couldn't help it. It had started the evening before, when I was practising alone with my booler. A song drew my attention, a kind of Salvation Army chorus with a sort of bagpipe hum behind it. I just had to stop to look. At first there was only the noise. Then out of the sunset blaze stalked a shadow, the chanting grew louder and the tinker appeared. Naked to the waist he was, but masterfully he stepped forward, shouting as he went and beating his chest. 'Ah'm the best, the very best,' he shouted; while the woman, coming behind him with a pram, chorused: 'He is an' aall, y'know; the best in aall the world!'

Seeing me he held up his arm and the procession stopped dead. 'Now here's a noticing kind of youngster, the kind with eyes in his head Ah'll bet. Is there any work for a mechanic round here?' Yes, I told him. Farmer Hutchinson had a broken reaper which had defeated every effort to repair it. 'Then lead me to it, Squire,' he said. In short order I did as he instructed. And he got his job.

I was about to leave when he stopped me. 'Let's see that booler of yours, lad,' he said.

'But what for?' I asked, and he gave me a funny look. Carefully he viewed it both ways, vertically first and then laid flat in his hands. 'Well, you want to win, don't you!' he said, and I nodded dumbly. Did I want to win? – more than anything else in the world I wanted! Only so far I wasn't so good – just better than mediocre. Which stands to reason. I've seen your kid's wooden hoops and they've nothing on steel. It's boolers makes boys into men, but steel must answer steel. My fear was that I hadn't enough of the right stuff in me. 'You'll never win with this,' he said. 'It's far too little and it hasn't weight enough.'

'Can you put it right, Mister?' I asked.

'You leave it with me,' he said, and he wasn't boasting. And that night I couldn't sleep. Why man, I was up and out the minute I heard my father close the door to go to the pit. The tinker and his woman were having breakfast. His fire glowed. There were blue scales on the anvil. 'There it is,' he said, and I picked it up, hardly knowing what to expect. 'You try it,' said the tinker, with a funny little edge to his voice. I took it for a spin. Down the bridle to Haggs Wood and back again and it handled better than a blood hunter. The tinker knew how I felt. 'You race it, kid,' he said. 'One day, perhaps, you'll fly, but Ah'm tellin' ye, kidder, ye'll never ride anything better.'

Well, the minute we pulled up the bank I knew that the man was right. It was the feel of competition – that and the blacksmith's art. Not that I pulled out the stops – not at first. But Charlie noticed. 'What got into you, Chris?' he says. Practice, I told him, but all the same I see him shake his head.

Well, the next thing I see is Willy, sneaking up behind the hedge with his kid-sized booler hung over his shoulder. Bobbie saw him as well, I'll swear, but pretended not to notice. I reckon he'd had enough.

By then we were too busy anyway. We were getting our boolers ready. I'd nicked one of Ma's old dusters and Bobbie Claxton had the oilcan and in no time at all those boolers – rings of three-eighths iron, each standing about three feet six, with hooks to match – had been well and truly oiled. Black as the ace of spades and true as a bell they rang, and now we were all set for going.

Only there weren't any aeroplanes. Clouds rolled by and their shadows played tig on field and meadow but apart from the odd skylark there wasn't a wing in view. Then our kidder saw them, far up, like three tiny bright crosses. They were the three right enough and they came round in a tight circle like they were making back from where they'd come from, swooping down and travelling very quickly.

But nobody panicked. Down zoomed the planes, coming closer and closer, and the minute they arrived six boolers leapt forward. Have you ever heard the song of a booler? It's the loveliest in the world. The hook cups the metal as it spins. Both sing. It's a duet of tempered steel. And it makes your blood pump and your body sing along with it. So from the word go I really put my back into it. Not that I pulled out all the stops – not at first. I did just what the tinker told me and the booler did the rest. It was the funniest feeling. There we were, racing aeroplanes, and I was damn near flyin' myself! And all this was without trying! Our kidder and Small John were easy meat; I whipped past each of them the way a wasp makes to a picnic.

Then a coal-cart hove in view and although it broke my heart I dropped back and resumed my usual place when – in order to pass – we broke away in order of single file. The order was Claxton, Parker, McCann, our kidder and me with Willy bringing up the rear, but try as I would I still slipped past our kidder when the road was clear and Bobbie turned and noticed. And this was bad. In our village nobody sets up a race; Nature has seen to that and the minute we started them rolling the race was on for the simple reason that all of us were demons for winning. But a man's handicap was important and it was half the battle to sharpen it up in secret. Now my two main contenders were wised up on me my chances were literally halved.

At the same time Bobbie had his mind set on leading us in, and that helped somewhat. Somehow – perhaps they'd a headwind to contend against – we kept those planes in view, so close we could see their landing wheels, so near that we could almost hear the eldritch scream of their slipstreams. This was thanks mainly to Bobbie. Once, when they went behind clouds, Bobbie with his eyes aloft, was so intent on keeping up with them that he went right through Dick Elton's garden and popped out by the side-gate to rejoin us again. Nor was this the only miracle. You know how it is with boolers; the way they sing, I mean. Somehow it seemed to bring out the best in people. Like the old woman in a white bonnet who ran out and clicked open the gate for us at Todhills Crossing. 'Gan on, me canny lads; give them gyp!' she screamed as we shot through, Willy Watson taking half her pinny along with him.

From then on for six hundred yards there was plenty of room where there had once been big sidings, then the line narrowed down to double track with only a footpath on the side. This was my chance, and I took it. I was lying third with Bobbie way out in front, and pushing up between Charlie Parker. Charlie was my biggest trouble. There was the six of us with Charlie and me fighting it out. The stretch was level, if anything a little in favour, but he sprinted hard and was hard to beat, boring in or out, whichever was needed to stop me. I was in a winning mood on that stretch and if only I could have beat him quick not even Bobbie Claxton could have done anything against me. Three times I tried to pass Charlie and three times he altered course in time, sending my booler bouncing. That kid had eyes in the back of his head.

Anyway, although I beat him, he lost me my chance that time. What I did was to bool straight at Charlie's heels, and, by consistently doing this, I eventually made him skip to avoid me. Then I drove straight through. But by then we were on the straight and narrow. For two long miles it went like this, until we reached the pit, but I can guarantee you that I kept close on Bobbie's heels. All the way I kept pressing. Now that he knew there was no sense in letting up. The funny thing is that once, when he turned, I saw his face. It was all twisted and distorted for want of wind, and at first I gloried in it – until I felt something thump in me, crack and tear me half apart. After that I knew it was going to be something more than just a tussle.

We passed the pit, where all the coke-works were, and the rams kept going in and out to tumble down the white-hot wall of coke. I didn't look, but the sound of that ram went right through me. I was just about ready to drop, and I suppose the others felt just the same, when suddenly something happened. All along the battery men stood up and cheered, and the locomotive blew its whistle. Why I don't know. The wagons there were ten times bigger than us and when all's said and done we were only racing boolers. But it put new life in me.

What happened is soon told. I passed Bobbie halfway along the wide and now it was me in the lead with him chivvying hard behind. All I thought I had to do was hold him off until we were onto the narrow again, and this is how he got me. The track was narrow and perched on top of a high embankment, you see, but what he knew was that every now and again it was broken by diggings for coal; and the very first I met brought me a cropper. I was up and off again in a jiffy, of course, but by then Bobbie had skimmed round and was way out ahead. And that was the end of me.

But I'm not kidding, we kept up with those planes all the way – wing to wing they flew and we were down on the ground, but always they were full in view. It's true they drew away from us in the end – but only after the long pull up Mount Slowly, with just a mile to go. We could hardly believe our eyes. First they drew ahead. Then we could scarcely see them. Then they'd gone and we knew it was over.

Bobbie Claxton just about cried. 'Now you'll be satisfied,' he says to me. 'You an' your jiggery-pokery! They've gone and beat us!' And he pitched his booler, away down the battery side.

'So what if they did beat us?' asks Charlie Parker. 'Them and their wings and big engines. But we gave them a run for their money.' Well, everybody liked Charlie, but it just didn't wash, you know. Nobody in the world likes to be a loser. If I *was* ashamed, I was ashamed of losing. But what I was proud of was the way we'd stuck together – I was proud even of Willy, who turned up a long time later so done-in that his legs gave way beneath him when he reached us. Only he looked dazed and happy.

'Look what Ah've brought ye, Charlie,' he says at last, reaching down into his shirt. I thought at first it was a baby whippet, then I just didn't know what to think. Except that his eyes were too big for his head and his ears lay back like little wings, he could have been that kangaroo that Charlie drew in the morning. The minute he set eyes on the creature Charlie not only knew what it was but stood there, tipped halfway between tears and laughter. 'Why, it's a champion young runner you've caught yourself, Willy,' he says. 'It's a baby hare!'

On spotting the baby hare Willy had promptly rolled down on top of it and the nettles it was among – the first so far as I know ever to get the drop on a hare, and so far as I know it's still a record. Charlie drew it then tore out the page and gave it to Willy as a present. Then we walked back to where he was caught and let him go. Talk about greased lightning – that baby drew sparks from those nettles. Then we went to the Flying Circus.

Admittance being a tanner – and us not having the price for one between us – we couldn't go in. Not that it made any difference. From where we were it was easy to see the planes take off and watch them come down again; and pilots, tall in boots and knee-breeches, slide out of the cockpit for a stretch and a smoke. When one gave us a wave, Charlier Parker said he'd recognised us for sure; that he knew us from our boolers. 'You wait and see,' said Bobbie Claxton. 'One day Ah'll fly up like them and kill Jerries.' But nobody took much notice.

We all had our dreams that day. Small John McCann wanted to follow Bobbie, but sure enough the day came when he couldn't – the day the roof fell in. Everything turned out different. Our kidder carried stretchers the long war through and saw another side of machine guns; Charlie went into submarines; and only Willy Watson went flying. I went into the pit. With Small John and Bobbie Claxton, the depths kept Charlie. The rest of us keep going.

And I keep asking myself: Why was Charlie, who was so clever and could do everything, taken, while I was left behind? The others were good too. Bobbie was always the leader and Small John could charm the birds down from the trees. Well, you can guess what I'm good for – nothing. 'But look at all the pals you made,' said Willy when I once mentioned it to him. 'Count yourself lucky.' Well, I see his point. Mine is harder to explain. Somehow after the day of the great race everybody lost interest in boolers. All of a sudden we grew up and never went racing again. I never did push my way to the lead. So all right. I know I made second the day we raced the aeroplanes. But I wish I could have been first... just for once, in a lifetime, bring home the gold.

[1968]

First Breeched

In the days when I was young we had nothing to learn about economy – it came naturally. I was the oldest of five, and, although we never knew real want, it was in the nature of things – and of the time – that we were always wanting for something or other.

Like the time I went tatie-picking. After one day in the fields my own boots went blotto and I had to fall back on Dad's pit boots. That week those boots were never cold: as fast as Dad came in from night shift, I was waiting to step into them.

Those whacking great pit boots went with a clatter and made me feel important, but they didn't go with short pants. This I found out at the end of the week as I walked home swinging a full pail of taties and jingling the money in my pocket, the way I'd seen the men do it.

Some lasses were skipping at the end of our street. As I passed by they stopped their pitch-patch-pepper and the rope, and stared. Then they shouted 'Ya, lobster legs.' What with the load in my pail and the load on my feet, I was no match for them at running, and so they gave me 'lobster legs' all the way to our gate.

So when I'd brooded all through my tea – and had been questioned about it – I asked for long 'uns. I tried, but knew that I didn't stand a chance.

'Time enough for long 'uns,' said my mother. 'It's daftness wishing your days away.'

'We'll think about it some time,' said Dad.

'I'll put my tatie-picking pay,' I offered.

'Now, just let it settle,' said my mother.

Well, how they managed it I don't know and daren't think, but come Saturday afternoon I had a pair of flannels. I put them on, paraded the kitchen, sat down with a hitch to keep the knife-edge of the crease, and said goodbye, for ever and ever amen, to bony knees and lobster legs.

Ten feet tall and dizzy with dignity I stepped out and along to my Grandma's to show off. There she was, rocking away and reading Christian novels, chewing the rice she picked up from the table with a damp forefinger. 'Why man-alive, look at the lad,' she said. 'He's gone and got himself breeched, and as proud as a turkey with it.'

'Aye, he'll soon be runnin' for the buzzer,' said Grandad, and I, who could imagine nothing better than to carry a lamp into the pit, wondered why he should pity me.

He had nothing to say as we walked up the garden together. The roses were blown and sloppy, but the show leeks stood to attention and the chrysanths were all autumn pride. Then we went into the shed where he kept his birds – linnets, finches, budgies and canaries – and whilst I tried to whistle them into song, he sat down on a broken chair and filled his pipe.

He was always a very quiet man.

At last he drew on his pipe and said: 'Ah was a lot younger'n you when Ah was breeched.'

'Did you get a thrippenny diddler?' I asked.

He shook his head, 'Ah was workin' when Ah was breeched,' he said. 'Your Great-Grandad was killed in the pit and from then on Ah was the man of the house. There was nine, and Ah was their bread and butter.'

'Ah wasn't a lad long,' he said. 'Nobody was in them days. Packed a lot into my life. Fetched two families up – carried a lot of men out of the pit – followed a lot of funerals – aye, and ate a lot of christening cake.' His eyes twinkled and a smile twitched behind his moustache. 'Had a lot of fun, as well, between times.'

Suddenly all the birds began to sing.

'Birds and lads,' he said. 'Let 'em sing, Ah say.'

He dug into his pocket. 'Here's a shilling – put it in your pocket and give yourself a treat.'

– And when I tried to refuse: 'Nay, celebrate the day. You'll soon wear your trousers out. You'll soon wish you'd never been breeched. But Ah'll warrant you'll never forget this day as long as you live.'

I spent the shilling that night: two seats at the pictures and two bars of chocolate for me and bonniest of the skipping-rope lasses. The trousers lasted a year and a week: my last year at school and my first week at the pit. So, within a year and a week I was wishing I'd never been breeched. And Grandad was right about something else. I've never forgotten the day, or the silver he put in my pocket, or the gold he gave me to the very end.

[c. 1967]

When at the age of 14 Sid Chaplin was first breeched, he went to work not down pit but at Howard's Bakery in Ferryhill, shovelling flour and mixing dough. He got five shillings a week and a bonus every Friday night – a sixpenny egg custard tart. But after only a year the young baker was forced to quit – the dust caused a persistent form of dermatitis. He went to the local pit, Dean and Chapter, where he worked with the other lads on the screens, sorting out the coals. It was a hellish introduction to pit life:

It was a kind of purgatory. You descended into a kind of inferno, with railway tracks leading from all the shafts, and conveyors, and tipplers going all the time and clouds of dust everywhere. Noise, terrible noise, so much noise that you couldn't hear yourself speak. The kids who picked the stones from the coal on the screens developed a sign language. There was a sign for everything. If the pit manager was coming someone would appear on the gantry and indicate a fat belly and a moustache. You could practically hold a conversation in the sign language.

This period in Sid Chaplin's working life is described in A Letter from Pancake Tuesday *(page 213). Eventually the boy began to learn a trade – he became an apprentice blacksmith, making tools for the men, horseshoes for the ponies. He learnt his craft – and much besides – from a man called Alex Wylie.*

Sid Chaplin's first job at the pit, sorting coal on the screens: 'a kind of purgatory'.

Seven Years in a Smithy

On leaving school I was lucky enough, after a couple of false starts, to get a job as an apprentice blacksmith. This was after the customary spell as a picker on the colliery screens, clanking iron conveyors along which the coal was carried for inspection and cleaning. About 100 boys were employed on two shifts to do this job, which consisted of sorting out the stone from the coal. I hated it. How I hated it! Since the first shift started at five o'clock in the morning, we were half asleep to start with. Even in summer the morning cold, the dust, the noise, the wind and the rain, were hard to bear; but harder still was the fight against sleep. Discipline – in a world where jobs were more precious than gold – was hard as well. The only kick we got out of the job was to make the stones fly in a continuous stream like jugglers, and converse, even make jokes, in the traditional sign language.

The smithy was better. It was big and warm and cosy. There was much to learn – thirty years on I can still fill a page with names of tongs, sets and swages and other smithy gear. We lads formed a tight little group, sticking up for each other as well as weighing in when the double hammer was needed on a neighbouring anvil. Our perk was a strictly unofficial trade in pokers, coal rakes, kipper grids and boolers and hooks, for which the uniform rate was 20 Capstans. In this way we learnt our trade. But we were all eager to get to the other side of the anvil; not that many of us took permanently to the trade – smithing is a dying craft, as well as a difficult one to master.

And it had its drawbacks. You might spend half a shift sweating away on piece-work, then be called to the top of the pit-heap to splice a broken rope – and always in the worst weather. Or you might be called from a repair job on the screens to the dripping depths of the washery, where they really do wash coal to make it clean, or sent underground to a 20-inch coalface to squirm and wriggle to replace a bolt in a machine half-buried in coal. If it was tough it was never monotonous – and there were other compensations.

There was skill. Like the other lads I could keep up a tattoo with my quarter hammer till the iron grew cold and the anvil hot. I served my time with a wonderful old Scotsman called Alex, who grew to trust my skill. Alex would hold a cold chisel with his bare hands and never flinch when I swung. I can never remember missing.

I inherited that much from grandfather and great-grandfather, both of whom were craftsmen before me. My grandfather had strength as well as skill. He was a big man, where I'm only middling as they say. A few years ago I met an old miner who told me that my grandad was the only blacksmith who had ever managed to cut through a pit rope with three bats of the hammer. But he could do all the highly skilled jobs as well.

Well, I learned to make links, shackles, hooks with eyes, wheelbarrows, pony limbers, rope sockets and such-like; but I stopped short of being a real smith. I've spoilt a bit steel in my time.

Alex did his best – and that was a lot – for me. He was patience itself as he explained for the umpteenth time how to calculate the length of iron you'd need to form a flange, or collar, for a driving shaft; or how to use the more complicated tools of our trade. But I was slow to cotton on. "By guess or by God" was my rule; but he *really* knew. I was a better pupil at other things. Stories for instance, theorising, or talking between heats. I can close my eyes now and see his hunched shoulders and red, sweating face as he told me the tale of his life and kept watch on the hearth – with him, talk was never allowed to stop work. He'd tell me about his days as a shoeing smith in a racing stable, silver shoes for bloodstock; or the troubles when he started the union; or the Christmas Eve he'd spent in a pit-shaft, 700 feet below ground and another 200 feet vertical drop below the platform on which he was perched. That was the time he'd crouched against the side while icicles fell like spears, and when his chisel had been so cold it had burned his hand.

The talk, or crack, was best when we worked alone on the night-turn. We'd work at top speed to get the better of our work, then sit down to a leisurely breakfast. I remember how quiet it was when we stopped the fan that provided the draught for the smithy fire and the compressor that provided power for the big hammer. We'd munch bacon sandwiches toasted on the anvil with a red-hot bar of steel – and that was food!

And we'd talk and talk. About people, politics, religion, and books, but mostly about people. Out of the seven years with Alex came two great gifts.

The first was an enduring respect for craftsmen and craftsmanship. I knew in my bones that I'd never be as good a craftsman as Alex or my grandfather, or as my father in quite another trade. I wanted to become a maker, and I was determined to search all my life, if needs be, to find something my own mind, or hand or eye, could shape.

The second gift grew out of my great admiration for Alex as a man. In the beginning I was always on edge to get *my* word in. Then I began to notice how much he knew. He didn't know everything, but he had a wide knowledge of three or four subjects – and he knew how to pass it on. He was something more than a great reader; he read, then he built on what he'd read. As we say in Durham, he knew his book. He could also "read" people; his memory teemed with observations and stories about men and women he'd met.

He was a very proud man. Although he'd been unemployed a long time, and although everybody else went in mortal fear of the sack, Alex was afraid of no man, nor of any gaffer, from the foreman to the colliery manager. He wouldn't be pushed. He spoke his mind. He demanded – and won – good manners. And that was quite an achievement in a rough pit and in rough times. Of course, he'd had a lifetime's practice. He'd followed his father as gardener on a great country estate. One day his master gave him an order. It was wrong, Alex respectfully told him, and got a minute's notice. That was his beginning. He was his own man to the end.

His big idea was that ordinary people had value. Never mind the history of Kings and Queens, he used to say. Look at the pit people. They have something special. They are the real aristocrats. This was news to me, so I started looking at the people I met, I mean really looking, and I found he was right. They were special in all sorts of ways. They had special skills, special words, special ways. They even had a special kind of humour. It was Alex who first told me that this brand of humour came right down from the Scandinavian invaders, and had been kept alive by the nature of the work. Just as the Norse invaders had braved the sea, the miner braved the hard rock, the darkness, immense weights and hazards of fire and flood. All the books I'd read had gentlemen as heroes, like Peter Simple,

David Balfour or Richard Hannay. I used to wish that I also could be a gentleman and a hero. Alex taught me that ordinary people could be both.

But it goes deeper than that. We all have something special. It belongs to our make-up, background and where we happen to be living. We have this – and at the same time, have something richer: the thoughts and feelings we share with all mankind.

Becoming a writer for me was discovering all this. First, there was my "something special". There was the countryside in which I lived. From boyhood I'd loved the long winding valley, with the Pennine moors hazy and half-seen in the distance. It was part of me. The microcosmos of the village, the fields and the farm, the river and the woods, provided new wonders every day. When the sun shone there was open country to run wild in. The high kestrel hung motionless, suspended in the blue like something hung there for decoration, till one noticed the blur of the beating wings – and the sudden swoop. The hare flashed through the meadow, passing the slow shrew, or mole, or field-mouse. Peewits wove invisible patterns over ploughed field and broke the silence with their melancholy note. It was Alex who made all this connect up with people.

People – my kind of people – had made the fields and planted the hedges. People had built the villages and sunk the pits. I was there because of the work that went on hundreds of feet below ground. I knew the landscape in daylight. What did it mean to become part of that other world, far below the soil?

There was only one way to find out. I left the blacksmith's shop and became a miner. Every day I dropped in the cage, or lift, a distance of nearly 900 feet, into a world which is carved out of the rock by men, where you are lost without a lamp. Work was at the end of a tunnel two long miles from daylight. Work was a seam of coal, a battlefront in which we fought lying on our backs, sides or bellies, whichever was the most convenient. It was a crack in the strata about 100 yards long, and our job was to work the machine like a ripsaw that under-cut the coal, drill holes for explosives to blast it down, then fill it on to an endless conveyor belt. At the same time we had to keep that little crack in the earth supported by props and planks, keep up the air flow which diluted and carried away the deadly gas and see to the cables, pipes, and other supplies.

Sometimes the movement of the strata shattered the supports or props, and tons and tons of rock came tumbling down.

Sometimes machines broke down and had to be moved and replaced by main force. Even when all went well the work was hard. There was slogging with the pick and shovel, lifting and heaving of heavy weights and a continual tug of war with time – whatever happened, the coal must be won. There were battles between men as well. As the dust worked in, the irritation worked out. A man was expected to do his share. There was no room for slackers. But you got something in return. You became a member of one of the oldest fighting regiments out of sight as well as under the sun. You had marrers – that's an old English word for a friend who is matchless. And you could depend on your friends at the coalface. Your marrer was with you. He would never leave you in the lurch. He would risk his life to get you out of danger. You would do the same for him. It was as simple as that.

Of course, the great things of this way of life, fellowship, endurance, courage and sacrifice, were grounded in necessity. We stuck together because we had to. The work itself was part of my "something special". But the loyalties and virtues we made in the darkness were grounded not in "something special" but in something which belongs to all men everywhere. They are my "something shared". You may have never seen a colliery, or worked at the coalface, but you can recognise the qualities they bring out in men. What counts is what you share in the inner life of the boy from the Bronx and the boy from Byker. You might even find a link between yourself and the boy of long ago, in the blacksmith's shop. Perhaps you are searching.

My search was for craftsmanship, and the first clue came from Alex the blacksmith when he told me that ordinary people had value. This formed a pattern, a kind of story, which brought together my kind of people and my kind of countryside. They were special. It was only slowly that I discovered that despite their differences they were part of a greater story, or pattern; the story and pattern of all living things who love and hate, who know joy and despair, who are capable of cruelty, courage and compassion.

Looking at people I discovered that there were no black and whites, no goodies and baddies, but human beings, and each was a world in himself; each was a story. Miners are great storytellers; down in the pit I've heard wonderful stories which I can never hope to tell as well on the printed page. Listening, I not only found stories, but found ways of telling them. Alex gave me good advice when he told me 'Always read what you've written. Read it aloud – and listen.' So I listen, and what I listen for is anything that is not true to the story, or true to the place and the people. And, since part of my own being must go into the story, I also listen to myself. It is hard to listen to yourself and truly report what you feel. Only a very good listener could have written the Saroyan story about a boy growing up; the pain, the funniness of it, the sadness and the wonder. That is why I can say 'This happened to me'. You may be able to see that some of the story is happening to you. It may help or it may not. That does not matter. What matters is being part of it, being able to share it. It is not telling alone, but the ability to bring about sharing which is the test of a writer – and the joy of a reader.

Many years after my days in the blacksmith's shop I made a story. It gave back to the place, and the people who had made me, something I had managed to make. I found myself using words the way my old friend Alex used his hammer. The story grew like the shape in the iron. It was like coming home. I wrote the story for Alex; and it was too late. But if it was worked, finished and tempered as he had taught me, it would bring him alive for others as he was for me, in the days when the great search began.

[BBC Schools, 1965]

To a Pit Pony

O blackbrowed beetling pony standing there,
In darkness standing, gulping in the air;
You are not more cold in heart than we,
For the green earth in shadowy dreams you see.

Those eyes, inured to night, have seen
Sparkling rivers, clouds, fields were green.
So in the dark you snuffle, kick the dust,
And stretch your weary head to take my crust –
Crunch steadily, while tremors rippling run,
Induc'd by visions of a half-remembered sun.

[1941]

As Sid Chaplin grew into maturity, the social structure of the Durham coalfield was under assault, not just from economic forces, but also from the insidious influence of the mass media. Over the next 30 years, this process was to accelerate and the distinctive way of life of the people began to wither and die. One small instance: who today knows anything of "laying out"? This was the process by which the loved one was prepared to meet his or her Maker, not by the undertaker, but by a relative or close friend. The body would be laid on a board and trestles in the best bedroom or parlour; dressed in white stockings and a fine white night-shirt, or night-dress, the eyes closed and covered with pennies and the jaw tied with ribbon to prevent the mouth opening; the body would lie on the best linen sheet (with another on top), the head on a thin pillow; and finally a napkin would be placed over the head, a corner over each ear. Naturally, the body would also be washed, and, if necessary, a final shave administered.

Half a Shave describes this loving ritual, not in a morbid way, but with a touch of innocent, affectionate humour; it's a typical example of how Sid Chaplin's work is peppered with nuggets of social history.

The young man, already bookish – and bald.

Half a Shave

My father sucked at his empty pipe with all his might. Then he laid it aside while he cut himself another pipeful from the dead-black bar in his tin. Then he smiled. 'That reminds me of old Ben Mallows, just before he died,' he said. 'I can see him now, a great hulk of a man sitting up in his bed, with his striped nightgown and tasselled nightcap, sucking away at his empty pipe...'

Ben was bed-fast for a couple of years; with one foot in the grave all the time. During that two years there were two or three false alarms; but he always managed to pull through. And practically to the end he stuck to his daily programme. He'd waken at eight, pull a shawl around his shoulders and yell out for his breakfast. Then Annie and Lizzie, his two girls would come running. It didn't matter how quickly they came Ben would still grumble. It was a matter of principle to him. He believed that a man had to be constantly grumbling to keep women up to scratch. Anyway, he kept his women up to scratch; they never argued back.

After breakfast Maria would put the kettle on for his shaving water and Annie would knock on the wall for Pa. For Ben insisted on his shave every morning. He was very particular about it; and to his mind nobody but Pa could shave him to his fancy. But he was a hard chap to shave. Always talking and shifting his head about. He had a big Adam's apple and it was fascinating to watch it jumping about as he talked; but it didn't make Pa's job an easy one. In spite of him taking a great deal of care Ben was always bleeding like a stuck pig after the job was completed. But Ben never complained. Pa could do no wrong in his eyes.

And he insisted on his daily shave until a couple of days before he died. You see, he was unconscious during the last two days.

The morning after he died Pa was sitting at breakfast when there came a tapping at the wall. Ma was in the shop but she

93

heard the tapping and came into the kitchen. 'Wasn't that Annie knocking?' she asked.

Now I fancy it had given Pa a bit of a turn. He said, 'I know. I heard it. But they can't be knocking for me. Perhaps they're hanging some crêpe up. Or perhaps one of them was pulling some coals down from the fireback.'

'It wasn't the fireback where the knocking came from,' said Ma. 'It was on the wall!' And to support her argument the tapping came again, a little louder this time, and it was definitely on the wall. 'There!' said Ma. 'It *was* you they were knocking for!' Then she said, 'Why, what's the matter Joe, lad. You're as white as a sheet!'

'Just feeling a bit off-colour,' said Pa. 'Wonder what they can be wanting me for?'

'Not his usual shave, anyway!' said Ma.

So Pa went in. And believe it or not, the first thing his eye lit on was the John Bull shaving pot. And beside it, neatly laid out as usual, the shaving-soap and brush and razor. And the old kettle on the fire, busily getting steam up.

It suddenly dawned upon him what was required, and he had to sit down without being asked. Maria was busy writing funeral cards. 'Good morning, Mr Castle,' she said without looking up. 'The kettle's boiling.'

'That's plain to see,' said Pa. 'But why tell *me*?'

'Ah'll pour it out in a minute,' she said, ignoring the question. 'How d'ye spell "interment"?'

Needless to say, Pa was a little relieved at this. 'I.n.t.e.r.-m.e.n.t,' he spelt. 'Is that why you knocked for me?'

'No,' she said. 'No, of course not. It's to shave father. It's all in the will. Annie'll tell you all about it. Annie!' she called. 'Annie! Here's Mr Castle.'

Annie came in from the other room. Her eyes filled when she saw it was Pa. 'He always thought the world of ye, Mr Castle,' she sobbed. 'That's why he put it into the will.' After five minutes she dried up, you know what women are, and Pa asked her what it was all about. And the long and short of it was that Ben had put it in his will that Pa was to shave him before he was coffined, so that he'd be all neat and spruce before his relations came to have a last look at him. And in return for this Maria and Annie were instructed to buy Pa a decent black suit for the funeral. A ready-made, of course. He also left Pa his shaving-tackle and his cups and medals. But

Pa was too stunned about the task to be delighted at getting these treasures.

'You won't mind shaving poor father for the last time?' said Annie.

'But I've never shaved a dead man before,' he protested. But all the same, he was sorely tempted. He needed a new suit badly, and after all, suit or no suit, Ben had been a good pal.

'It's never too late to learn, Mr Castle,' said Annie severely. And added, 'It says in the will that if you don't shave him we've to get someone else. And whoever shaves him gets the suit.'

That decided Pa. 'What! Let some stranger shave my old friend for the last time! Not likely! Pour me some hot water into that pot!' But all the same, he was feeling a bit shaky when he went into the sitting-room where Ben was laid out. He was lying in the old bed, just as Pa had seen him many a time. His hands were crossed over his chest and his face was a beautiful ivory colour.

'Beautiful, isn't he?' said Annie softly. 'But he does look a bit rough!' And indeed he did. The bristles seemed an inch long; a regular forest of them. Maria tucked a towel under his chin, had a long look at him then burst into tears. Pa waited until Annie had taken her out of the room, then he ranged all his tackle on the little table, which stood beside the bed. Then he sat on the bedside to make a start. But the moment he sat down he decided it wasn't decent to do so, so he stood up again. He bent over the still face and started to lather it but his hand shook so much that he had to stop. He put the brush on the table and went back to the kitchen.

'You don't happen to have a drop of brandy?' he asked.

'Get the bottle down Maria, the one that's broken into,' said Annie. 'Ah was wondering how long it would take him to think about that!' She said in a sharp, sarcastic kind of voice. Pa was a bit put out but he said nothing. It was just the kind of remark you could expect from Annie. She'd knuckled into old Ben all her life, but now that he was cold in death she was soon showing who had stepped into his shoes. But Pa was in need of something bracing, so he only said thanks for the first glass and shot it down his throat quickly before Maria had time to put the bottle away again. He needed as much as he could get of that brandy.

He went back in fine fettle and put a lovely lather on old Ben, then started to shave him. He didn't feel at all frightened. By the time he'd shaved one side and was starting on the chin he was having a one-sided conversation with Ben. 'Aha, ye old champion!' he said gaily. 'You can't jigger your head about this morning, same as you used to do. No talking back today, old pal! You won't bleed this time!' And so on. I can just imagine Pa, his eyes shining as they always did after a glass, joking and jesting with the poor dumb corpse.

'Aye,' he continued. 'This is the last shave, me old shaver, and no answering back –' That was when Pa stopped short. For old Ben moved, or at least, his arms did. They fell apart from his chest. Pa didn't wait for any further motion; he just yelled and ran for his life. Maria and Annie gave a good display of screaming when he ran into the kitchen with the shining razor in his hand and a wild look on his face. I fancy they jumped to the wrong conclusion, because they ran for the door too, and the three of them were jammed together there.

Well, it was a proper mix-up until Pa managed to convince them that he didn't intend to cut their throats. Then they asked him what was really the matter. Before he answered he wiped the sweat of fear from his brow.

'You won't believe me,' he said, 'But he moved; as sure as I'm sitting here, he moved! And it wouldn't surprise me to see him walk through that door!' The two girls registered disbelief; but for all that they watched the sitting-room door pretty closely. But there was no sound of life in the sitting-room. Annie soon grasped the situation.

'Mr Castle,' she said. 'Ye've had too much brandy!'

Pa was justly offended at this. 'Let me tell you this, Annie Mallows; me and your father's many a time supped half a bottle of brandy and ten pints between us and walked home steady and sure, both of us, afterwards. And I'll not have you tell me that two thimblefuls of brandy can turn *my* head!'

'Fiddlesticks!' said Annie. 'Ah thought at the time that it was a trifle early to be drinking brandy. We'll soon see if he's alive again!' And with that she marched into the sitting-room with a look on her face that said plainly he'd better not be.

And, of course, he *was* safely dead. His arms had moved; but Annie soon put that detail right. Then she ordered Pa to go back and finish his job. But Pa's mind was made up; he flatly refused. He was determined not to go back into that room at any price – even the price of a new suit.

'Very well,' said Annie, 'Have it your own way. But you've only shaved one side and part of his chin. So you don't get the suit, that's flat!'

'But that's not fair!' protested Pa.

'The will says that you've got to give him his usual shave,' said Annie firmly. You could see that she was thinking of saving the expense of the suit.

'He just wanted to look his best when he was laid-out, poor man,' said Maria. That gave Pa an idea.

'Listen, lasses,' he pleaded. 'Let's keep our heads. Fair's fair, the world over! All that we need do is to change the bed round so that the side that isn't shaved is in the shade. And nobody'll ever notice.'

'And let my father go into eternity with half a shave! Never!' shrieked Annie.

'Now Annie, the Lord doesn't take any notice of little details like that,' he said piously. But it was no use arguing. Her mind was made up. And so was Pa's. He was determined never to enter that room again. He realised Ben was truly dead, of course; and he knew that if Ben did come back from the dead he'd be the last to harm his best pal. But there are some things which can't be stomached, and half a shave was enough to convince Pa that as a shaver of corpses he was just no good.

The end of it was that the undertaker shaved the rest; so Ben was able to make a clean-shaven exit after all. Coming back from the funeral Pa told the Minister all about the will and the shaving. And after the Minister had finished laughing he promised to have a word with Annie. It says a great deal for the persuasive manner of the Reverend William Macpherson that Annie finally compromised. Compromised, I said. For Pa never got the suit. Only the trousers. But it was always something. And as Pa said afterwards, when you're working behind a counter nobody can see that you're wearing an odd pair of trousers.

[1946]

97

*During the mid-1930s, Sid Chaplin began to pursue a literary edu-
cation. Much of it was self-administered, but first of all he needed
the necessary direction and encouragement and, of course, copies of
the books themselves. All of these commodities he was given by the
Workers Educational Association and by the Spennymoor Settlement,
a kind of artistic institute run for the benefit of the local people by
Bill and Betty Farrell and Jack Maddison. Here he discovered poetry;
he read Browning, but preferred Walt Whitman. Sometimes, however, inspiration came from an unlikely source:*

I remember, after one meeting, saying to a fellow called Enoch
Goynes, who was an engine driver down pit: 'Boy, have you
read *The Everlasting Mercy*? Absolutely marvellous.' Masefield
you know. 'Tha come down to our house,' he said, 'and Ah'll
give tha a book that knocks Masefield into a cocked hat.' He
took me to his house, and he gave me a paper-covered first
edition of a D.H. Lawrence, *The Widowing of Mrs Holroyd*. I
can remember setting off at about six o'clock and stopping at
a street called Cobbler's Hall, and dying to look at this book,
you know. I just sat down and read it, there on the dyke side.
I'd never come across anything like this before. I knew about
Cronin and had read *The Stars Look Down* in the *Daily Herald*.
But all that paled into insignificance. It was a major event in
my life.

*But as well as literature, the young blacksmith was also deeply
interested in politics and religion. He became an activist in his union
– the Colliery Mechanics – and later an official. Once, he threatened
to bring out his men on an issue which he felt was important to their
dignity – dirty cutlery in the pit canteen.*

*He also became a Methodist lay preacher, first at Dean Bank in
Ferryhill and then at Kirk Merrington. It was there – in the pulpit
– that Rene Rutherford first clapped eyes on him, late in 1938. Her
first opinion of him was that he was a rather cocksure fellow, who
needed cutting down a peg or two. This she achieved the following
Whit Monday, when they both went on a chapel picnic along the
Wear by Croxdale. He tried to kiss her; she slapped his face. They
were married seven months later, on New Year's Day, 1941.*

*Sid Chaplin remained a lay preacher for another ten years or so:
he was, by all accounts, rather a good one.*

In Blackberry Time

Tom Greenaway was burning stubble in the Top Five Acre when he noticed the girl working slowly along the far hedge, the sun flashing on her milk-can. Some child, he concluded, who must have slipped unnoticed through the farmyard, since his mother never allowed brambling. He decided to deal with the girl when his work was done.

Soon the red line of leaping flames was advancing into the golden stubble the full length of the field, crackling fiercely and leaving a brittle black desolation in its trail. In front, though, the stubble was alive with panic-stricken life. As well as field mice scurrying hither and thither and often climbing over each other in their efforts to escape, there was the odd shrew or two. With their reddish-brown pelts and pointed little snouts they looked for all the world like blind little elephants of the stubble. Being a kindly lad, he picked up as many as he could with the intention of releasing them in the hedge, and soon his poacher's pocket was alive and kicking with the little creatures.

The intruder was still methodically brambling, taking not the slightest notice of him. Angrily he whistled and threw out his arm in a commanding gesture. The child, turning, cheekily waved back at him. Such cheek! He strode angrily over the field toward her, the stubble crackling underfoot, a covey of partridges clapping up, two hares bounding in wide opposing circles. He'd show her!

But it was he who was given the first surprise. That she was no child was stunningly obvious as he came up behind her, stretching to reach one of the topmost branches. He quickly collected himself. 'Now, Missus, what d'ye think you're up to here!' he demanded, unnecessarily loudly. Taking her time she plucked every berry. The branch snapped back with a vibrant flutter, like a young partridge learning to fly. Then only did she turn.

'Why, I'm gathering blackberries, Mister Cleversides,' said

she.

'Now less o' that!' frowned Tom, but finding it difficult to stay severe, she was such a pretty little thing, dark with snapping black eyes and lips redder than the red of her vivid skirt, and soft and kissable.

'Less of the what?' she asked with deceptive sweetness.

'Less lip, my lass!' he remonstrated, having noticed the absence of a wedding ring.

'We – ell!' she said, 'I must say, you're the first young man ever to tell me that...' Tom had the grace to blush.

'You're trespassing,' he said gruffly. 'It's the biggest wonder in the world how you ever got past my mother.'

'Oh, I didn't,' said she. 'She turned me back, but I sneaked round another way.'

'You've certainly got a cheek!' said Tom. She looked him critically up and down. 'So that was your mother? Well, I must say, you're better-favoured. You're almost good-looking – *and* kind. I saw you picking up those mice.' Pleased with the compliment he was appalled by her frankness and nettled at the reference to his mother. She needed bringing down a peg or two, he thought.

'They're for the farm cats to play with,' he said mendaciously. 'Nothing's wasted on a farm.' Giving her a stern look. 'Now are you going, or must I lead you away?'

'You'll have to carry me!' she said defiantly.

'We'll see about that!' he laughed. Pulling out a tangled mass of grey and reddish-brown pelts and tails he placed them at her feet. Instead of screaming she bent down and scooped up a protesting shrew. It ran over her wrist and sat in the crook of her elbow. The girl sat stock-still. The shrew twitched his whiskers and after a precarious descent down the red skirt scurried away into the hedge. Tom was amazed. 'You're a rare 'un,' he said. 'Most girls would have run a mile at the sight of all those mice – and you let one walk all over you! Weren't you scared?'

'Of course not,' she said. 'I've helped the Professor with his flea circus and the performing mice. They're quite harmless.'

'Well I never!' said Tom. 'That explains it. You're here with the show-folk!'

The girl flushed dangerously. 'And what's wrong with show-folk, may I ask?' she challenged.

'Only one fault,' said Tom quietly. 'They move on much too quickly.'

'Ah! Then I can stay and fill my can?'

'You can follow me,' he said masterfully. 'I'll show you where there's real blackberries for the picking – in the Fox Covert – that's the place.'

The covert was three fields, two gates and one stile away, only the nether step of the latter was almost engulfed by a thick invading growth of nettle. 'Ups-a-daisy!' said he, and without as much as a by-your-leave lifted the girl bodily through the air. 'You know, if this were my land, I'd have those nettles cut down sharp enough,' said she. 'Is it yours or must you do as you're told?' she asked outright.

'I work it for my mother,' he said, a shade defiantly, and it struck her that he was younger than his years and had been "kept back, knulled-down" as they say. But well-made and open-faced, a big handsome lad who only needed a guiding hand. She sighed. What a pity show-folk were always moving on. They walked uphill, over humps and through hollows and at last came to the brow. Here they washed their hands at a spring. The Fox Covert was a tumbling strip of land that fell gently, then steeply, to the river far below. There were regular leaning hawthorn trees heavy with scarlet haws and a great green cascade of furze, or gorse, some of it still in flower. But there were no blackberries. 'It doesn't look very promising,' she said doubtfully.

Then she gasped with excitement as he went down on one knee and pulled up one thick tendril of many threaded through the grass and laden with large purple berries, each one crafts-man-made, it seemed. Everywhere you looked the network of tendrils ran and each tendril was thick with fruit nurtured in the hothouse provided by the long grass. Soon the thrill of the chase had both in its pull. Oblivious of damp grass or thorns or the thin lines of migrating spiders that spun out in the breeze they picked and picked, often picking toward each other until their hands brushed or snatched or fought. True, they were too busy for talk, but their eyes conversed – and once, very briefly, their faces touched. Then they laughed and moved apart and started picking again; and again they met.

It seemed a shame when the can was full. They rested on a fallen tree. 'Such beauties – such a pity to pick them. They're almost jewels,' she said.

'Father used to brag about 'em,' said Tom. 'He used to say you could roll one home and there'd be enough for a pie and a pudding in it.'

'Your father used to say?' she asked. He nodded. 'Aye. He went. He went too soon. It was a happy farm with my father.'

'That's strange,' she said. 'You lost a father. It was a mother with me. Who'd have thought when we met that we had so much in common. We're both in the same boat, in a way.'

They sat in silence for a while. A shadow spread across his face. 'Well, not exactly in the same boat!' he burst out at last. 'Here am I, tied down to the land, ploughing, over with the harrow, buying cattle in, haytime, reaping corn, tatie-picking, turnip-snagging...'

'And burning the stubble and keeping the bramblers out!' said she with a smile.

'The same thing, year in, year out. And I'm sick and tired. Now at least you're on the move all the time. New places, new faces, always on the road.'

'What I'd like is a country cottage,' she said with dreaming eyes. 'There'd be some hens and a vegetable garden. And a lovely kitchen of my own with a Welsh dresser where the dishes stand all in a line. And really getting to know people in a place, instead of living in a caravan behind the Giant Bingo stall...'

'You mean you'd like to live on a farm!' he cried incredulously.

Her eyes had stopped dreaming. 'In any settled place. Only it would never do for Dad – he's a showman to the core.'

'And I'd give anything to get out of it,' he groaned. 'Anything!'

'Well, we are a pair and no mistake, aren't we?' said she very briskly.

She was rubbing her hand. 'Are you any good at getting thorns out?'

'Where?' asked he, bending over. She pointed out the place. He took her hand to his mouth. 'There,' he said, 'That's done it.' Their eyes, their lips, were swimming near. 'Well, I've kissed your hand...' he said, and kissed her full on the lips. He drew back with a puzzled frown. 'Well, I'll be damned!' he said. He kissed her again. 'I'll be jiggered!'

'And I'm going home,' she said.

'B-B-But I've got something to tell you,' he stammered. 'I'm in love. I'm in love with you.'

'And I've a blackberry tart to bake for Dad,' she said. 'While you've a mother to look after.' Then she ran away.

Tom ran after her. 'But don't you understand? There's the hind's cottage standing empty. It has a vegetable garden and a linden tree and there's room for hens. And you shall have a Welsh dresser as my wedding present.'

'Ah, you make it all sound so simple – but then you're such a simple lad,' she said. Her voice was half-sorrowful, half-loving. 'I told you we were in the same boat, but I put it wrongly. We're in different boats, drifting different ways. And it cannot be mended.'

'I think it can,' he said, man-like. 'We can try.'

'Ah, lad,' she said. 'You may walk roughshod over your nettles, but not your own. Aren't they all we have?' Indeed she was so determined that his heart almost failed him. Still, that night when the milking was done, he washed and shaved and put his best suit on.

'Where are you going?' asked his mother.

'D'ye know the brambler you turned back today?' She nodded. 'Well, I'm going off courting her. D'ye mind?'

'Are you determined to have her?'

'Yes. Yes, I am.'

'Can she cook and bake?'

'She can bake a bramble tart.'

'That's something to start with. What else?' asked Mrs Greenaway, and he knew what she meant.

'She refused me out of loyalty to her father, he's a widower,' he explained. He grinned. 'So I suppose I'm courting the two.'

'Good enough, lad,' she said, her needles busy again. She also was a woman that knew her mind.

So to the shows he went, he went two nights running, playing bingo with a little plastic board and hardly ever bothering to watch the numbers flash on the electric panel. Tom was too busy looking at her. Despite this carelessness he won a tea-service on the second night. Distant and cold she handed the parcel over to him. Shyly he pushed it back. 'You keep it, Polly,' he said. 'It'll do for your bottom drawer.' Colouring, she turned her back on the boy and his present. 'Never mind, Polly. I'll keep it by,' he called after her.

In the end it was her father, Billy Larkin, who invited Tom down for tea on the Sunday. Billy was a friendly man, and observant too. Polly, indignant at first, gradually simmered down. There was a lovely spread. There were thin slices of brown bread nicely buttered, hot scones with strawberry jam for those who wanted it, home-baked ginger-bread, fairy cakes and a beautiful bramble tart. Then the two men settled down for a smoke while Polly washed up the dishes in the little kitchenette.

'Marvellous, I envy you the life,' said Tom, looking appreciatively at the caravan's interior – everything found, including television, fridge and cooker, wardrobes, cupboards and drawers, and seats that transformed into beds in a twinkling, not to mention the canary in the handsome gilded cage.

'You try forty years of it,' said Billy Larkin, with feeling. 'Too much racket and too many faces – never a resting place. Sometimes . . .' With the pause his eyes were dreaming. 'Sometimes wish I could settle down, in a nice little cottage, with a hen-run and a vegetable garden and an orchard with apple trees. I've the money to do it.' Leaning forward confidentially he whispered. 'But it's Polly, you know. She'd never settle, never!'

Tom looked up and nodded at Polly, then turned to the father once more. 'Depends where the cottage happens to be,' he said. 'I've got a cottage that's going for a song – and she loves it – a case of love at first sight. I think she'd try it if you asked her; in fact I'm sure she would.'

'Would she now?' asked Polly's father, and something in Tom's expression made him turn. 'Well, I'll be blowed. I'll be jiggered!' he said.

So that was settled. The two walked back to the farm, taking the longer road. Such was their trepidation. But Tom's mother simply asked: 'Can your Dad mend tractors?'. That was after she'd cried, of course.

Soon all was planned. The retirement and the wedding will take place at the back-end, in blackberry time. There will be a knife and fork repast. There will naturally be a wedding cake. But bramble pie will also be available. The bride insists.

[1965]

Just married: Sid and Rene Chaplin in the backyard of their home in Gladstone Terrace, Ferryhill, July 1941.

The Bed

The Reverend William Macpherson regretfully put aside his unfinished sermon. It was on his favourite theme of the sheep and the goats, and he had been working it up to a grand climax when Ranter had been shown in by his housekeeper. 'Sit in front of the fire and get yourself warmed through a little,' he said to his visitor. Ranter gingerly worked himself into the easy-chair. He was a big man with a red face and stubbly jowls. His overcoat was obviously a gift and was too short for him. He had lost something of his usual confidence. And no wonder! thought the Reverend. In the camp of the enemy. Aloud the Reverend said, 'Now . . . I'll be with ye in a minute.' Ranter nodded dumbly and warmed his big paws at the fire, an excuse to hide his face from the Minister.

'There . . .' said the Reverend at last. 'I'll know where to start from, now . . . What was it you wanted to see me about, Mr Ranter?' His sermon, his theology laid aside, it never occurred to him that Ranter was one of the goats – 'Then the Lord, shining in His Glory will take his crook and separate the sheep from the goats' he had written – was, indeed, a man of evil repute. And worse. Ranter didn't like parsons of any kind; didn't agree with the church; was a confirmed boozer and blasphemer. There were strange stories about the man. He'd worked on the railway at one time. Until one morning, walking along the track he'd found the decapitated body of Lowrie, a local tradesman who'd taken the short way out of bankruptcy. The head had bounced like some overripe pippin, some several yards further along the line. Ranter picked up the head by the hair and walked into the cabin where his mates had already started their midday snack. He held up his trophy. 'Any of ye chaps ken this lad?' he had asked. This somewhat thoughtless action had caused no little dismay. Two strong men had fainted; the rest were violently sick. The foreman reported the matter to the District Office and Ranter got the sack. Since then he had served as odd-job man for several local farmers during his sober periods. Ranter didn't believe in the conventional long weekend booze. He would work for several weeks without touching the beer; then devote a week to it. He liked long arguments and he liked to win them; and he wasn't above winning one with his fists.

But the Reverend had no thought of these matters as he waited for Ranter to speak. Long ago he had considered Ranter and found one thing to his credit. He lived in his own cottage on the crest of Half-Mile Hill, just outside Gomorrah. The Reverend had a healthy respect for thrift. Ranter wasn't married. A Mrs Corrie kept house for him. She'd been his housekeeper for many years. And she never had any complaint to make of Ranter. The Reverend had visited the cottage several times, and it was always as neat as a pin, clean and comfortable, with the fire glowing and the irons shining. And Mrs Corrie was a big cheerful woman who attended chapel. In the Reverend's opinion Mrs Corrie was a testimony to something good in Ranter's character...

'It's like this,' said Ranter. 'A man doesn't live forever –'

'True,' agreed the Reverend.

'– And when a man feels he's gettin' on – it's time he was making preparations.' continued Ranter.

'Quite so,' nodded the Reverend.

'Saw Doctor Graham last night. Told me there was something wrong with me old ticker. Won't take me much further.'

'I'm sorry to hear that,' said the Reverend.

'So Ah thought Ah'd make a will. There's the house and a few sticks of furniture. And a bit money in the bank; not much, mind ye.'

'Very sensible,' said the Reverend.

'Aye, but trouble is that Ah don't know how to start writin' a will out. And Ah thought perhaps ye'd help me.'

'I'd be honoured,' said the Reverend gravely. Ranter struggled with his gratitude, which found expression at last in an expressive grunt. 'Ye would? That's a load off me mind. Y'see, Jean – that's Mrs Corrie – she's been wi' me nearly twenty year. And Ah'd like to leave everything to her.'

The Reverend took a will-form out of his drawer. He always had a few handy for it was a job that often came his way. 'First of all,' he said, 'we'd better make a list of all the separate items. You're sure ye want to leave everything to Mrs Corrie?'

'That's right. Ah've no kith or kin.'

'Well, then, first of all, the money.'

'There's ninety pund in the bank.'

'Right. Then we'd better make an inventory of all that's in the house.'

'A what?'

'That's a list. We'd better start with the kitchen.'

'There's three chairs . . . a sideboard . . . and a deal table. Then there's her bed. It's one of them cupboard beds; the kind that folds up durin' the day.'

'What about upstairs?'

'One room's damp an' draughty; so we've nowt in it. There's a wardrobe, a chest of drawers, a kist and some chairs in t'other.'

'There'll be your bed, surely.'

'No, that's all.'

The Reverend looked up from his writing . . . 'Then where d'you sleep?'

'Where d'ye think!' said Ranter defiantly.

The Reverend laid down his pen. His face was as hard as flint. 'You're trying to tell me that you share your house-keeper's bed?'

'Ye don't expect me to sleep on the floor?'

'I expect nothing of ye,' said the Reverend. 'I'm merely drawing up this will for ye. But I've got to say this, Ranter; it's my duty. It's a black, shameful sin to treat a good woman that way.'

'What d'*you* know of women?' said Ranter, then hurried on. 'Never mind that. Ah've no time to be gettin' married if that's what ye're hintin' at.'

'Yet ye've time to be making a will and leave her all your worldly goods. That's a kind of insult. Tell me,' said the Reverend, 'd'ye love her?'

Ranter turned his face to the fire again. 'Ah don't reckon much to this love business,' he said slowly. 'And what's the odds? It's too late now. Ah'll be dead an' buried soon. Marry-ing wouldn't alter anything.' This was said in such a tone of finality that it silence the Reverend for a moment.

'All right; let's get on with the will,' he said at last. 'But if I know her, she'd prefer your name to any of these goods and chattels!'

So the will was drawn up, and Ranter departed. The follow-ing day the Reverend made his way to the little cottage on the

109

crest of Half-Mile Hill. He was made welcome by Mrs Corrie. 'Ah'll have the kettle boilin' for a cup of tea in a minute,' she said after she had seen him comfortably seated.

'Ah, now,' he said. 'I could never refuse a good cup of tea, Mrs Corrie.' But his heart almost failed him. Then his eye lit on the cupboard bed. Tall, angular and ugly, its high polish seemed to reflect an insult to him. He hardened his heart. 'Ranter was down seeing me yesterday,' he said casually, as she handed him his cup.

'Ranter down seein' you!' she exclaimed. 'That *is* a surprise. The awful things he says about religion, too. But his bark's worse than his bite!'

'He came to ask me to draw up his will,' said the Reverend.

Her cup and saucer crashed to the floor in a litter of white fragments. Her eyes were fixed on the Reverend's face. 'What - whatever for?' she faltered at last.

'Because he thinks he's going to die,' said the Reverend, slowly, hating himself for it.

'Oh . . . it's just one of them daft ideas he keeps getting into his head,' she said, but her hands trembled as she picked up the broken pieces of pottery.

'The doctor told him so,' continued the Reverend ruthlessly. 'Ranter thinks a great deal about ye, Mrs Corrie. He's leaving all to you.'

'And he told you all about us.' Her eyes turned to the cupboard bed.

'He did.'

She shook her head slowly; sighed. 'Robert Ranter's got the name of bein' a hard man, Mr Macpherson,' she said. 'But Ah've known him for nigh-hand twenty years, and Ah'll tell you something about him. He's only got one fault; he opens his mouth too much!' She took a handbrush and swept the smaller fragments up, and the Reverend marvelled at her composure. Then she poured herself another cup of tea. 'Ah well,' she said. 'That's the end of chapel-goin', Ah suppose. After a time Ah got to forget that we weren't married. Nobody knew, Ah thought. There was no harm done. But ye can't hide anything frae the Lord.'

'Indeed not,' said the Reverend gently, 'but there's still time to make amends.'

She shook her head. 'Once Ranter makes up his mind he never shifts. If gettin' married would open the gates of heaven for him he'd still take hell.'

'He thinks a lot of ye,' said the Reverend softly. 'He'd listen to you...'

'Little ye know of my man, Mr Macpherson,' she said scornfully. 'Ranter's not the sort to change his mind... And ye'd better be on your way. He's due in for his dinner any minute, an' if he sees ye sittin' there he'll put two an' two together in less than no time.'

The Reverend had been a widower for some years, but he was still domesticated enough to take an order. He rose from his chair automatically and turned to leave, conscious of failure. He lifted the latch, then turned. 'I'm an old man, Mrs Corrie, and my memory isn't what it was. The moment I leave this house I want to forget what we've talked about. So I'll say good afternoon; and I'll be expecting to see ye at chapel on Sunday.'

But Mrs Corrie never passed through the chapel doors again. Death gave Ranter good warning, then grinned as he took her without any warning at all. Exactly a week to the day of his first visit Ranter came knocking at the Manse door again. Mrs Corrie had took a stroke, he explained, and was in a very poor way. Kept askin' for the Minister. Would he go to see her?

For answer the Reverend took down his overcoat and trudged once more up Half-Mile Hill, with Ranter by his side. For a long time both men were silent. Then Ranter spoke. There was a note of fear, almost panic in his voice. 'She's got something on her mind, Mr Macpherson. Talked about it all through the night. She's like a bairn. There's no tellin' her it's impossible ... Doctor says we can expect t'end any time now...'

'Ranter, what have you got against marriage?' asked the Reverend, quite irrelevantly. Ranter jumped. There is no other word for it. At last he said, 'Ah've been married once. She was a – a bitch.'

'That's a strong word.'

'Not strong enough,' said Ranter grimly.

'She led me a dog's life. Ah thought the world of her till Ah walked in one night and found – well, that's enough. Ah gave her a second chance. Can ye imagine it, me that's got the heart of a Pharaoh now – or so they reckon. Well, it was her that gave it to me...'

'Oh...' said the Reverend. 'Then what happened?'

'She's dead now,' said Ranter. 'Dead and buried. An' the

best part of me wi' her.'

'And the sins of the first fall on the second,' said the Reverend.

'Ah'd give my life if it would ease Jean Corrie one little bit. But what she wants –'

'Leave it to me,' said the Reverend. 'But mind ye, Ranter, not one word of it to a living soul. This lies between the three of us.'

An old friend of Mrs Corrie's was watching by the bedside. The Reverend greeted the dying woman, shocked by the change in her. 'Now, Mrs Corrie, what have ye been doing with yourself,' he asked with gentle raillery. He had to bend his head to catch her answer.

'That's all right,' he answered. 'Everything's settled.' He turned to the friend. 'Just a word wi' ye,' he said. They stood at some distance from the bed. 'Well, what's your opinion Mrs Castle?' he asked.

'Poor lass! She hasn't much longer to go.'

'I thought so.' He pondered for a moment. Then he asked her if she would mind slipping down to the village with a note for his senior deacon explaining that he wouldn't be able to get to a concert. Naturally, the woman thought it a little strange, sending her, and a man in the house, but the Reverend had an easy way with him and she went without any argument.

That woman was my grandmother. When she returned Mrs Corrie was dead. The secret of her last hour might have stayed with the Reverend and Ranter but for one thing. The dead woman wore two wedding rings, the second one plain and heavy and loose on the finger. It was a man's ring, and starting with this clue it didn't take my grandmother very long to explain to her own satisfaction what had happened during her absence.

But she never knew, and even if she had known, would never have explained the significance of another incident. The day after the funeral Ranter asked a friend of his to help him to carry the cupboard bed into the garden. His friend stayed for a glass of whisky and some enlightenment, but Ranter was dumb, if generous with the bottle. But looking back from the bottom of the hill this man saw the black spiral of smoke rise which marked the beginning of the end of the old bed.

[1946]

112

The writer at work. In those early
days the poems of Walt Whitman
were never far away.

Sid Chaplin had started writing when he was in his teens. At 16 he had a letter published in the 'Hear All Sides' column of the Northern Echo: *it vigorously argued the case of the cyclist against the motor car. He always used a pseudonym; one letter, taking the political writer J.A. Spender to task, was modestly signed Socrates II. Eventually he began to write longer articles and short stories; but his family only got to know about this solitary pursuit when a postal order for half a crown arrived for him from the* Northern Weekly Gazette. *The news did not go down well with his family; his mother disapproved in particular. But she wasn't alone in thinking there was something odd about a pit lad writing stories:*

When I started writing short stories in the privacy of my bedroom it wasn't just the modesty of the beginner that made me shut the door, and shove the pad and pencil under the pillow if anyone came. It was shame. The same confusions made me hide my real name under a nom-de-plume.

The reason for all this was that I was going against the grain of the social mores – bucking the system which laid down that son should follow father and so ensure that the brood was kept going. It was OK to go into the union, politics, or even religion, or take over an insurance book, because they were all part of the set-up. But writing books! What's the lad coming to! It was like a pitman riding to hounds. It was like going into a restaurant when there were fish and chip shops around.

My mates were kindness itself, but there was no disguising their attitude: I must be some kind of holy idiot. This meant I had to work twice as hard as anybody else. Not that it did me any good. 'Well, he's all right, you know' – you could almost hear them thinking, as if I'd got by with some terrible disability. I was better off than most. I could check up. I used to hear what they had to say about my friend, the artist Norman Cornish. It was a pound to a penny that they said and felt the same about me.

And yet most of these men were born story-tellers with a biting, mordant wit and a lovely sense of fun.

Despite this, Chaplin persevered with his writing: and with his WEA classes. Eventually, a golden opportunity came his way. At the age of 22, he won a place at Fircroft College for Working Men, at Bournville in Birmingham, to study economics. Once he'd finished his one-year course, he planned to launch a career in the trade unions or the Labour Party. So in December 1938 he left the smithy at Dean

and Chapter for the last time, a set of Coleridge's Biographia
Literaria *under his arm. His marrers gave him the additional honour
of a "tinpanning" – every smith and striker striking an anvil as he
went on his way.*

*At Fircroft he learned how to apply himself to research, how to
make a bed; he read Bede's* History of the English Church and
People, *'the only classic piece of literature to come out of Durham'.
Eventually he switched to literature after his tutor told him that his
economics were inexact, but jolly entertaining. Then all his plans
began to fall apart: he was offered a place at Ruskin College, Oxford,
but had to turn it down because he simply did not have the money
to support himself while on the course. Then, with war looming, it
was announced that the Fircroft course was to be curtailed. It was a
strange, disturbing time:*

And all those last few weeks the burden of impending war
hung heavy upon us. On May Day, 1939, the Fircroft contin-
gent marched through Birmingham chanting: 'Down the drain
with Chamberlain, and don't forget to pull the chain.' Three
years before I had signed the Peace Pledge. Less than a year
away a brother of mine would just make it to the last troopship
of all to cast off at Boulogne.

Jock Saul and myself stayed on to work through the holidays
at Cadbury's, with lodgings near the factory. I remember
cleaning out the Aero-chocolate department and eating blocks
of the stuff until I was sick. Then I was sent to assist an old
boilersmith from Birkenhead in repairing miles and miles of
ventilation tubing, a kind of semi-mining job, crawling yards
along in the chocolate-smelling darkness. It was during one
of these sessions that my boilersmith told me how he had
been taken along in a naval pinnace to open out the salvaged
submarine *Thetis* after it had been lost with its officers and
crew aboard. His description of the charnel-house smell which
emerged confirmed my growing unrest, part homesickness
and part war-fear. I was no longer a pacifist, but I wanted to
get home before it all started. Seeing the Frenchman André
Parrot off intensified this feeling. I caught up with him at
Fircroft just as he was on the point of leaving, walked with
him part of the way; then, after we had clasped hands he
jumped on to his bike and pushed off without a backward
look. It was then that my sense that all was well in "the best
of all possible worlds" collapsed. Alone of all of us at Fircroft

he saw himself as a soldier to the wars returning.

All of us had been inculcated with the idea that aerial warfare (vide Wellsian books and films) would be sudden, brief and totally devastating, and Spain had confirmed this view. All that summer we lived with the fear of Hitler's aerial armada.

Then, one Sunday, lunching with friends not far from Fircroft, we heard Mr Chamberlain's announcement: 'You can imagine what a bitter blow it is to me that all my long struggle to win peace has failed. Yet I cannot believe that there is anything more or anything different that I could have done that would have been more successful...' Along with another guest, I picked up my spade and we started to build an air-raid shelter. Shortly after the broadcast the air-raid sirens wailed, and, lacking a shelter, we took cover in the house. A few weeks later I returned home via a heavy lorry, sleeping overnight in a transport café at Bawtry, resuming my journey the following morning with the same driver, who dropped me off outside the pit wall from whence I had started some nine months earlier. My vintage year was over – but not the good wine.

In fact this episode marked not an end, but a kind of beginning. As soon as he got home, Sid bought himself a typewriter and began to write in earnest. He returned to work at the pit, though this time, since the smithy was full-up, as a belt-fitter, underground. It was his job to maintain the huge conveyors, which took the coal from the face to the shafts.

The job took him into every corner of the pit and he got to know hundreds of pitmen, many of them with tales to tell:

Men would put their lamps face down in the dust and say, 'I mind once...' and you'd get a story. It was absolutely great. Taking my material from miners like that strengthened my resolve to be true to the spirit as well as the letter of what I was writing.

Sid Chaplin did a lot of his writing underground, during bait-time, drafting poems on the back of report forms with a stubby pencil, the paper illuminated by his pit lamp.

Conveyor

Conveyor, run
With you
My life.
Rubber smell
Dust cloud
Dark dooms
Endless
Running, rubber ribbon.

[c. 1941]

Dead Drunk

Ah, dead-drunk mate of mine!
Laid in your vomit like a swine;
You cast off grandeur when you left the mine.

There, naked, black and battle-scarred,
Human wedge in the planet's bone,
You were supreme, my mate, unmarred;
While here, the usurpèd king does moan,
Bereft of his kingdom of stone;
And lies in the gutter, alone.

Ah, dead-drunk mate of mine!

[1943]

Sid Chaplin began to submit these poems, and some of his short stories, to the many magazines and periodicals publishing new work which flourished during the war years. At first all he received was a flood of rejection slips. One of them was from Horizon; *but fortunately, its editor, Cyril Connolly, passed on the submitted work to his friend John Lehmann, the editor of the prestigious* Penguin New Writing. *Lehmann liked the work very much and over the course of the next few years published many of Sid Chaplin's poems, articles and stories. He began with a poem, which appeared in May 1941, for which Sid Chaplin received the not inconsiderable sum of £5. Most of it – £4 10s – went on a present for Ike and Elsie Chaplin's silver wedding, a dinner service from Binns in Darlington. It was a good buy; the service is still in use.*

The poem which made its purchase possible was 'A Widow Wept'.

A Widow Wept

When they carried my comrade
Out of the pit,
Cold, silent, and crushed,
We knew that the price was paid.

Silent the wheels, and hushed
The conveyors. No bugle sound
For him was heard,
But only the signal bell
Pealed out in mournful tone,
When they carried the body to bank.

The sunshine greeted him,
The wind caressed him,
A widow wept for him,
When they carried the body to bank.

[Written underground at Dean & Chapter, June 1940]

FOLIOS OF   THE PENGUIN

NEW WRITING

601,Carrington House, Hertford Street. W.1.
23.3.43.

To Whom It May Concern:

I have known Mr. Sid Chaplin personally
and have studied his work for some years.
I consider him to be a person who has a deep
and genuine interest in literature and has
already shown, in a number of short stories
some of which I have published in New Writing
considerable promise as a writer. His work
seems to me particularly valuable because he
can describe working-class life from inside
knowledge and yet is not tied down by any
preconception about reportage or bare realism;
the stories I have seen, in fact, often have
a strongly lyrical and humourous strain.

John Lehmann

Diamond Cut Diamond

Big Mitch and Corn Miller were the sportiest, drunkenest, brawlingest, most powerful pair that the village of Little Gomorrah ever produced and they hated each other, consistent and earnest, till death did them part. There were never two men fought so hard and wicked, or respected each other more than Big Mitch and Corn Miller, and there was never a better pair to watch bowling or batting, running a race or wrestling, flinging a penny or tossing a tumble matched against each other. But it had to be a match. Their blood was up every time they met: it was square up and square in and no giving in until somebody turned a hose or half a dozen slops on them.

They were a noble unforgiving pair and this is their history – and my drink's mild and bitter, so don't stop me to ask.

Miller was the eldest of ten. His Da was fore-overman at the pit: straight-laced, straight-faced, hard-faced, the meanest man that ever sent hewers into thin coal, wet coal, rough coal, blackdamp and firedamp. He was worse in the house than he was in the pit, and he ruled with a rod of iron till Corn Miller was 13, and felled him with an iron poker; ever after the old man carried the crease and a twitch. But even before this Corn was king of the kids.

Big Mitch wasn't a native of our village. He came from Bishop's Batts. His mother was widowed when his Da, a big ginger hawker, got rolled flat by a cast-iron boiler he was stealing single-handed from the pit-yard. She married the fireman they sent to break the news, and that's how Big Mitch came to Little Gomorrah.

First time the two of them met was in the school-yard. Corn Miller walked up to Big Mitch and said 'Ah'm the boss around here.' Big Mitch just laughed. His hair was cut short all over except for a long topping over his brow. Miller got hold of that topping and pulled hard, then clouted Big Mitch across the lug-hole.

This was one place – across the ear – where one lad never clouted another – and Big Mitch was mad. He let out with his boot and clicked Miller's ankles. Simultaneously, he landed his right on Miller's nose. Miller was wonder-struck for a minute, then went into action. He laced Big Mitch round the school-yard. He cut his eye and bent his nose. He swelped him standing up and hammered him lying down. I can still see Big Mitch lying on the asphalt with the blood spurting from his nose, and Corn Miller pummelling him fifty to the dozen. Big Mitch got a hammering that day, but he never gave in. Once, when Miller slowed up he shouted: 'Go on, go on! You lace me – but it'll be my turn next time!' And it was. The next time they met Big Mitch got a hold on Corn, squeezed the wind out of him, then threw him into a bed of nettles.

Big Mitch always got the better of it when he got a hold on Corn Miller. Mitch was as broad as he was long. He was like a gorilla. He was stubborn and slow, but he was strong; stronger than Miller. Mitch wasn't a moron. He was only slow. You'd never get a flash of wit or a smart quip out of Big Mitch but he could tell a good story when the mood was on him. He wasn't a sociable man. Mostly he went on his own, a wandering man, a born poacher, and a melancholy drinker. Funny thing, although he wasn't good-looking he went through a lot of women.

Corn Miller *was* good-looking. Stripped, he was as nice a lad as you could wish to see, and he kept that way, in spite of the drink. Another five years might have made a difference but he didn't live that long. Had a mind on ice, never lost his head, was a natural boss. Cold as a snake one minute, he was your best friend the next – and you believed it. Could have you rolling under the table with the things he said. But he never held Big Mitch any way.

Half the trouble between Big Mitch and Corn Miller was that Corn had all the things that Mitch lacked – smoothness, science, speed. I once saw Miller clean bowl Big Mitch. Mitch turned and looked at the scattered bails. His face went red. Then he turned and threw his bat at Corn Miller. If it had hit him Corn would have been a dead man. But it didn't. Corn just moved his head without shifting from the spot where he'd let go of the ball, and the bat whizzed past him and broke two of the stumps. That's how hard Big Mitch could throw. That's how mad he could get. 'That'll learn you to bowl me out!' yelled Big Mitch. Miller smiled coldly, picked up the bat, then threw it back. Mitch went down like a big tree. It took six men to carry him home on a gate. He was out for an hour.

That was when they were both working at the pit. Of course, the manager knew all about them. They were always hettled in different shifts and working in different districts. But they still managed to meet at shift-changing times. Big Mitch would jostle Miller, or Corn Miller would say, 'Here's the hairy ape,' and they'd be at it hammer and tongs. We'd stop them, but they'd always fight it out later. Big Mitch once waited for Miller coming off the afternoon shift. They fought in moon-light, till two o'clock in the morning. We carried both of them home that morning.

Sport was the one thing they had in common. Miller was a decent middleweight. He beat Jonathan Jackson and he held Dominic Jones for three rounds. Big Mitch was a wrestler. I never saw him in a big competition, but he did well at Stanhope and Appleby, and I've heard tell he won Keswick one year. But Corn Miller soon saw where the money lay, and got himself a job as bookie's runner. Big Mitch was a runner too, but a proper runner. He won the big ten mile run three years running, and would have won it the fourth, but Miller stopped him.

Miller was running a gang by then, and they put up a chap called Slinger, from Branksome way. Slinger was a good run-ner, but nobody knew it, and Miller and his gang spread a lot of money on him. Corn Miller should have known better, but he offered Big Mitch 50 guineas to lie back. He took half a dozen of his pals along when he put the question. Big Mitch laid two of them out with a chair leg and chased the rest – Miller included – out of the house. Corn Miller swore he'd get him for this. He had to, anyway. There was too much money involved. But he was a fair swindler, you can say that for him. He walked up to Big Mitch before the start of the race. 'You'd better lie back,' he said. 'Not for you,' says Big Mitch. 'Ah'll stop ye then,' said Corn. 'Not for fifty, not fifty thousand, not for you or any of your floppy-trousered lot,' says Big Mitch. 'Have it your own way,' said Corn, 'but ye'll lose.' 'Get to hell out of here,' says Big Mitch. 'Right,' said Miller with a faint smile. 'Be seein' you then.'

Big Mitch was so mad and determined to win that he went to the starting-line stripped to the buff and the starter made him go back and put his shirt on. He did so, and was off like a rocket with the pistol. He'd more wind than any man I ever knew and he was leading by a quarter of a mile at Corner's Wood.

This was what Miller had reckoned on and a dozen of the gang were waiting there. They tripped him with a wire rope and one of them bounced a beer bottle over his head. Then they sat on him for a couple of hours. Slinger got the cup and the prize money; Miller and his gang collected over £500 from the bookies; and Pony Jones, Big Mitch's trainer, got a horse and trap and went back along the route. He heard Big Mitch groaning in the ditch where they'd left him. An ordinary man would have taken to his bed but Big Mitch got washed and changed and went out to look for Miller and his gang.

He found the gang in the back room at the Bull. I was there, minding my own business, and I saw it all from start to finish. The lads were laughing and singing and flashing their cash. The waiter had just come through with a trayful of pints.

There was a pint for me among that lot, but it never touched my lips. The door had hardly closed when it opened again, and there stood Big Mitch. The waiter just stood – the way he balanced his tray was an act in itself – knowing there wasn't another way out but looking for it anyway. He'd have been glad of a mouse-hole, and so would Miller's boys – big as they were they'd have tried to pile in; but they were boxed, and they knew it. They just sat where they were and froze. Everything froze. Their mouths were still open; a couple of laughs and a song hung fire among the cigarette smoke.

Big Mitch got hold of a bench. It was about nine feet long but he handled it the way a schoolmaster handles a cane. 'You come out of there,' he said to the waiter. That waiter came to life quick. He put his tray down on the table and went weaving back of Big Mitch, but I was out before him. Then the bench landed among the bunch of them, and there was an awful noise of heads cracking, glass flying, the wash of seven or eight pints on the floor, and the yelling of desperate men (those still conscious) as they rushed Big Mitch. He wiped the floor with them and you couldn't tell blood from beer when he was finished. Then Mitch went looking for Corn Miller. But he never found him. He was on the train for Blackpool with 300 quid in his pocket half an hour after the end of the race.

Big Mitch said he'd get him the next time he saw him. As it happened he didn't. For the next time the pair met was in High Street. Corn Miller was carrying a couple of suitcases and there was a girl with him. Big Mitch shot across the road and stood in front of Corn Miller. 'Put them cases down,' he ordered. But Corn kept hold of the cases. He turned to the girl. 'Meet Big Mitch,' he said. 'An old school pal of mine. Best wrestler an' runner around here – and practically the best fighter.' Big Mitch's left hand took hold of Corn's shirt front. The girl said: 'I'm very pleased to meet you, Mr Mitch.'

Big Mitch looked at her. She was a beautiful girl, and she was holding out her hand. He took hold of it, 'Meet Mrs Miller,' said Corn. Mitch looked blankly at him and became aware that his big left hand was still grasping Corn's shirt front, and almost flushed. Then he managed a smile. He released Corn and put his left hand behind his back, and said, 'Well, Ah'm sure Ah wish ye both the best.'

'Thanks,' said Corn. 'Well, we'll be on our way.'

'Ah'll see ye at the Bull tonight,' said Big Mitch, meaningfully.

'Way, Ah don't know about that,' said Corn earnestly. 'You see – we were just married this morning.'

Big Mitch swallowed. 'Some other time, then,' he said.

But after this Corn Miller and Big Mitch didn't tangle together for a long time. For one thing, they both left the pit. For another, Big Mitch kept out of Corn's way.

Miller set up in business as a bookie. Finding it was too much like real work he collected his gang together again and followed the meetings. He used to go the round of the bookies, with the boys a step behind, and hold out his hand. He never said anything and there was rarely any need for rough stuff. He also organised a few schools, consisting of anything up to a hundred adult scholars, who met in the woods or on the moors to investigate the laws of probability through the medium of spinning pennies. Miller got ten per cent of the money wagered, plus twenty per cent of the big wins. The latter wasn't strictly legitimate, but since the disappointed scholars were never concerned about the welfare of the lucky ones, Miller invariably coined again, unless the winner was one of the big boys from Newcastle.

The Miller gang got to rule the roost around our way. Miller never paid a bus fare, or bought his own drinks. Landlords and customers used to fall over themselves to treat him.

Big Mitch got the sack. The manager hated doing it because, left alone, Mitch was a genius with a pick and an artist with a shovel, and could win more coal from the solid than six men shovelling it loose. I've seen him swing his pick and the coal crumble out of sheer fright before the point landed. But Mitch got tangled with an overman named Horace White, who was always picking faults in his work. Horace came into Mitch's place one day and said it wasn't properly timbered. Big Mitch picked him up, dropped him into a barrel of tub-grease, then knocked out all the timber outbye of the barrel. The roof came down, Horace yelled blue murder, and Big Mitch walked out of the pit. It took six men as many hours to shift the fall of stone and rescue Horace, which gave him plenty of time to scrape off the thickest of the grease. Big Mitch got three months for that.

Afterwards he went into the quarries and pretty nearly worked them out. Then he got a job as keeper on Marlowe's estate. It became the best preserve north of the Trent – the partridges and pheasants were as thick as flies, and the rabbits were so tame they'd sit up and beg for lettuces.

The rarest bird on Marlowe's estate, after Big Mitch took over, was a poacher. I remember once a poaching gang came down from Tyneside. They came in a van and had enough tackle to stock a zoo. When they got back from the woods their van was upside down at the bottom of a quarry. After fighting about who'd left the brakes off they decided to try to put the van to rights. Big Mitch gave them time to break both hearts and backs, then walked on top of them with Sergeant Slack and his men. Slack says it was the funniest thing he ever saw, those fly boys trying to climb the quarry walls, crying and swearing with frustration and fear.

It looked as though the two had settled down. Big Mitch had a cosy little cottage on the edge of the estate. He kept pretty much to himself, excepting the odd time or two when he went on to the spree. Miller got a little heavier and made – and lost – a lot of money. If he'd paid his rent he'd still be alive. But Miller never liked to pay anything. The landlord had him thrown out, paid for it with a fortnight in hospital, and Corn moved into a caravan on the edge of the Marlowe estate, not far from Big Mitch's cottage.

Peggy Miller never complained, but I reckon she was a lonely woman. Corn was away most of the time, and she had no friends. Nobody wanted to have anything to do with Corn anyway; but on top of that he was a jealous man. She was his property, and she couldn't move.

I remember she once got into arrears with her insurance. The company sent an inspector down to collect. He was a big, pleasant man, and he talked to her like a father. Then Miller walked in. He accused the inspector of trying to run away with his wife. He pulled out a big razor. The inspector ran for his life. He got the first bus out of Little Gomorrah and was never seen again; in fact, he was so afraid of Corn Miller that he paid up the arrears himself rather than come back again.

Corn Miller joined up with a Liverpool race gang. He had big ideas. He thought he could rule these Liverpool boys and run every race course in the country. But they were too tough for him. The gang jumped a bookie at Aintree and passed the wallet to Miller. A few hours later they met at a pub. Miller pulled out the wallet and showed it to them. Except for a return ticket to Manchester it was empty. Miller tried to bluff them. He said the bookie must have got wind of the jump. For once Corn Miller was a fool. He should have split fifty-fifty, or he should have bought off the worst of the Liverpool boys. But he was too greedy. They never said anything, but three months later they jumped him one night as he was walking home to his caravan. They jumped him and belted him. They took his wallet and his money belt. Then two of them held his head and two sat on his legs and two held his arms while the boss-man carved his face with a razor.

It was the yells of Corn Miller that brought Big Mitch running through the woods. Big Mitch says he's heard a hare crying in a spring-trap. He's heard a bitch-fox cry for her cubs. But he says he never heard anything worse than the yells of Corn Miller when the Liverpool lads nicked him.

They were so interested in their work that they didn't hear him coming. They must have thought it was the end of the world when they saw Big Mitch loom out of the night. He kicked the razor out of the hand of the man that was using it, then picked him up and threw him into a ditch. He kicked another under the chin, then used him in turn as a punch-bag, shield and club. He let go of this one when he saw a second razor click open and shine sharp in the moonlight. Big Mitch snatched it. A split-second, the lad who had lost the razor lost an ear also. The wounded man gabbled a lament of pain and complaint, scrabbled in the dark for his missing ear, then took to his heels. Those that could followed suit. From the ditch came a slithering, sucking kind of sound as the first casualty dragged himself away, not knowing where he was going but glad he was capable of going somewhere. Then Big Mitch knelt beside Miller.

He couldn't do much for him out there in the woods, so he put him over his shoulder and carried him home. He carried Corn Miller all the way without stopping, and he laid him down against the side of the caravan. Then he tapped at the door. First thing Peggy Miller said when she saw him was: 'Why Mitch, what brings you back so soon?' He took hold of her hand. 'Take hold of yourself, lass,' he said. 'He's been in trouble.' Then he moved aside and the yellow glow of the oil-lamp lit up the face of Corn Miller; and she knew what he meant.

They got him inside and dressed his face as best they could. When Big Mitch left Corn Miller was conscious, but he never said a word of thanks. Not that Big Mitch expected any thanks, but that silence made him uneasy. The last thing he saw, he says, was the face of Corn Miller swathed in bandages and the eyes following him. Big Mitch knew those eyes. He'd seen them at close quarters more times than he could remember. But it was only later that he remembered the way those eyes followed him, the way they were the night he left the caravan. They weren't the eyes of the Corn Miller he knew any more.

Nobody knows what Miller thought, or said, that night, because Miller never talked at the trial excepting to plead guilty. He never said a word at the trial, never opened his mouth to lawyer, judge or chaplain, except to say he was guilty. Maybe he talked on the eight o'clock walk. Maybe the last thing he saw as he swung was her face when his razor flashed too quick for her even to say goodbye.

But Big Mitch talked at the trial. That girl was Corn Miller's girl. She was scared for herself, but she was scared more for her man when she heard about the Liverpool lads. She asked Big Mitch to keep an eye on the caravan and the woods. That's why he'd called the night the Liverpool lads jumped Corn Miller. But Big Mitch had never been over the doorstep of that caravan. Big Mitch talked hard and fast at the trial. He did the talking and Corn Miller stood quiet as if there was nothing in the world to hear but the scream of a lovely woman when a razor flicks open. He never said a word, but his head went down when Big Mitch told the judge why Corn Miller killed his wife. Because she said: 'Why, Mitch, what brings you back so soon?'

I sat up with Big Mitch all through the last night. We drank whisky mostly. We drank a lot and it was still a long time waiting. You can imagine me and Big Mitch watching the hours stretch and counting the years from dawn to eight o'clock, and not far away, not five miles, Corn Miller seeing the hours slip through his fingers like minnows.

The last hour Big Mitch stopped drinking. He just sat at the table, hunched over it, his big hands clasped. His face was hard and yellow and his eyes saw nothing at all. He looked like a man praying. He looked like a man waiting for the rope himself.

At a minute past eight he stirred. 'Ah hope it wasn't too quick,' he said. 'He'd die hard.' I never said a word. He was talking to himself. 'First time Ah met him Ah knew he was no good,' he said. 'Ah wouldn't let him best me. He hammered me all ways, but he never ruled me. Perhaps,' he said, 'if Ah'd liked him less we'd never have clashed.'

He stood up and swept the bottles from the table. He stumbled to the door and flung it open and the raw hard morning swept in upon us. 'Proves how near we were,' he said, 'when we both loved the same woman.'

He stood there with his back to me, blocking the doorway, with the hard cold light around the black square shape of him. 'Ah hope there's a heaven and hell,' he cried. 'If it's true, there's one battle coming up that neither God nor the Devil can stop. There'll be all hell let loose when Ah catch up wi' that Corn Miller!' It was something in his voice told me. There was one man mourning a crook and a murderer. There was one man weeping for Corn Miller kicking at the end of a rope. There was one man breaking his heart in the cold morning for Corn Miller dead, and Corn Miller gone, and Big Mitch was the name of that man.

[c. 1948]

The publication of other pieces soon followed; and the young writer received encouragement not just from Lehmann but from such diverse literary figures as the poet Geoffrey Grigson, who later commissioned a book – The Lakes to Tyneside – and George Orwell. During the war, Orwell was literary editor of Tribune, the Left paper. He took articles on poetry, once giving over the whole of the back page to a piece on Wilfred Owen and Synge. Orwell also asked Sid Chaplin to take over his 'As I Please' column in Tribune while he was away on holiday.

Other commissions began to arrive at the little house in Gladstone Terrace, Ferryhill, where the Chaplins lived. He gave talks on the radio for the North of England Home Service, beamed out from Pontop Pike; and some of his stories, The Man Who Nearly Walked to London among them, were broadcast. (The inspiration for this story was the grandfather of a friend, George Woodrough, who really did set out to walk to London, so that he could see Buckingham Palace before he died).

As the years went by, the stories accumulated and publishers began to sniff around. The first collection, The Leaping Lad, was published in 1946; it included the story, The Pigeon Cree, despite the fact that its portrayal of petty council officials and self-righteous parsons worried Penguin's libel lawyers. But Sid Chaplin was anxious to try out new forms; and two novels, The Thin Seam and My Fate Cries Out, appeared in the late 40s. Various other novels – a detective thriller in the Chandler mould, an ambitious book about coal nationalisation – were finished but never published, because the author was not happy with them.

The flavour of the stories began to change as well: Weekend in Arcady is almost of novella length, a slow-burning evocation of a Durham town at night. The Arcady of the title is clearly Shildon, the coal and railway town where Sid Chaplin was born.

The Man Who Nearly Walked to London

The man who *nearly* walked to London? You may say why, if he *had* walked to London it still wouldn't make a story. Even though London happens to be 250 miles from Little Gomorrah, if the old stone in the market-place tells the truth. But the substance of the story is in the fact that the man who eventually went to London, whether by foot or train, it matters not, was a very unusual man. My Grandad, in point of fact. Eighty-five next Christmas Day and still going strong. Sixty of his years spent at the coal-face. Fifteen years ago they said he was too old and had to finish. He'll never forgive the man that had the painful job of handing him his notice. 'Too old!' he still snorts at least once a week.

'Ah'll show him. Ah'll live *him* out, mark my words!' My opinion is he'll live us all out. But never mind. London's the story.

I wrote my cousin Sam who lives in Wimbledon. I told him that Grandad and me were coming to London for a week, and could we stay at his house? His reply came back by return of post. 'Delighted to have you both,' said cousin Sam, 'it's ten years since I saw the old man. I suppose he'll survive the journey. Anyway, he's welcome to my easy chair for a week! Fancy wanting to walk all the way at his age!'

That bit about the easy chair made me smile! Sam should have known better. He does now. And I'm willing to bet that Grandad *could* have walked to London and back again. If it wasn't for the trifling matter of a drop of water he'd walk to America, coming back by way of China and the South Sea Islands. Itching feet, that's his trouble. Take him on a bus and the only man he envies is the conductor. 'That's the life for me,' he once said, 'give me a punching machine and a double-decker and Ah'd be set for life.'

This was how it started. My father came to see me. 'What's the trouble, Dad?' I said.

'Another bee in his bonnet,' he said, 'he's not content with

131

rising at six-thirty every morning; looking after three gardens, and walking an average of a dozen miles a day. He's talkin' about walkin' to London! Do it easy, he says. Nothing to it. When Ah told him he was gettin' too ould to be gallivantin' off to London, he told us to shut up or he'd clip me lug! There's nae dealin' wi' the ould demon!'

'What d'ye want me to do, Dad?' I asked.

'Just try to talk him out of it,' he said, 'Ah'm not disputin' that he can walk to London. But he'll likely sleep in barns and hedges an' get his death of cold.'

As luck would have it Grandad walked over to our house the next day. It was a blazing hot day, ninety in the shade, but he was as fresh as a daisy. Me and the wife were half-dead with the heat, he was as cool as a cucumber. 'Sit down, Grandad,' I said.

'Haven't much time,' he grumbled, 'Ah'd like to walk back by Arn Fell an' gather two or three pund of wild rasps. Might as well make the best o' the fine weather!'

'Walk over Arn Fell on a day like this!' protested Milly, my wife.

'Aye, it is a bit hot,' he admitted.

'What's this about walking to London?' I said.

His face brightened, 'Good idea, eh? Niver been to London before. Got a fancy to see it once before ould age come creepin' on.'

'But it's too far to walk,' I said.

'Too far!' he said, 'why, Ah can walk thirty miles a day easy. Should do it in a week.'

'Why not go by train,' I said.

'Cooped up in a box!' he said scornfully,.'three pun' return, an' cooped up in a box like a tame rabbit! *That'll* come soon enough without payin' for it. No thanks; Ah'll walk!'

There was only one way out, I could see. So I gave Milly the wink. 'Milly an' me's going for a week's holiday,' I said, 'why not come with us, keep us company?'

'Why, that would be grand!' he said. Then a look of horror came into his eyes. 'But sittin' down for seven hours! Ah couldn't stand that. No, Ah'll walk. Ah'll set off a week sooner an' we'll meet in London. Then we'll walk around and see all the sights.'

'Grandad,' I said firmly, 'if we go to London; we go together. And as for sittin' down all the way – that's not true. The train'll stop at York and Grantham, an' you can stretch your legs on the platform. And anyway, it'll be a corridor train; you can walk from one end to the other if you want.'

'Never in the creation,' he said, 'a train that ye can walk along! Ah dinna believe that one.'

'It's true, Grandad,' said Milly, 'furthermore,' she added cunningly, 'if you do walk to London you'll be too tired to see the sights when you get there.'

'Well,' he said, 'there's a bit sense in that, Milly, lass. After all, it's London Ah want to see. Bow Bells, St Paul's, the Tower of London, the Thames Embankment where they're chuckin' themselves off every night, an' Dick Whittington's cat.'

'All but the cat, Grandad,' I said.

'Ye're wrong there,' he said. 'It's bound to be in that Madam Chesards.'

So in the end we managed to persuade him, and we all went by train. I'll never forget that journey as long as I live. He was like a caged lion. He paced the length of the train, having a look in every compartment. The third trip, three cardsharpers threw their marked pack out of the window and started talking about the weather, thinking he was a plain-clothes man. He made friends with a dozen bairns playing in the corridor, cured a baby of the hiccups, repaired a milk-bottle teat, and entertained a compartment of chorus girls with whistling solos. He had a chat with the guard, and left him, having proved they were cousins three times removed. Some-how or other he got into the mail van and devised a new system of sorting letters. He met a big chap smoking a stubby pipe beside an open window, ferreted out the fact that he was one of the Big Five returning from a big murder case, and convinced him that the wrong man had been arrested.

That was before we got to York Station. At York the train stood ten minutes, and we had a job stopping him from pop-ping out to see the Minster. We convinced him there wasn't time, so he walked twice round the station, found seats for six old ladies, and helped the guard to pack sixteen bicycles and three prams into the van. Then he had a chat with the driver and fireman, shook hands with the station-master, who still can't make up his mind whether Grandad was the Duke of Aberdeen or the Marquis of Montreal, and just had time to jump on the train before it left.

He consented to sit down a bit and eat a sandwich. Then

he took some assorted articles out of his pocket and asked Milly to take care of them. There was a card admitting him to Scotland Yard and a look round the Black Museum; six bars of milk chocolate presented to him by grateful old ladies in lieu of a tip; a toy soldier and a copy of *Alice's Adventures in Wonderland*; six complimentary tickets to the show *Ladies in Waiting*, and a packet of Giant Runner Beans Seed. Then he returned to the corridor, presumably to fill his pockets again, to organise games among the bairns, and to make several dozen more friends. At Grantham sixteen awed porters and a packed platform watched him make the circuit of the platforms with easy grace. The second time round they broke into a cheer, thinking he was an Olympic champion. At King's Cross a dozen children broke away from worried parents and gave our taxi a right royal send-off.

He talked like a brother to our taxi-driver. There wasn't a dry eye in the taxi. The driver promised to sell out and take up some honest occupation – become a postman or a tramp – and would only take his legal fare when we said goodbye to him at Waterloo. But Grandad slipped tuppence into his hand and earnestly requested him to call at Little Gomorrah for a slice of bread and hunk of cheese when he was reformed.

We were glad to get to Sam's house in Wimbledon. The table was set with the best of everything. Milly and me were too tired to do that magnificent spread full justice; but Grandad didn't need any help. When every plate was empty he sat meditating a while. Then he said, 'Ye haven't a tin of treacle by any chance?' Given half a loaf and a tin of treacle he was happy for another ten minutes or so.

Then there was a touching scene. The easy chair pulled up in front of the fire, with a pair of slippers on the carpet to tempt tired feet. They got Grandad to sit down. Sam junior knelt down with commendable thoughtfulness to unloose Grandad's shoe-laces.

Grandad roared like a bull; young Sam ran for safety. 'What's the idea?' yelled Grandad.

'The lad was only goin' to take your shoes off so's you could rest a bit,' said Sam senior.

Grandad gave him a look of utter contempt. 'Why, man, it's only five o'clock,' he said, 'feel like stretchin' me legs.'

That was the beginning of Sam's education. It was ten o'clock when we got home, having beaten the bounds of Wimbledon

Common and all. The following day Sam startled the foreman at their place by asking if he could work a couple of hours overtime to get a little bit of ease. On Wednesday I had to call the doctor in to have a look at the finest selection of blisters my feet have ever possessed. Young Sam was worn out, and thought of running away to sea. Night and day Grandad tramped the streets of London, stopping to talk with every policeman on point duty. He was invited to a Chinese wedding in Limehouse and reviewed the Yeomen of the Guard. He went to the Zoo and had lunch – treacle to hand – with a Fellow of the Zoological Society. He had tea on the Terrace of the House and was introduced to the Prime Minister; then excused himself to keep his appointment with Scotland Yard. He was offered a job as door-keeper at the theatre, and one of the young ladies of the chorus proposed marriage.

The week came to an end at last. A police car took us directly to King's Cross. We ran a smash and grab gang down and arrived at the station with five minutes to spare. Two young ladies of the chorus were waiting to say goodbye. Ignoring Grandad's blushes they kissed him tenderly and departed for rehearsal. 'Let's hurry,' I said, 'or we'll miss the train.'

Grandad shook his head. 'Ah'm walkin' home,' he said. No amount of argument would persuade him. At last I cried, 'but your return ticket'll be wasted!' I thought this was one argument he couldn't answer. He shook his head. 'Ah gave it away last night,' he said, 'found a bit lassy frae Newcastle crying her eyes out on the Embankment. Gave her the return ticket.'

What could I do? I was broke, and there was only two minutes to go. We left him at the barrier. 'Don't worry about me,' he said, 'Ah'll walk it in fine style. Me legs need stretching after a lazy week like this.'

We had a card from him last week, posted in Manchester. He says he's coming home by Carlisle and Berwick. Milly says I've got to end with an S.O.S. You never know, she said, some farmer's wife up Cheviot way might see him. A big chap with a long stride and a wonderful way with women and bairns. They might get him to stay for a cup of tea, especially if there's a tin of treacle on the table. If so, as a favour to me, they might wash out his socks.

[1946]

PHOENIX HOUSE LIMITED

EDITORIAL AND PRODUCTION : *38 William IV Street* ·
Charing Cross · *WC2* · ACCOUNTS AND DISTRIBUTION :
Dunhams Lane · *Letchworth Garden City* · *Hertfordshire*
'PHONES : London TEMple Bar 0525 · Letchworth 1043

Dear Sid Chaplin:

      Have you ever been approached by a
publisher or thought of collecting your stories for
publication as a volume?

      You will see from the heading above
that, apart from RU, and with the friendly co-operation
of our parent, J.M.Dent & Sons, we are venturing into
the publishing world.

      Your stories have always impressed me
and, with our publishing scheme in mind, during the last
year or two, I have always promised myself that I would
ask you, when the time came, to let us see a bunch of
your stories. Is that possible?

      Sincerely yours,

      John Baker

Sid Chaplin Esq.,
9 Gladstone Terrace,
Ferryhill,
Co.Durham.
                       January 17 1946

PUBLISHERS OF BOOKS

DIRECTORS: *John Baker* (MANAGING DIRECTOR) · *E F Bozman* · *A J Hoppé* · *A E Pigott* · *W G Taylor*

The letter that led to the
publication of Sid Chaplin's first
book, *The Leaping Lad*.

Weekend in Arcady

As the bus turned down Church Street he saw that there was a change. The orchard in the Vicarage Garth was gone; apple trees replaced by council houses. But the grass grew tall around the tombstones in the churchyard. The blacksmith's shop was closed, boards nailed across the windows. The little patch of green, once carefully tended, was now criss-crossed with paths and bore the marks of football playing. The ash trees bowed despondently; still sheathed in protecting iron frames, they seemed to have given up the fight. But the one chestnut flaunted its high candles. He was glad of that.

The first thing that struck him when he got off the bus was the smallness of everything. It seemed as though the place was shrinking. The buildings that had towered above him in boyhood were now small and drab and dirty. The narrow, busy railway crossing had disappeared. Gone too, the tall signal-box and its winding stairs. There were walls instead of the great gates. The pit wasn't working. It was difficult to remember how those gates used to miraculously open and close for the fussy little loco coming down from Datton with its twenty clanking trucks winding behind. He looked over the wall. All the way up to what had once been the pit-yard was a patchy sort of a field. You could barely distinguish the scars of the old track. The grass wasn't good, growing from slag and coal-dust it couldn't be, but the place was a riot of dandelions, an army of dandelions marching any old how, wave after wave of them, right up to the ruined base of the old engine-house.

How often he'd awakened to the sound of that regular thud, to run barefooted to the window to see the pulley wheels spinning fast, and dust and smoke rising slowly, and the little shaggy pony pulling the tubs of waste to the tip-end, with the lads shouting encouragement; and when you leaned out of the window and waved, they waved back. Now the engine was silent and the pulley wheels stripped, the pony to dust

137

and the lads – probably among the men at the corner-end or queueing up for the second house at the Hippodrome. There it stood, the old Hipp with its ornate front and bare backside. Something was missing: that was it, the chush, chush, chush of the gas-engine at the back, the thin grey jet of its exhaust. When he was a boy there was more magic in its regular throb than church bells.

'Can Ah go to the pictures, Grandma?' He used to hang about the house for hours before he dared screw up courage to ask. She'd pull open the table-drawer and take out her purse. That was *her* drawer. There was a pin-cushion in it, and boxes with buttons and cotton and hooks and eyes, and a little box inlaid with a fancy pattern, in which she kept her treasured jet beads and brooches. She'd take out three pennies and drop them, one by one, into his hand. Then he'd wait, and she'd say, 'Well, what are ye waitin' for? It's thrippence to go in, isn't it? Now go and get washed, and *don't* forget your ears! Then we'll see...'

'Ah'm washed, Grandma.' 'Turn round... Um.' Out with the purse again. 'Here's tuppence for spending money.' 'Thanks, Granny.' Tearing down the street as if there wasn't a minute to lose, knowing perfectly well that there was an hour to go yet.

Those old pictures! They were worth waiting for, sitting in solitary spendour in the dim light until the place began to fill up and the rows of empty seats became rows of people. Those old pictures! There was one about a journey to the moon, and there was Two Gun Bill, and Tom Mix and Bill Hart and Charlie Chaplin and Buster Keaton. Sometimes there was a serial with Pearl White or Harry Carey. You used to sit with beating heart waiting for the pictures to begin. There was a big safety curtain with advertisements on it. Waiting restlessly, you used to read them with rage and contempt, for the safety curtain and the advertisements stood between you and the screen, stood there like some blatant ugly guardian with its family butchers and Groceries and Service and Satisfaction and New Hats – *When it's a new hat you need, try Smith's* – and the latest designs and so on in a weary jumble. The two rows nearest the curtain were for the kids. Shouts and catcalls and fights, paper pellets and orange peel and apple gowks flying until the curtain went up and the virgin white screen was revealed. There were no bad films in those days – they were all good – provided there wasn't too much love in them.

Home from the pictures to find Granda getting his supper. Onions and chops disappearing beyond the walrus moustache. 'Umph!' Another mouthful, 'Pictures, eh?...Was it good? How many got killed?' And that was all. Granda was a man of few words. Articulate only when the talk turned to welding, angles and t-bars, sheet metal and ropes and sockets. Or roses and canaries...

Now he was gone. It had been a bitter day when they buried him. Bitter cold, with the rain driving hard across the green mounds with their leprosy of white marble, bitter cold, and the memory of his gaunt, sick face.

Someone else was in the old house now. No use turning that way. Other pictures on the wall. There had been a text: *God is our refuge and strength, a very present help in trouble*, a picture of the bridge at Arkingarthdale, and another of Buttermere. He used to stare at the lake and the clouds, until, in a kind of dream, he was there, floating down, light as a thistle seed, among the crags, walking on the water. Then the smell of frying bacon, newly cut from the ham that hung on the hook in the passage, would come drifting upstairs. No dream could resist that smell. The shining booler hoop that Granda had made himself hung in the yard, and after breakfast he'd run with it twice round the street. Saturday mornings he'd watch the men playing quoits. Or climb the deserted pit-heap with the others and make Indian fires in treacle tins, swinging them till they glowed red-hot.

Those days had gone for ever.

There weren't so many butcher's shops now. Johnson's the cobbler's was now a newsagent's. Cat's Nest, with its narrow streets and leaning houses, was demolished. The Latter Day Saints still met above the ironmonger's shop, if the weatherworn notice was to be believed. Remember the shock when Fatty said they were Mormons? But don't they have twenty wives! he said. Fatty shook his head. Not in England. They save up and emigrate to America where they can marry as many as they want, he revealed; and ever after he kept an eye on Mr Longstaffe, who every Sunday wore a white carnation in his button-hole; but he never went.

Going down the long curved street, Sand Street, where Uncle Joe lived, he saw a tall man limping towards him. There was something familiar about him. The man stopped, stared.

'It's Nick, isn't it?' said the man. 'Yes, it's Nick all right...
but I don't know you...' The lame man flushed. 'It's a long
time since we met. Ah'm your cousin Sam.'

'Well,' he said. 'I didn't recognise you. It's a long time,
though.'

'That's all right,' said Sam, 'Ah've changed since you left,
Ah suppose. Ah'd only be a lad in shorts when you went
away.'

They stood a moment, an awkward, fidgety moment of
silence, while they shot half-shy glances at each other. It had
to stop. Nick said: 'You've been in the Army?'

'Aye, till Ah got this.' He motioned to his leg.

'That's bad,' said Nick, 'I was in the Navy. Minesweeper
took us from Dunkirk. A bit cramped.'

'We didn't mind,' said Sam. 'Were ye goin' down to Uncle
Joe's? Ah've just been down to see him, but he's out. Took
Aunt Rose to the bingo, the people nextdoor say.'

'He expected me coming...' said Nick.

'Aye, he did, but not so soon. Expected ye comin' wi' that
last bus. Tell ye what, how about having a look up to my place
till the bingo comes out?'

'Righto!' said Nick.

They walked back into Church Street, past the demolished
houses in Cat's Nest, and turned in to Chapel Row. Sam's
house stood alone. 'It's not much of a house,' said Sam,
'should've been pulled down long ago.' Inside, it smelled
strongly of damp and decay. Sam's wife made a cup of tea
while Sam talked on about the house. The last time Nick had
seen him he'd been a harum-scarum lad with torn breeches
and a cheeky face. It was hard to believe that this serious man
had grown from the cheeky lad.

'We were lucky to get this house,' he was saying. 'But it
was in a hell of a mess when we got it. Some Irish folk lived
in it – well, perhaps it was just a place to sleep in. They hadn't
any furniture. No mats or carpets. Kept cats and allowed them
to muck all over the place. The rooms were filthy. Had to hold
our noses when we came to have a look at it. And the floor
was heavin' wi' the damp. We set to and started to clean it
from top to bottom. We swilled the walls, and the floors and
the ceilings. We were tired of carrying water. Then we started
scrubbin'. And after we'd scrubbed once, we scrubbed again.
It was a fortnight before the house was dry enough to live in.

And then our troubles started. It rained in, and wi' the floor lifting all the furniture was topsy-turvy and Annie kept trippin' up and hurtin' herself.

'So Ah told Annie to tell the feller that came for the rent that it was time he was seein' about some repairs. Well, the next time he came she told him. And got nothin' but a lot of impitence for her trouble, didn't ye Annie?' 'He was terrible,' she said. Sam chuckled: 'The next time he came Ah was waitin' for him. Ah was sittin' in front of the fire readin' a book when he landed. He never knocked, just walked in! How did you get in? Ah says. Through the door, he says, kind of snappy. Six foot three he is, a retired slop. Ah eyes him up and down: Ah was brought up to knock at the door and wait till Ah was asked to come in, Ah says.

'He flushed up. Ah happens to be collectin' rents, not payin' social calls, he says.

'That makes no bloody difference, Ah says. You'll knock the next time ye come for the rent, or ye'll go out a dam' sight quicker than ye come in. So put that in ye pipe and smoke it!

'So Ah goes back to me readin', and Annie gets the rent book and the money. He starts fillin' the book in, mutterin' like this all the time: A week in arrears, and this week, he says, that'll be twenty-one shilling.

'Beggin' ye pardon! Ah says, shuttin' the book Ah was readin'. Ye call for the rent once a fortnight. So it's not in arrears. It's you that's in arrears. Come once a week and ye'll get it on the dot. Yer come fortnightly for your convenience, not mine, and he grunted something about it havin' to go down as arrears to keep things right.

'Be then me blood was up. All right, Ah says, Ah'll do ye out of a job. In future Ah'll send the rent to your boss by registered post, less postage! There's no need to do that! he says. Then shut up about the bloody arrears, Ah says.

'He's just about to go, and glad to go Ah'll bet, when Ah says: Oh, and what about the repairs? No men or materials, he says. Ye'd better get it done or Ah'll take it further, Ah says. Take it as far as ye like, he says. We can't do the job without men or materials. And he shoved off.

'So the next day Ah went to see the Sanitary Inspector, and he backed the landlord up. So Ah went to see the M.O.H. And he came up wi' me to see the house. Terrible, he says. This house is a death-trap for children. Ah'll shake your landlord up a bit.

'And he did, because a week later we had to move out while they put a new floor in and repaired the roof. Kept poppin' in and out to see how the job was gettin' on, 'cos we were livin' in with me Ma, and not getting on very well with her, either. Took them a week to finish the job, and the foreman says we should wait another week before we moved in again.

'But we never lasted that week. Annie had a row wi' me sister, and Ah had a row wi' me Ma, and after the row Ah says, Aw, to hell wi' this, and packed the suitcases and staggered outa the house. Annie was helpin' Aunt Rose to do a bit cleanin', and Ah intended callin' for her on the way home. It was a good job Ah met her comin' back to Ma's. That was about the roughest journey Ah ever had. There was a strong wind blowin', Ah had a suitcase in each hand and a parcel under me arm, and a kettle hangin' from me little finger. Ever time me little finger got tired the kettle dropped and the wind blew it away helter-skelter. And Ah had to run after it, still holdin' on to me cases, and try to pick it up. When Annie met me Ah was cursin' like a trooper.'

'That he was!' said Annie. 'He was glad to hand me one of those cases! Have a cigarette, Nick?' 'Thanks,' he said. She gave him a queer little smile as she held out the packet. She was tall and dark. Her legs were good. Her eyes had a bit of the wanton in them. 'You don't remember me, do you?' she said.

'Can't say that I do,' he said apologetically, lighting his cigarette. 'Ye should,' said Sam. 'She's a Datton lass. Her dad had the cobbler's shop in Church Street. Johnson's.' Then he remembered. She was smiling. She had reason to. It had been one of those school romances. It had been a mixed class and they had sat at the same desk, walked to school together. After tea he used to hang about outside the shop, waiting for her coming out. It had been chalked on the school walls and on the street-ends: *Nick Dempster goes with Annie Johnson.*' Well! He'd often thought of her, but not like this. She was different, changed. He knew that kind of smile, the way she crossed and uncrossed her legs with a careless pulling of the skirt. She was...'

'Yes, of course, Annie Johnson. We went to school together,' he said. She smiled, satisfied. 'That's right Nick,' she said. Her eyes surveyed him, cool and fathomless through the haze of her cigarette smoke. Sam caught the look, flushed, glanced at his watch and said, 'Well, Nick, the clock's gettin' round. Let's have a look down Sand Street.' 'Right you are, Sam,' said Nick. 'Thanks for the cup of tea, Annie.' 'Don't mention it,' she said, 'should have something better to celebrate your visit.' She walked to the gate with them, 'Call again,' she said.

There was something wrong at Uncle Joe's. Nick couldn't place the feeling, but there was something wrong. And yet Uncle Joe and Aunt Rose were just the same. Uncle Joe as fat, a little thinner on top, Aunt Rose as thin and miserable as ever. They greeted him warmly enough, but there was an undercurrent of uneasiness. 'Shall Ah make ye a cup of tea?' said Aunt Rose, 'there's not much to go with it, but what there is you're welcome to.' 'Don't bother, Aunt Rose, thank you,' said Nick, 'I've just had a cup of tea and some biscuits at Sam's.' 'You're sure,' she said, relieved. 'Jack and his wife and the bairns landed without a word of warning on Thursday, and Ah'm sure they've eaten us out of house and home.' So that was it! They'd invited him to stay with them, and now, other visitors had arrived unexpectedly! Uncle Joe was speaking. 'Ah've got some chaps to see,' he said, glancing uneasily at his wife. 'At the usual place, Ah suppose!' she flashed. Uncle Joe grinned. 'Well, they might take a bit findin'.' They went out.

As soon as they were in the street Nick said, 'I think I've come at an awkward time, Uncle Joe.' Uncle Joe made an expressive gesture with his hand. 'Her relations, Nick lad. They come like locusts ye might say, without warnin', and when they've gone the place is as bare as a badger's backside. But don't worry lad, we'll manage somehow.' 'Listen, Uncle Joe,' said Nick carefully. 'I don't mind sleeping out. I can fix up at one of the pubs.' 'Ye'll do nowt of the sort,' said the little man, a trifle weakly, though. 'It's better than sleepin' on the couch,' said Sam. 'Well, ye might be right at that,' said Uncle Joe. 'They'll be goin' home tomorrow night, anyway. But it goes against the grain. Oh! them bloody relations of hers, they'll be the death of me!'

They walked in silence while his passion simmered. 'Ah well,' he said at last, 'as long as ye don't mind, Nick. We'll have a look at Top-end Club first. Ah want to see Joe Banting about a bit business. But we'll not stay there long, just long enough for a drink and a bit crack wi' Joe; then we'll move onto the King Willy.' 'Why move on t'd King Willy,' protested Sam, 'Top-end beer's good enough for me!' Uncle Joe shook his head decisively: 'Nick wants a night's board at the King Willy, and we want to be along in good time. There'll be no pleasure at Top-end tonight. Kirby's been playin' Datton today, and there'll be a busload o' them in Top-end, pinting to their heart's content. There'll be a bit of a concert, if ye like concerts, but Ah've had some.' Sam shuddered, 'You're right as usual,' he said.

Top-end Club was full to overflowing. They had to squeeze through the serried ranks at the bar. A sweating waiter, tray above his head, forced his way through the crowd. The way he balanced his tray was as pretty a picture as Nick had ever seen, but there was nothing pretty about the words he was using. 'Seen Joe Banting?' asked Uncle Joe. 'Make way there! Make way!' cried the waiter, and more impatiently, 'he's upstairs.' They went up some creaking stairs into a long, low room full of people and noise and smoke. A piano was playing at the far end, you could hear it if you listened closely, little keys tinkling vainly against the ebb and flow of voices. 'There he is!' cried Uncle Joe, and darted into the maelstrom. They made their way to a man who stood among the rest like a rock. He was a big man. He wore loose-fitting tweeds that looked as if he'd slept in them. There was a grey covering of ash over his waistcoat. The only time he removed his cigarette was when he wanted to drink. When he was talking it waggled grotesquely in his lips. He stood there, like a rock, a little distance from the bar, with the unending traffic of men and beer brushing against him but never disturbing his anchorage. His eyes were hooded, but when he smiled they became deep pools amidst the crags of his features. An unusual man.

'Ha, Joe! Now, Sam!' The hoods lifted and the deepset eyes took in Nick. 'This is Nick, me nevvy, Jake's lad.' 'Pleased to meet ye!' said Banting. His cigarette was the merest stub, almost level with his lips. He took it out, looked at it, sighed, and let it drop to the floor. 'Packed tonight,' he said. 'Look at them! Look at my brethren!' 'You're not at the piano tonight,' said Uncle Joe, 'what's the matter?' The hoods lifted for a second and the pools flashed fire. 'Some fool from Kirby's playin'. He's murdered every tune so far. Not that it matters. It's only what the wireless calls incidental music.' 'Er . . . about them leeks . . .' said Uncle Joe. 'Shut up,' said Banting, speaking from the corner of his mouth. 'D'ye want everybody to know where ye get your show-leeks from? We'll talk about it somewhere else.' 'All right,' said Uncle Joe, 'Ah'll get some drinks in and then we'll move on.' He thrust his way to the bar. Banting drained his glass quickly. 'Make mine a bitter, Joe,' he called.

They had a drink and left. Once outside Banting heaved a sigh of relief. 'Ah'm glad to be out of that!' he said. 'A lot of bloody lice, that's what they are. Where're we goin' now?' 'King Willy.' 'Good!' He pulled a battered Woodbine packet from his pocket. It was empty. 'Have one of mine,' said Nick. 'Thanks.' He lit up and puffed luxuriously, 'Dam' lice. Played 'em a piece and they ignored me. Ah might have been playin' a tin-whistle for all the notice they took. So Ah stopped halfway through and left them to it.'

'They've got a poor idea of music, Joe,' said Uncle Joe. 'But what about them leeks?'

'The leeks? Plenty of time for the leeks!' He turned to Nick. 'What did ye say your name was?' 'Nick Dempster.' 'Oh, Dempster. Any relation to Joe here?' 'Ah told ye once he was me nevvy,' said Uncle Joe patiently. 'Mustn't have heard ye. Them lice made too much noise. Music! They don't know what music is! Why, Nick lad, Ah can play sixteen instruments. And Ah'm a composer, too.'

'You must have a talent for music,' said Nick.

'Talent? Ah wrote a hundred and fifty songs, set 'em to me own music. The publishers sent 'em back. No good, they said. So Ah took one of their own songs, reversed the tune and made a lyric for it, and sent it in. It was a raging success. Made three hundred out of it. Whenever Ah get short of cash, that's what Ah do. Reverse a tune and write a lyric. Burnt me own songs.'

'You shouldn't have done that,' said Nick. 'They might have published them after you were dead.' Banting stared at him, wide-eyed. For a moment Nick thought he was going to strike him. Then he was doubled up with laughter, and the tears streamed down his cheeks. 'Oho,' he chortled, 'that's a good 'un. Why haven't we met before lad.' He was still chuckling when they entered the snug at the King Willy. There were pictures of horses on the walls. Derby winners. Cap colours and crop in a glass case. An old-fashioned life-sized photograph of a jockey with a walrus moustache. 'That's Ned Garrick, the landlord, when he was in his prime,' explained Uncle Joe.

'Give that bell a ring, Nick,' said Sam, 'Ah'm thirsty.' Banting winked, 'Born without a clack to his throat,' he said. Uncle Joe smiled, 'It's the family malady. Nick'll be the same Ah expect.' 'I can knock a few back when I'm in the mood,' said Nick modestly. The landlord came in. Shorn of his colours and moustache he looked small and commonplace. All that was left of his racing days were his bandy legs. And his shrewd, keen eyes. ''Lo Joe, 'lo Sam. 'Lo Banting . . . How d'ye do?' This last to Nick. 'That's my nevvy, Nick Dempster,' said Uncle Joe. The landlord nodded. 'Make it four of the best, Ned,' said Banting. As the landlord turned: 'Oh, Ned,' said Uncle Joe, 'can ye put my nevvy up for the night?' Garrick smiled thinly. 'You should know better, Joe. This is a pub, not an inn.' 'Sorry Ah mentioned it,' said Uncle Joe, a bit huffed. 'That's all right, Joe,' hastening to mollify a good customer. 'Ah'd have put the young man up, but we've got relatives here for the weekend, and there isn't room for a cat to swing his tail.' He departed. 'Well, that's that,' said Uncle Joe, 'we'll have to try somewhere else.' 'Are there any inns?' asked Nick. 'Plenty,' said Banting, 'there's the Green Tree . . .' 'The Ship,' announced Sam. 'And not forgetting the Sportsman's,' said Uncle Joe. Nick laughed: 'It looks as though we're in for a night!'

They were sampling their second pint when Major Domo arrived. He was a little man lost in a loud suit of plus-fours. He wore brown shoes inlaid with fancy patterns in white. He had shifty eyes. Nick saw his companions eye the man disdainfully and wasn't surprised. He rang the bell like a visiting lord, and pulled out a wad of notes to pay for his drink. Nick noticed his hands. They were a dirty brown. His nails were too long, each had a black fringe, black as the dead black of Hangman's Cap. Each knuckle had a little tuft of hair.

'Cheers!' he said, and tipped his head back to pour the beer in. That was the measure of the man. He didn't lower his head until the glass was empty. The way his Adam's apple bobbed you'd think there was something alive trapped in his scrawny neck. 'Ah!' he said, and gazed into the empty pot. Not quite empty. There was a bit froth left. His tongue, slick as a humming-bird's, popped in and out, flicking the froth from the inside of the jar until it was as clean as any barmaid's apron could make it. 'Ah!' he said, in deep satisfaction again, and pressed the bell button. 'Have one with me, gentlemen?' he enquired. Uncle Joe and Sam grinned assent. Nick stared. 'You can count me out!' said Banting disdainfully. 'Suits me,' said Major, carelessly. Two more chaps came in, respectable looking chaps, with spats and pin-striped trousers, but Nick was hardly aware of them. He was too busy getting an eyeful of Major Domo. The man wore rings. Several of them. And he'd opened his jacket to reveal a great gold watch-chain with a heavy seal attached. 'What does he do for a living,' whispered Nick to Banting. Banting didn't whisper. 'Ah don't know for sure – but the Divil does, nae doubt!' he said loudly.

Major flashed a deadly look, like forked lightning, but it merely glanced off the man of flint. 'So you grow leeks...?' said Nick, in a desperate attempt to change an unprofitable subject. 'A double-dyed scoundrel if ever there was one!' said Banting. His voice rang like a bugle. Major lifted his glass as if to hurl it at his enemy, but luckily for Mr Banting, Garrick arrived with a loaded tray, and Major was not yet in that condition where you throw the landlord's glasses about while he's watching. There was a couple of hours hard work to put in before he reached that happy state. It took many pints to forget that Garrick had the disposition of a weasel. Garrick took Banting's empty glass and looked enquiringly from glass to man.

'Mr Banting's wearin' the ribbon tonight, Ned,' said Major. 'Keep ye trap shut or ye'll be wearing lilies!' said Banting. His voice was cold, his eyes unhooded and bleak as he stared at the Major. 'About leeks...' said Nick. He'd been in too many pub brawls. 'Leeks is educated scallions,' said Banting. 'Just as Mr Major Domo is an educated scallawag!' Nick never saw anything so quick in all his life. The Major was over the table like a monkey, his face contorted into a snarl, gibbering a seemingly endless stream of unpleasant words. What he intended to do, no one will ever know. For Mr Banting merely grabbed him and held him at arm's length. 'Lemme go...' sobbed the Major. 'Lemme go.' 'What about the money ye owe me?' said Mr Banting. The Major stopped sobbing. His face cleared. 'Is that all ye were worrying about?' he asked. 'It's a fortnight since the race was run, and the winnin' horse was mine, and ye were the bookie. But ye've never been seen since.' 'Did you back that horse, too,' said Major. He pulled out his wallet, 'How much was it, now?' 'Ah had a quid on,' said Mr Banting, 'a twenty to one shot.' 'It was, it was,' said Major. 'Here you are, Banting old boy!' Banting grasped the notes as if it was a dream. He folded them, opened them out again, held them up to the light, did everything but smell them. Then he walked slowly over to the bell. The company sighed a massed sigh of relief.

Nick pulled out his mouth-organ. He felt like letting off steam. 'Needn't ring the bell, Joe,' said Sam, 'here's Ned.' 'Ah, Ned lad. Drinks in for everybody.' 'That's better!' said Garrick, reversing his decision to order one of the two out.

That was the beginning of a very pleasant evening. Nick played jazz until round about nine. Then Mr Banting asked for *Daisy*, and when they'd finished with that they asked him to play some more of the old ones. Then, a little later, one of the chaps with spats leaned over and asked Nick if he could play any hymns. Nick said he could, and what would he like? He studied a bit. Nick thought he was trying to choose between *The Old Rugged Cross* and *Abide with Me*. But he didn't; he asked for an old chapel hymn. Nick knew it. He'd been brought up chapel and knew all Charles Wesley's hymns. And he knew this one. It was *What shall I do my God to love, My loving God to praise*. Nick played it over. 'Is that the right tune?' he said. The chap nodded. So he played it, and the chap started to sing. He hadn't a bad voice, either. Nick guessed he must have been a choirmaster or something sometime or other. Until Nick started playing this hymn the man had seemed dead to what was happening. His companion had done all the talking which was mainly restricted to ordering the drinks. Although, it goes without saying, the dumb one's elbow had been pretty eloquent. Now, he forgot his beer. So did the others. Even Major. He tried to take a sly drink once, but Banting stopped him with one look.

He sang half a dozen hymns and they all joined in the choruses. Then his voice went, so they stopped singing. The singer started his elbow work again, and Nick had two or three quick while he had the chance. He'd got behind with playing the mouth-organ so much, and there were half a dozen jars standing in front of him.

Major was soon busy talking to the two chaps. As usual the singer didn't talk much, but his pal seemed to have plenty to say. After a while Major went out.

Five minutes later he came back, leading a whippet. He

must have been home for the dog. 'He's run all the way there and back,' commented Banting. 'Unless he rode back on the dog,' suggested Uncle Joe. And certainly the dog was almost the size of a small pony. Nick didn't care much for whippets. They're all right outside. There's nothing more exciting than to watch a rangy whippet run a hare down. But they're too big for rooms. They don't fit. This one had a muzzle on. He was a big brute with a great lean body. You could count his ribs. He had large liquid eyes. Whenever he got near a boot he cringed. There was a big sore under his left ear. Major dragged him over to the two chaps. 'This is him!' he said, 'and here's his pedigree.' He handed the talkative one a roll of paper.

Major started a line of selling talk. He thought it was going down well, but it was obvious to Nick that it wasn't. The singer kept bending his elbow, completely ignoring the sales talk. The other man seemed to be having a job to keep his face straight. 'No,' he said at last. 'There's nothing doing, Major. Somebody's sold you a pup! This pedigree's a fake.' 'A fake!' cried Major. 'Don't tell me it's a fake! That chap owed me twenty quid!' Banting laughed scornfully. 'Ye need laugh,' said Major. 'My God, there's no honesty left in the world. Me, Major Domo, dipped of twenty quid!' 'And about time you were dipped, too!' said Banting. Major was nearly weeping. 'My God,' he sobbed. 'When Ah think of what Ah've done for that dog! Ah've fed it on the best. We sacrificed our rations to feed him. He slept at the bottom of our bed. Ah got a vet in last week about that sore under his ear, cost me two quid. He walked about the house as if he owned it, this dog, he knocked the bairns over if they were in his way, be dam' he'd knock me outa the way, never mind the bairns! He used to stand at the door like an old man, watchin' the folk go by, and Ah used to watch him and think next year's Waterloo was in me pocket. And he was a fake all the time, a fake!'

'Dry yer eyes Major,' said Sam. 'Buy a little cart and he'll pull ye to the tracks. He's nearly the size of a pony anyway.' 'But he don't eat hay!' cried Major. The whole company roared. Then the singer of hymns came to life again. He clicked at the dog. 'Come here, lad!'

The dog whined with an eager note, wrenched away the leash from the Major's hand, walked over to the singer and laid his head on his knee. The singer spoke with difficulty, which was not surprising, since he had consumed about eight or nine pints in just under an hour. 'This dog...' he said, 'this dog...is a...gentleman.' 'Accordin' to this paper he is,' said Major. The singer shook his head, 'Thassa fake,' he said, 'but look at the way he acts...walks...can't fake...these marks of gen'leman.' 'No,' said the Major, thoughtfully. 'Tell you what...tellyouwhat...I'll take him off your hands.' 'How much?' asked the Major, eagerly. The singer jumped as if he had been shot. 'Not offering price...just take him off your hands.' 'Ah'm not *giving* him away,' said Major. 'Keep him then!' said the singer, and reverted to his elbow. Major was shocked. He sat down opposite the singer and tried in vain to catch his eye. 'Ye don't expect me to give him away, d'ye?' he said.

The other man beckoned Major over to him. 'Give it to him,' he urged. 'You'll not regret it.' Major stared at him. 'You'll not lose on it,' promised the man. Major went back. He looked long and intently at the singer. You could see it was the hardest decision of his life. 'All right, Mister,' he said at last, 'he's yours!' The singer held up a protesting hand. 'Not so quickly, sir. Why d'you give...give me...this dog?' ''Cos ye want him,' said Major mournfully, 'and 'cos Ah'm sure ye'll give him a good home.' 'And what else?' asked the singer of hymns. His wandering eye for once met and held the Major's. Now what will he say, thought Nick. ''Cos yer pal said it was worth me while givin' it to ye, sir.' The singer sat up, electrified. 'And you took a gamble, eh?' Major nodded. The singer took out a notecase and extracted five notes. 'Thy faith shall be rewarded thee,' he said, and handed them over. 'Ta,' said the Major. He seemed to be a little dazed. He went into a corner and examined the notes. Then he put them in his wallet beside the others. The whippet still rested his snake head on the singer's knees. 'Come on, old boy. It's time we were going,' said the talkative one. The singer got up without a word, and made his way to the door. The dog followed, trailing his leash. The talkative man took a pad out of his pocket and scribbled something on it. He handed it to Major. 'Here, sign this,' he said. Major signed it. 'And Ah might as well have the pedigree as well.' Major handed it over. The man said 'Good evening all,' courteously, and walked out. A few minutes later there came the sound of a car starting up.

Major emerged from his daze. 'Hell's bells!' he said, 'did ye see that bit play, lads? Did ye see it?' 'Ye were lucky there,' said Sam. 'Lucky! What d'ye mean?' said Major. 'Why, that he was tight,' said Sam. 'Ah, that was a bit of luck, wasn't it!' said Major. He patted the bulge where his wallet was. Mr Banting was smiling. 'He wasn't tight, Major,' he said. 'How d'ye know that?' said Sam. 'Ah know that feller well – by sight,' said Banting. 'It takes more than nine pints to make him tight. He's got the biggest belly for beer of any boozer Ah've ever met!' Major came out of his corner like a bouncing ball. 'Who is he, then?' he demanded. Mr Banting lit another cigarette, 'Being as he's in the same line as yourself, Major, Ah thought ye'd know him.' 'Not from Adam,' breathed the Major. 'No!' said Banting. 'Ye mean to tell me ye didn't know him! Why, that was Jack Prendergast, him that runs the Stadium at Kirby!'

Major rushed to the door. 'Where are ye off to now?' asked Banting. 'Off to get that dog back off them dirty low-down double-crossers,' shouted Major. Banting shook his head, 'It's no good,' he sighed, 'for one thing, they went off in a car. They'll be half-way to Kirby now. For another, ye signed the dog away, y'know.'

'My God, Ah did,' said Major. He sat down again. 'Then that pedigree wasn't a fake?' 'What d'you think?' said Mr Banting. 'Ah well, Ah got a fiver out of it,' said Major. 'If Prendergast gave ye a fiver, then he was worth fifty,' said Mr Banting pleasantly. Major Domo made a valiant attempt to keep his passion under control.

At ten o'clock they turned out, or were turned out, one of the two. The houses danced and the moon was giddy. They stood at the corner-end saying their fond farewells. Passers-by disgracefully lurched and staggered. Three times Sam and Uncle Joe had to pursue Major Domo who had an idea that somewhere up the road Prendergast was hiding with his dog. The fourth time they gave him up in disgust. He passed rapidly from their limited field of vision, tearful and gesticulating, shouting down the wrath of heaven on the singer of hymns. 'Well, Ah'm away home!' said Mr Banting, 'enjoyable evening. Better than the pictures. Glad to have met ye, Nick.' And he too passed out of sight, an unsteady rock.

The three linked arms for greater safety. For half the population of Datton was drunk. Street corners were toppling, telegraph poles and gas lamp standards grew in plantations, bent by a crazy wind. They passed the waterworks. 'Y'know, when I was a boy, I always wanted to swim in the waterworks,' said Nick. 'Too late,' said Uncle Joe sadly. 'Too soon,' said Sam, 'the sun's not up yet.' Nick stood stockstill. 'To swim in the moonlight!' he cried, 'what an adventure!' 'Sleepin' in bed's a better,' said Sam. 'C'mon, Nick.' Nick laughed. 'Did Ah crack a joke there?' demanded Sam, a little hurt. 'The joke's on me,' said Nick, 'I've got no bed to go to. I'll have to find shelter in the waterworks.' 'By gum, he's right! We forgot all about goin' to The Sportsman's and the others,' said Uncle Joe. He was thinking of Aunt Rose, and the thought nearly sobered him. 'Think of all the fun we've missed,' said Nick, 'the Green Tree and the Ship...' 'And the Sportsman's,' said Sam, sadly. 'Nick, will ye sleep on the couch at our house?' 'I'd sleep on the floor if it pleases you,' said Nick earnestly. 'Good enough,' said Sam, and collapsed. They stared at him for a while. 'He must be drunk,' said Uncle Joe, 'he always loses the use of his legs when he's proper tight. We'll have to carry him home. It's always the same,' he complained, 'Annie'll tell Rose and Ah'll get the blame.' 'Never mind. Let's get him home,' said Nick.

Home seemed a long way away. Streets went a wandering and houses were divorced, Sam's legs dragged behind like fishing hooks, catching every obstruction, shadows wrenched themselves from their moorings, and the moon, riding a tipsy sky, laughed to see such fun.

At last – 'Here we are, this is it!' said Uncle Joe. 'It doesn't look like Sam's place to me,' said Nick, doubtfully. Uncle Joe looked around uneasily, 'Hell's bells, ye're right, Nick. This is Sand Street. Right about turn!' A slop walked out of the shadows. 'Hello, what's this?' he said. 'My friend's had a fit,' explained Nick. The slop looked at them a long time. Then he put his hand under Sam's chin and had a look at his face. 'You're right,' he said. 'Get him home sharp. D'ye want a bit hand?' 'We'll manage, thanks,' said Nick. 'Give him some black coffee when you get him home,' said the slop, 'it's good for that kind of fit!'

They found the house all right, this time. Meeting the slop had sobered Uncle Joe up a bit and he didn't tend to drop his side of Sam so much. The kitchen door opened as they dragged Sam down the yard. It was Annie. 'He's had a drop too much, lass,' said Uncle Joe. She only said, 'Take him upstairs.'

'Wouldn't a cup of coffee do him good,' said Nick. 'It wouldn't,' she said, 'he'll sleep it off. Take him upstairs.' They laid him on the bed and came down again. 'We didn't take his clothes off,' said Uncle Joe. 'That's all right, Ah'll manage,' she said. 'Goodnight, Uncle Joe. Goodnight, Nick.'

And they found themselves in the street again. 'But you were goin' to sleep on Sam's couch,' said Uncle Joe, 'Sam asked ye!' 'I was,' said Nick, 'I thought of it when we were comin' out, but she didn't seem too pleased with us, some-how!' 'Oh, take no notice of women!' said Uncle Joe. 'You go back, lad. Ah'll find me own way home. G'night.'

He felt badly about it as he knocked at the door. After all, she had plenty on her plate when she had Sam. She opened the door, 'Oh, it's you, is it,' she said, looking him up and down. 'Sam asked me to stay here for the night,' he explained. 'Don't you think Ah've got enough to put up with?' she demanded, 'there's plenty of trouble wi' one drunk without havin' another on me hands.' 'I'm sorry,' he said. She flung her head. 'Oh, all right, come in. Don't stand there with your bottom lip hangin'.' So he went in.

'And where d'ye think you're goin' to sleep?' she said, 'we've only the one bed...' 'On the couch,' he said meekly. 'Good enough.'

Sam had also said 'good enough', but the way she said it was different. Two small words drifting on a sea of sorrow. He sat on the couch while she poured him a cup of tea. She asked him if he wanted anything to eat. He was hungry, but said no, he didn't feel like eating. So she poured herself a cup of tea and sat in the chair beside the fire. For the first time he noticed that she was wearing her dressing-gown. She brooded, cup in hand, over the fire. Then she looked at him. 'You're not so drunk after all, are you?' she said. 'I hadn't so much,' he agreed. 'Perhaps you'd like something to eat, then?' 'Well, I wouldn't mind,' he said. She brought him some sandwiches, then returned to her chair. 'Funny,' she said. 'You comin' back like this. Remember when we were young, Nick? Remember school and the fun we used to have? Walking out together, two kids without a care in the world?' 'I remember,' he said, 'they were good days.' She sighed. 'Yes, they were good days.'

'Then you went away,' she said, 'I never forgot you Nick. That's the reason I married Sam. He was your cousin. He reminded me of you.' Nick wanted to say something but couldn't. He felt as she did, the enormous weight of the years. They sat in silence for a long time. Then she said, 'Ah'm going to bed now, Nick, if you don't mind.'

She got some blankets from a drawer and laid them on the couch beside him. Then she sat beside him and took hold of his hand. 'You can give me a kiss for old times' sake,' she said.

The kiss lasted a long time. She was good to kiss, she had been before, but this was different. Everything she had was poured into her lips. Then her lips slipped from his, and she was weeping like a lost child, her face buried against his shoulder.

'Ah don't know why Ah should cry like this,' she said. 'For the same reason that I'm not, honey,' he said. 'Ah'd better go to bed,' she said. 'There's no hurry.' 'Ah'd better go.' 'Well,' he said, 'you haven't finished your tea yet.' He went over and picked up the cup. But when he turned round she was gone.

He shrugged his shoulders and started making the bed, spreading the blankets over the couch. Then he heard a noise from the street and pulled the curtains aside. It was Major Domo, weaving his lonely way home, holding threatening converse with an invisible company. Behind him, like a fantastic mime, danced a shadow Major. The real Major shook his fist at the moon, and the shadow Major shook his flat fist at the real Major. He wandered in a circle, became giddy, lost his balance and his shadow, and fell in the gutter. He cursed, he wept, he called for his whippet. Then he was still. He had fallen asleep.

And Arcady slept with him.

[1947]

The joker, striking a pose for the camera, with some of his family. *Left to right:* Sid Chaplin, sister Kathy, mother Elsie, brother-in-law Walter, father Ike, brother Fred, sister-in-law Margaret; *at front*, daughter Gillian and son Christopher. 1950.

As well as being a flirtation with a different form, Weekend in Arcady *represented a kind of coming home for Sid Chaplin. In fact, it was written at a time when the writer was actually leaving the county of his birth for good.*

His writing had been noticed by his new bosses at the National Coal Board and he'd been asked to contribute to a new magazine for the industry and its workforce, Coal.

In 1950 he joined its staff and so left Dean and Chapter and took his young family south to London. He became Coal's *roving reporter, criss-crossing Britain during the early 50s in a little light aircraft piloted by his photographer Harry Smead. Many of the jobs were routine – profiling managers, writing features on new machinery and old pitmen. But he also came to expect the call in the middle of the night: the times when he had to hurriedly pack and take himself off to a far corner of Britain. And steel himself for what was to come. There'd been another disaster.*

Twenty years later – when water flooded the workings of Lofthouse Colliery, Yorkshire, in March 1973, killing seven men – Sid Chaplin recalled these times.

Over: On assignment for *Coal* magazine: Sid Chaplin with his photographer Harry Smead.

The Life a Miner Gives

In forty years I have been underground in every part of Britain, from the Mull of Kintyre to the coast of Fife, through workings in Lancashire, North Wales and down the deep shafts of Yorkshire. I know the miners of the Potteries, of Notts, Derbyshire and the bright clean Dover coast, South Wales from the close valleys to the wide open spaces of Carmarthen. Betimes I've crawled my stint in Irish, Italian and American mines as well.

But I've never forgotten the first great lesson of the mining life. I was 15, pint-sized and wide-eyed, setting off on my first pit-shift. The time was 4.30 a.m., and I'll tell you something – I was privileged. My mother got up with me. The first thing a miner learns is to get himself up and out, but this first morning my mother was there. 'Now look after yourself, lad,' she called. I was halfway down the street when I discovered that I'd come without my bait or breakfast. So I went back, picked it up at the double and turned. 'Now just you sit down,' she said. 'Sit down and consider – never mind the rush.'

And always ever after while I was at home she would make me do just that – sit down for a while when I returned in a hurry for something. Just one of her little foibles. Then one morning the screens ground to a halt. The word went round, 'Two men buried in a fall; they're fetching them out.' And we waited, and waited. The first party came up. The man on the stretcher was very white. Another party took over and carried him away. The other fellers were plain dog-tired. Then the cage came up again. This time the blanket went right over. It was a plain brown blanket with a red band round the edge, and it covered the whole of the form on the stretcher. I can see the face shaped now to the brown material. The shape of the nose, the lips and the chin. The hollows of the eyes. Eyes that would never again see wife and child, darkness and daylight, pigeon and sky again. And I knew what my mother had meant when she made me sit down, and when she called after me, 'Now look after yourself, lad.' It was spelled out plain on the stretcher.

Still to this day I get the same feeling. It might be Italy, it could be Africa or Illinois or it could be Lofthouse in Yorkshire. But it's exactly the same feeling.

It's a strange feeling because it's such a mixture. Fear, yes – because I know the score when the man says on the box or over the radio that water broke through at half past two in the morning in Lofthouse Colliery, some 750 feet below the surface.

Some pits go nearly three quarters of a mile, but never mind, 750 feet straight down through solid earth and rock stratum is a long way down to be. But that is through the solid. Between the coal-face where the coal is won and the shaft, life-line to daylight and freedom, is another 2½ miles of tunnels and creeping darkness. That and the wall of water.

And because you might have been there you imagine. Of all the imponderables, water is the most devastatingly unexpected – pray God there were air pockets along the cracks in the rock. Pray God they made it in time.

And with the fear derived from knowledge is something else. With the lead in your stomach, and the sickness, your first instinct – almost a compulsion – is to get there by any means whatsoever, and pitch in and help. A disaster bonds all pitmen together, come hell and fire and water. Two hundred and fifty miners were standing by ready to assist the rescue brigades, said the announcer, adding later that Derek Ezra, Chairman of the National Coal Board, had flown up to the colliery. Well, of course! All were true to the mining instinct. If you can help, then you get there. At Knockshinnock, the first great disaster I ever experienced, pitmen cycled, hitch-hiked, bussed and legged it to offer their help. They were there, scores of them, in the rescue gallery – once it had been cleared of gas – one at each side a yard apart all the way out, waiting to receive the entombed miners. Thirteen they snatched from the jaws of death.

When Easington, County Durham, blew up, a rescue worker on hearing the news, thought: 'My God. This is the test. I've got to go – but will I stand up to it?' He went and he passed the test. At Knockshinnock, Easington, Creswell, each in turn, I saw a whole community bereft. Memories jostle. Of looking down from Easington's headgear, high up on the platform beside the iron pulleys. East the sea rolled, infinitely blue. West an empty village suddenly full of folk in black with the band playing the dead march and the lodge banner billowing like a great sail on the sea of mourning folk. That was one day I unashamedly wept.

The next time was at Creswell, and this was remarkable. It was on account of a smile – the forced smile of a widow. 'But there it is, we shall just have to manage,' she said. 'He wouldn't have wanted us to fold up, I'm sure.'

Men go down into the depths. They take a little light and they go down into the most terrifying darkness. For them it's a life and the weekly pay packet, chance and a pint to wash away the clinging dust. Some become victims, and others to you may be heroes. Often the hardest-hit and most heroic are the men who have the task of command. But always for me in the aftermath of disaster I see the face of a miner's wife. Sometimes she speaks. 'Be careful,' she says. 'Now mind what you're doing.' That is the woman I am thinking about today.

[1973]

Jam Twenty

It happened like this. I looked down the face one morning and saw lamp after lamp on the wag. Up and down they flashed in a kind of zig-zag, and I knew that trouble was brewing. So I dropped my shovel and crawled down to see Jack Ramsay, our lead-man. 'Trouble, Jack,' I panted. 'We've got the bosses.'

'Then put the kettle on,' he retorted, and went on working. Like a great big tank he was, his shovel going in and out. The dust lay thick upon his face and arms. 'Just let them,' he continued. 'Ah'm ready for them.'

And he was still at it when the manager and old Bill Elgey, the undermanager, appeared, breathing like broken-winded ponies, and flopped down beside us. Even I felt irritated. There were we and there was this big half-naked machine of a filler digging a ton of coal a minute and taking no more notice of us than if we were flies. Only when the gaffer was forced to speak first did I begin to get a glimmering of an idea of Jack's tactics – this was his parish, and he was going to keep it that way. 'Now come on, Jack. For God's sake leave off a minute!' said the gaffer. Dapper he was, and sharp into the bargain, but this time he was well and truly out-manoeuvred.

'So long as you don't stay too long,' said my partner. 'We've got work to do here.'

'Ah'll say one thing,' said the boss, looking around. 'She's looking very pleasant.'

'If it isn't a flash in the pan,' said Jack. 'But same as me, no doubt you've seen the plans?'

'Plans – what plans!' comes back the gaffer sharp.

'The plans I have,' said Jack, fixing him with his eye. 'You know as well as I do that Jawblades worked the same coal as us. I'll bring it along if you like... when we negotiate.'

'That's two miles away,' said Major Chilton.

'It's the same coal,' said Jack Ramsay. 'Average twenty-two inches thick and a rotten rambly top plus rolls galore. You know all about it, Major.'

'It looks all right to me,' said the Major.

'And so it should,' said Ramsay, 'the way my lads have worked at it.'

'Part that and part that the seam's got through bad ground,' said the gaffer. 'Ah doubt we'll have to ask for a reduction.'

'Aye, your percentage'll have to come down,' said Bill Elgey, in his regular His Master's Voice.

'And you can bugger that for a tale,' said Jack, so quickly that I almost missed hearing Elgey's bit. 'A pig of a face she's been, and a pig she'll stay; that's my reading. The worst face and the worst travelling in the pit. We'll be asking for an increase.'

'Wake up, Jack. We're not in the Promised Land yet!'

'No, we're not, and we never will be – but one thing we will have, and that's a bit of justice,' said Jack Ramsay. 'Do you know what they call us lot – the Chain Gang, on account of the distance we've got to travel and the rotten conditions before we even get to our work.'

'So all right; what are you going to do?' asks the Major.

'Well, for a start we want an increase.'

'That's a laugh,' said the Major. 'What else?'

'A new travelling road,' said Ramsay; and even I was taken aback at his temerity. I knew what he asked. You never saw anything like the way we came. You dropped down nine hundred feet to the Brockwell Seam and then you climbed hard for more than a mile to get out of it. Our seam was above, you see; on the top of an underground mountain; and West Twenty was the furthest, a kind of tropical Siberia. The last stretch was the worst of all. It was more a rabbit hole than an underground railway, hot as the hobs of hell and dusty with it, and the roof timber was broken to smithereens. In some places it was barely four feet high... and great dirty greasy bags like nanny goat's dugs kept gently swinging, to give you a sort of pat after the jab of a broken plank sticking down from the roof like the spear of an attacking Zulu. It was duck and duck again with your head cricked to one side and the sweat pouring like the falls of Lodore. There was an alternative way in; but it would cost thousands.

'A bloody new travelling road!' said the gaffer – even he was astonished. 'You must be kidding, Jack.'

'Ah'll give you a word you've forgot and it's safety.'

'You'll what!' said Major Chilton.

'It's worth taking to arbitration.'

'You haven't got a hope in hell,' said the gaffer. 'Why man, you'll be laughed out of court.'

Ramsay stretched out on his side, and played soldiers with lumps of coal. 'There'll be referees, Inspectors even, Major. We mightn't get our increase – but I'll tell you something. You'll be in trouble. You'll get the caning of your life.'

'Oh, come off it, Ramsay,' says the gaffer, and with one swipe Ramsay shifted his platoon of coaly little soldiers. His lips were white under the muck, and he was shaking with passion. 'No, Ah'm not comin' off, Major, and I'll tell you why. My men have worked hard, and you're not goin' to do them down. I'll crucify you first.' All this time his face was right up to the gaffer's. He was like a hurricane and a thunderstorm wrapped up in one and ready to burst; and every word came out like a sledgehammer. For the gaffer it must have been like the world falling in on him; and had he been able he'd have scurried away. 'Why man,' he said with a laugh that was all right, except that it ran out of confidence. 'You haven't a leg to stand on. You'll be asking for free baccy next!' And he crawled off, laughing as he went. But he foxed me. 'Well man, it looks as though Jack's bitten off more than he can chew this time,' I thought. All this was passing through my mind, when the boss squirmed round; only this time he wasn't laughing. 'You take it to your bloody arbitration, then. But Ah'll promise you one thing: Whether you win or lose makes no odds, just leave it to me. Ah'll see to it that you're paid, by God I will.'

But Jack was never lost for a word. 'With respect, Major – it'll be out of your hands by then. That's the point of arbitration.' That finished the boss. Out he got – you never heard such a scuffle and his language was terrible. 'That's fettled it,' I said. 'Now he'll have our guts for garters. We'll have to go to arbitration.'

'Isn't that what we want?' asked Jack, and from then on I knew there was something brewing. I mean, there was eyesight in it. Not only did I see Jack Ramsay start, but I saw him a champion. I watched him win and knew how he did it. It wasn't only the punch he packed in his gloves. He was faster always. He was always three moves ahead, and it was a ploy of his to get his opponent angry. So naturally, when we met a stone wall when we negotiated with the Major, and inevitably our case went forward for arbitration, everybody wondered why Jack Ramsay was smiling when the lodge chairman – in giving us his blessing – said we didn't stand the chance of a cat in hell.

Meanwhile, up at West Twenty, the travelling worsened, and with it the work at the seam, as Ramsay had prophesied. We were what we were, and that was that; thin seam men all our lives, fillers who'd learned to shove in and belly-flap or work on our sides; and before ever we'd set eyes on the place we knew that it would be rough. But even at that West Twenty became intolerable.

The coal-face is a slot in the coal-seam with the rock below and above stopped from crushing by steel and timber; a kind of ant-hill gallery with one moving wall from which the coal is extracted. Ours was 24 inches thick and 80 yards long. It dropped two to three inches in places – the difference between comfort and slavery. A bad roof and a soft floor came as a sort of free gift with these manacles to involve us in constant striving and double-propping: all unproductive work. In the end West Twenty became for all of us a kind of treadmill on the level (imagine, if you can, this crack in the earth packed with cutter, endless conveyor, timber and sweating toiling men). Some of us even got to the point where we wished that war would break out immediately, and a bomb put pay to all of us. The only one that managed to keep his end up was Jack – and not underground either, as it transpired.

I remember the day. It was Friday – and that it wasn't the 13th didn't make one iota of difference – when who should turn out of the engine-plane or travelling road but the gaffer. Wringing in sweat he was, and from a wild black face stared the red eyes of a man not far short of madness. He'd been out all night with the black gang supervising operations along the roadway, which had at one point 'closed like a box'. It's no joke, I can tell you, when a main roadway (used for coal transport as well as to get men in and out) drops roof to floor; and this was a different man to the beaming, genial Major Chilton of only the day before – the smiler who'd made mince-meat of our case.

Jack Ramsay was the first man he let eyes on. He charged. I tell you, even I shut my eyes. He reversed his yardstick and charged with the rounded end at Jack's midriff. The next thing

I heard was a grunt as they met. Jack held that stick firmly with one hand and it was embedded in the Major's stomach. 'Now what?' asked Ramsay.

'So you defied me!' yelled out the Major. 'You went and took it to arbitration.'

'The lodge did,' said Ramsay.

'You pressed it,' said the gaffer fiercely.

'And now we'll wait for a decision,' said Ramsay.

'But you'll not,' said the gaffer. 'You'll work for coal – you'll work like slaves for me.'

'Coal?' asked Ramsay.

'Coal – to pay your wages!'

Ramsay jerked the stick. It came away out of the Major's grasp like a knife out of hot butter and Jack politely handed it back. 'Beggin' your pardon, but there's something else.'

The Major was already turning. 'What's that?' he asked.

'There's men's lives. Twenty of us, and a deputy. What if the whole of that travelling road had closed this morning after we got in?'

'You attend to your own work,' said the Major. 'And mind, Ah'll be watchin' you.' And with this he left us.

'Things *are* bad,' said Painter Reynolds.

'And they'll get worse,' said Jack Ramsey. 'Come on, let's get started.' And we set off along that roasting hell of a road-way to the face that lay beyond. And there we found our deputy, Charlie Nelson. He was lying stretched across the kist face downwards. 'Now what?' said Jack, tapping him on the shoulder, and for answer Charlie groaned. Then he sat up. His brow was damp and his face was fish-belly white. 'Sorry, lads, to let you down,' he said. 'Ah'm sick and bad; Ah'm pained all over.'

Jack took me down the road a bit. 'You know what's the matter with him?' he said. Well, I hadn't a clue, and I told him. 'It's sympathy labour pains,' he said. 'His wife's expectin'. Ah've seen others bad this way, but never so prostrated.' He knew I'd done football training. 'You'd better have a look at him,' he said. 'And mind you find something – he might be a soft berk but he's still the best deputy we've got!' So I laid him over the kist again and massaged him, using a drop spare oil from the conveyor engine. Then I made him stand up. 'My God, no wonder you were feeling rotten,' I said. 'Your big bowel muscle was in a knot – I've never felt anything like it.' And it worked like a charm.

We stripped down and made for the face. On the way in we met the cuttermen. Three hours late they were. Their heads were down, and they'd barely list to speak. Those men came out like walking wounded. 'How is she?' we asked. They regarded us with lack-lustre eyes and passed on. 'You'll find out,' they said. 'My God, it must be bad,' said Charlie Nelson. 'When they won't talk about it.'

But we knew all right when we looked at it. Even the twenty-two inches of yesterday was a Grand Canyon on edge compared with this nipped crack, almost as thin as a hairline in the stratum. It would have gladdened the heart of a Grand Inquisitor – the way the floor yearned upwards to the roof, and the metal of the conveyor rang bell-like. And not only did the face move – it talked. You just had to stop whatever you were doing to be frozen by those sounds. Firedamp bubbled and chuckled as it pushed out every last drop of moisture. Then would come the starting piston and a chariot race of rock panels shoving and rubbing and leaping over each other, or maybe cracking like china plates. That was our main job – waiting for the sudden depth of tone that would give warning of a total pincer movement.

But what was real hell and purgatory was being in a world of only one dimension and no horizons. The face spread laterally, a chink of blackness which you knew only too well would resolve itself into obstacle after obstacle . . . the moment the roof came in and you tried to get the hell out of it.

So we contained ourselves. Knowing it would come sooner or later, you watched and waited and above all you listened, while all the time you worked on – and for what and why and who? It's a question I've never answered. 'We'll cope, lads,' said Jack Ramsay; it was his favourite expression. Only this time nobody believed him. We worked on out of sheer force of habit. Call it bigotry or pride, we weren't going to give in. And in the end you could see right down the face. We all put our lights out and the first man looked down the double line of props and saw the shine of the last man's lamp. What's more, the quiverings of the roof had been silenced.

That's why the end, when it came, was so surprising – it was so unexpected. One minute we were laughing and joking and the next the top dropped down again. Not all the way. Just two or three inches; but down it came as silently and smoothly as the lid of a sea-chest. In the middle of all this Charlie took a fit. Back he fell, kicking like he was swimming backstroke, out came a couple of props, and with a huge sigh or a wheeze the top squeezed down.

We dived; but Charlie was caught flat on his back. We couldn't see each other. 'Oh, my guts!' he shouted. We worked round towards him. A panel of stone had pinned him. It had just toppled that bit, then dropped with a thump. There it lay, flat on his legs and belly, like a pie in an oven. We pushed it clear with our boots. He cursed us, then he yelled blue murder. Then the lads pulled him out with his own shot-firing cable, while we crawled behind him. We made it just in time. Then the entire face closed behind us, like the proverbial vice. Only a vice doesn't blow dust. It was minutes before we could see each other, or talk.

Nor was that the end. From the tailgate to the shaft, from the cage-deck to the first aid room, it took eight of us spelling each other in turn to carry him out to daylight. And half a mile of it was little more than four feet high. He weighed thirteen stone without his boots on – imagine carrying a man half a mile in that height. It doesn't bear thinking about. But it's funny, you know. I never felt so happy. The sun was shining, and carrying Charlie was easy. Call it a kind of thanksgiving.

Perhaps we all felt that way. All I know is that nobody complained when they asked us to carry him home. This was after the doctor passed him. 'He's all right,' he said, 'but he's shocked. Will you carry him home?' Mind you, Charlie wanted to walk it. He knew that nothing was wrong with him that a week's rest wouldn't put right. 'You lie down,' said Jack. 'You're our responsibility . . . till we get you home to your missus.'

We bore him home. It was Pay Friday, I recall, and the village was thick with people. Women buzzed everywhere. Shaking mats, cleaning doorsteps or polishing knobs they waited for their pay . . . and men to come home. You could see them turn as we approached, wondering – was it their man on the stretcher; almost hear the hush that followed in our wake. Then the whispers. 'Poor soul, who is it?' 'Who can it be?'

Then along came the boss. Immaculate as always – in knee-breeches of blue, his white silk scarf contrasting with helmet and shining black boots – he smiled on all about him; especially the prettier daughters. I can see his yardstick now describe its perfect arc. We broke it. He knew who we were all right. 'Lower,' said Jack; and we rested. We opened out as he arrived. 'Now, Nelson – how do you feel?' asked the boss. 'Ah'm glad they've got you out all in one piece.'

'Well, I like that!' said Ramsay, unable to contain himself. *'You're* glad – it's no thanks to you that any of us got out alive today.' The women began to drift in towards us. 'Now come on, Ramsay, calm yourself down a bit,' said the boss, with the corner of his eye on the women. 'It's all part of pit-work, you know – it's all part of the life.'

At which Jack really got stuck into him. 'Don't you talk to me about pit-work,' he said. 'You don't even know your own business. In your system the product is everything – everybody knows that, even the bit lad who goes down pit for the first time in his life. So why don't we make it easier for the men to get at the product in the first place? I've heard tell of pits where they do it.'

'Mining,' said Major Chilton, 'is a science and an art. It takes a lifetime of study. A man has to have qualifications.'

'But oh no! that would be the reasonable thing to do – it would be treating workmen fairly,' said Jack Ramsay, ignoring him. 'By making it easy for men to win coal we might make it easy for men to work – and that wouldn't do, would it! So we get men that couldn't organise doll's houses, let alone pits and coal seams.'

'Ay, now; that's putting it a bit hard,' said the Major.

'Look at him!' said Ramsay. 'This man – who's the head and chief of them all! Do you want to know what happened when we went to reason with him? He sat and laughed in our faces. "Get back to your vomit, you dogs!" he as good as said. Which we did. Because we'd wages to earn and bairns and wives to keep. We went back... and a good man nearly died. This man; the man you see here – whose wife's expecting their first babby.' There he stood. His face was black as the ace of spades and full of fire, and as he pointed the finger the words rushed forth. But what stands out in my memory is the way he pointed his finger. The air crackled betwixt man and man. Jack spoke and the boss stood rigid. Even when Jack dropped his arm the boss kept standing still. Somehow he seemed lost. Only when we lifted did he stir himself... at least that's what

I heard. So we got young Charlie home. He walked in. There was nothing else for it. Because we knew then. She'd had twins.

I wish I could say that the boss conceded, but in fact he didn't. We had to fight every inch of the way, and although the terms agreed weren't much to sniff at, at least we got our new travelling way. And West Twenty, when it was finally won out again, proved a sight better than it had ever been before. Not that it was any great shakes... but it was paradise compared. It was the one face in all the pit that never failed to turn, the tonnage came off and our pays went up; we were in clover. And it was jam easy. That's how it got its nickname: Jam Twenty. 'Plenty Jam,' we used to say. We should have known better.

Nothing good ever lasts. That's the scheme of things in a coal mine and it could be the same everywhere. Maybe it's our destiny. The next time West Twenty came down it got a man. Our champion – and a champion in his own right. Nothing dramatic. Just three yards of roof came quietly down and buried him, and only one arm was free – his good right arm. They say Charlie Nelson wept like a bairn when he heard it. As for me – I lay over the rock that crushed his body and cried. So take warning you pitmen. However good your coal may be, never give it boastful titles. The coal will not be mocked. And there'll never be jam in my life again.

[1979]

Sid Chaplin (*at front, right*) with his team of mechanics from Dean
and Chapter, on a trip to Blackpool in the 1940s. Sid is without his
glasses; he'd made the mistake of making faces at a chimp at
Blackpool Zoo. The chimp swung down, snatched the glasses away
and broke them in half. Brother Jack is third from left.

Sid Chaplin lived and worked in London for seven years, commuting from a spacious London County Council house in the flatlands of Essex (with not just one, but two toilets, and inside the house) to an office block overlooking Buckingham Palace Garden. He explored the big city:

I have the village instinct to walk the bounds, and in my seven years in London assiduously walked the City, finding it a conglomeration of villages. Indeed Victoria is, or used to be, known to its natives as 'the village', but the great high-rise buildings have changed all that by becoming daytime townships. As such they are fascinating, but also blood-chilling. I put some of this in a village book called *Sam in the Morning*, but not the murder – the ruination and desolation made in the name of redevelopment. I still love places like Islington and Greenwich, but much of the rest I find unbearable.

Although London fired a later book, the seven years down south were a barren period for the writer; and when he was offered a job as a public relations officer with the NCB in Newcastle in 1957, he jumped at it. He told friends he was moving because the job was better and he couldn't stand the heat in the humid (and centrally-heated) metropolis. But there was something else; there was something about the windswept city on the Tyne that really fired his imagination:

Newcastle is still that kind of city you can touch and feel, and despite the ruination of traffic all the inhabitants converge on the centre and have a fellow-feeling for each other. It rises in steps and stairs from the Tyne, and its suburbs are, for the most part (even the swankiest), mining villages which have lost their shafts but not their individuality. This is something of a miracle, this people continuing stubbornly to be people, and it fascinates me as a writer, because I happen to believe that the problem of modern times is the problem of keeping individuality intact against the great invasion of the dead urban sprawl. I don't know anywhere in Britain where they do it with any more grace, wit or sweetness than on Tyneside...

The city is like an old glove, and again it's like one of those great houses which has been handed on from one generation to another and then suddenly is inherited by the stranger from over the hill, myself. The sensation is delightful. I feel like a free man with such richness of people around me. It is a dream come true.

The decade spanning the late fifties and early sixties was the era of grandiose public planning and Newcastle was right there in the forefront of it: Tyneside was to be 'the Venice of the North'. The optimism of the period seems sadly splendid in retrospect, but to Sid Chaplin, it had its dangers, as well as its benefits; and in a series of stories, articles and novels, he spelt them out, along with his ideas about how they might be avoided. The writer, now in his full maturity, had found his subject.

Black River

She's all things to all men, the bonny hinny or a noble flood, a twisty-faced old drab or a pay packet that's never quite fat enough. If no longer that 'cursed horse pond' of Captain Phipps, or the universal provider of hostmen and merchant adventurers, or the limpid stream known to generations of boozy singers and brawling keelmen, she still does us proud. Stuck in a traffic jam on the Swing Bridge or at the foot of Pilgrim Street we never pause to think that she's at the bottom of it all. Without her we'd be lost; indeed we wouldn't be here.

Lining up on the Low and High Lights for a clean run into the crab's legs of her piers she is home at last; and it doesn't take small sailors only to know that the Prior's Haven and Shields' sands are gifts of the gods. At the same time, perched on a catwalk in freezing rain and jockeying so many square yards of ship's belly into place, or morosely considering an empty order book, or despairingly looking for one bit of grace in the chewed-up battlegrounds between the yards, slipways and workshops, you wouldn't give a couple of megs – that's a Tyneside tuppence – for her.

But she can be a beauty, especially by night, all of the 18 miles from the Boundary Stone, where an infusion of Cross Fell porter and Cheviot peat buffs against a tide probing all the way up from Spar Hawk and the open sea. Being at the bottom of the Tyneside cellar she pours on, inexorably, like lava, molten glass, or black treacle, under a triumphal arch of light and reflected light. Sentinels mark her way: cooling towers and the standards of transmission lines, the big brick cone of Lemington glassworks, pubs with impossibly high flood markers, cokeworks, gasworks, Armstrongs and the long lurch of Scotswood Road, the Shot Tower, then a concourse of bridges, including the big bow of the New Tyne all radiant in floodlighting. Stumps of Norman teeth look down on her, and the lantern of St Nicholas is warm against the sky, softer than the blazing portholes of multi-storey flats and big ships awaiting a tide. Shields way, beyond the crackle of electric arc-welding, there are huddled villages of ships, tugs and trawlers. The lights sweep round, and mast lights move like fireflies intent on business, not fun. You can only judge from the wash what kind of ship passes by, collier or butter-boat, grain-ship or coaster; looking down from the Spanish Battery all you get is an impression of one kind of darkness cutting through two others of air and water.

She can also be a beauty in daylight, best of all on a rare summer's day when sky, cotton wool clouds, and smooth water shimmer together, and when ships, buildings and buoys grow identical twins below a waterline of outrageous Mediterranean blue. Ships endow her with a momentary splendour – for instance when the drag-chains settle in a cloud of red dust and a host of figures borrowed from a Lowry paint-ing throw up their arms and yell themselves hoarse at the sight of busybody tugs slowly turning another one of her bairns in line with the channel. Or when a luxury liner decked out in white tropicals sails over the bar with her nose in the air. But simpler things will achieve the result – one rowing boat alone in the wastes off Bill Point. Or the sun setting on a packed congress of shipping at Shields. Or a pack of seagulls going up with a clatter as the Swing Bridge begins to turn on its axis, directed by a man in a glass conning-tower – facing upstream the Swing Bridge looks like a ship, the water cutting away from a bow that's anchored in Pons Ælii and maybe three other bridges. At these times you feel that there's some-thing in being a son of the Tyne.

But beware sentimentality, the curse of this river. The noble old dame has a questionable past. For Ptolemy she simply didn't exist, or wasn't worth a stroke of the stylus. And with what name the Tigris boatmen cursed her as they ferried pro-visions to troops building some kind of Wall or other is open to conjecture. It was only when Bede was sent back to his native Jarrow (really Monkton, but we can stretch a point) that the old dame was christened, churched and named in the one great book to come out of County Durham. Then she became the moat behind the Marches; then another army marched in (or came as human ballast in the collier boats); and literature and learning gave precedence to millstone and grindstone (a friend of mine once saw a Kenton grindstone in the middle of Russia), salt, iron and ships, glass, coal and chemicals.

They couldn't help making a mess of it (we can) but those chewed-up bits of Sandgate, St Anthony's, Friar's Goose, Felling Shore, Wallsend (where miners dug the first tunnel under the Tyne), Hebburn, Percy Main and Chirton, are enough to make a point: it must have been beautiful once, it could be beautiful again. The river needs not only landscape planners but men with green fingers. And noses. It would be grand to see children bathing bare-pelted, in tributaries where salmon and sea-trout run once again.

This is not all. To see the river you have to foot it, and to see it is to realise how a great port has been strangled for want of good roads. The ground on both sides falls steeply, sometimes near-precipitously, ideal for the waggonways that ran down to the staithes with coal for the keels plying down to the colliers at the bar – sometimes as many as 500 hand of sail. Then the problem was to get coal out and nobody was bothered much about stuff coming in. The legacy can be seen in a criss-cross of moderate roads – the steep, cobbled outlets from the quays must have killed many a good horse, and a good lot of trade. The ferries are splendid (and one is splendidly free of charges) but too far apart and too slow, while the post-war foot tunnel at Howden amounts to little more than a toy, especially when you look at the steep escalators and the tiny echoing passage then remember that this is the age of the car. So the new bridges and the new big tunnel can't come too quickly. They will truly marry the two shores, but it's a pity the nuptials had to come so late in the day, especially in a region that grows miners and bridge builders like apples on the tree. What will she look like when all these plans have matured? As different again. We have discovered at last that even a black river can be coaxed into being something incomparably better. This one could be the wonder of the world.

[1966]

A Credo

When I was young I had a succession of ambitions – and all before I was sixteen. I had ideas about myself, and none of them was frivolous. I believed in turn that I could be scientist, a writer, a preacher, a political leader. In the end, I settled for writing. I've always been happy in my choice of a calling which has been entirely – or almost entirely – private; but I've never quite been reconciled to the loss of the other callings. I wanted to mention this because I think my work has been influenced by an intense interest in science. I used to collect fossils and then I started collecting people and stories with an equal passion. Theology and philosophy and politics have one thing in common: they attempt to discover or impose a pattern on that very disordered thing we call life. Whatever the pattern it is never completely satisfying. The human story is a story of individuals. The mere fact that they are born and die shatters the pattern, whatever it is. Perhaps it was this frustration that led me to fiction, in which you create your own people and your own world and impose a pattern, or a plot, and sometimes a happy ending, although everybody understands that the ending is only happy for the time being and not for ever and ever.

You can tie up the ends in fiction and that is something you can never do in real life. Fiction is compensation as well as entertainment. Here are the characters, the problems and the values which fascinate you, without the trivia which clutters up ordinary life, and existing in an artificial kind of time, a kind of contracted time, so that you can attempt to show what in your opinion it's all about. I don't pretend to know what it is about, but it's fun trying to find out. And I don't want to make any bones about this – it is about something, it isn't meaningless. This is my anchor although basically, I'm a doubting sort of man. As a novelist I don't take up the position of the callow young preacher who said 'In the opinion of God and myself...' Neither do I take up the position of the man who says 'In the opinion of Karl Marx and myself', nor the man who states categorically: 'Vanity, all is vanity'. No, I prefer to say that I'm continuously fascinated, obsessed, appalled, amazed and delighted by the infinite variety of human beings, especially ordinary human beings, and especially by their capacity for courage, nobility and compassion.

They are gullible and teachable, ordinary and extraordinary – and if you think they are shallow, just talk to any ordinary Joe and find out just how deep an ordinary Joe can be,

In many ways I'm an ordinary chap myself. I have no intellectual qualifications and have never been in demand by the posh weeklies or Sundays. I'm a poor critic of other people's work and I don't have an organised sort of mind. My reading has been very limited and I project myself totally and uncritically, so that what I have learned from other writers has been absorbed subconsciously. This is a great drawback technically, I know, but that's the way I am.

I suppose you could say that I'm the last of the self-educated men; though I *am* educated – I've read the basic stuff on economics, sociology, political theory and philosophy. More important, I've read people and, along the way, had a shot at just about everything. But my period of hit and miss is over. I know exactly what I want to do as a writer: capture the last chapter in the history of the old working class, from 1916 when I was born, to the 1960s. All the values I respect came from mining villages and mining folk, not other writers, provided with whatever gifts for story-telling I possess. But the future lies in the cities, great masses of roads and houses and factories, great masses of newly affluent people. How will the old working-class virtues stand up to city life? What will wither and die and what, on the other hand, will flower? How will the individual stand up to it? The last is perhaps the most important of this set of questions.

I'm not going to quote Chekhov, Henry James, or Beckett to you, but a politician. 'The Multitude is the people of England: that eighty per cent (say) of the present inhabitants of these islands who never express their own grievances, who rarely become articulate, who can only be observed from outside and very far away . . . How will they expand or degenerate in the new town existence, each in the perpetual presence of all?' That was written 50 years ago by C.F.G. Masterman. We know the answer in terms of statistics. I'm interested in the in the answer in human terms. That's why I've tried to write what I call social thrillers. Those millions in Coronation Streets and multi-storey flats and council estates constitute a great unexplored continent as far as fiction is concerned. I'm intrigued with every feature of this continent, its scenery, its people, its aspirations. Intrigued is an understatement – I've a passion for it. It's this passion which provides the drive to write the kind of books I write.

[1964]

Over: Enjoying street life along
the Scotswood Road, Newcastle,
in the early sixties. These streets
have long gone; so have the ships.
In the disintegrating
working-class communities of
Byker and Scotswood Sid Chaplin
found a story that needed to be
told.

A Pint or Two

'Bet ye've never had a pint before,' said Fisher.

'Well, Ah've tasted it,' said Arthur with an uneasy laugh.

'Now where was that?'

'Once when we went campin' – in a little country pub.'

'How did it take ye?'

'To tell the truth, Ah didn't see very much in it.'

'There ye are – ye've never had a *real* pint – after a day's hard work holdin' down a windy pick wi' the sun belting down till your skin's full of dryness an' your body chock-a-block wi' dust. That's the time to stand at a big comfortable bar entirely surrounded be glass an' what it holds; that's the time to have a big wet glass in your fist, full o' the stuff that cuts through iverything – like magic.'

As if to demonstrate his unbelief Arthur rubbed his eyes: 'Not through this it won't. This stuff stays with ye.'

'You haven't tried it yet. You'll see!'

'It's paynight an' Ah promised to be in on the dot – Friday night Ah always take the old man to the pictures.'

'Won't take a minute or cost ye a penny – Ah'm treatin' ye.'

The offer to pay resolved his doubts, for the truth was that he didn't have money to pay his turn. True, his pay-packet was in his pocket and two pounds of it were his own, but the simple ritual demanded that the packet be handed over intact. This was something he could never explain to Fisher, who was a married man and master in his own house. But if Fisher were kind enough to treat him –

'We'll go to the Vulcan; by the time we get there they'll be open.'

'Ah'll not want to stay too long, mind.'

'A couple of minutes – then ye'll ride the trolley home refreshed like a king.'

Twenty minutes later, the car safely parked, they walked into the Vulcan. To reach it they went through an arch and along a cobbled chare – a narrow crack, almost a tunnel, cutting through tall buildings. There was a swinging sign of an ancient smith in sandals wearing an unworkmanlike gown, then a dark landing with a flight of stone steps leading down on either side.

'Into the pit,' said Arthur.

'Aye – the pit of paradise.'

The Vulcan consisted of two rooms – one in darkness, the other containing the bar and a landlord polishing glasses. Giving them a sharp glance – 'Now Jackie; early start tonight, eh?'

'One long shift deserves another . . . make it two Scotch ales – pints. An' draw one for yourself.' They drank off and Arthur was pleasantly surprised. Unlike the other stuff in the country pub, it didn't set his teeth on edge; it had a tang and it cut his thirst. 'Like it?' asked Fisher.

'Not bad at all.' The landlord had turned his back to drink off his pint. Now he turned, drawing his hand over his mouth and eyeing Arthur sharply.

'How old's your pal?'

'Younger'n me,' said Fisher with a wink.

'A dam' sight over young – Ah don't want any trouble.'

'Rest content, Dick,' said Fisher. 'Ah went to his twenty-first party – an' what a night that was!'

'Fair enough,' said the landlord. 'Sorry to ask, but ye know how it is – ye never know when a slop's goin' to drop in.'

'A quick pint – then he's off . . .'

'But not you – ye'll be bringin' your bed one day!'

'An' where better?'

'Where's your fat friend – the one ye had on the treat last night?'

'That's me pal, Norman . . . he's due at seven; it's his night tonight.' Turning to Arthur he explained: 'Bumped into him last night – he was skint. Canna see a pal skint. So Ah paid his turn all night. What's a pal if ye cannot pay his turn?' Draining the last of his pint he shoved the glass towards the landlord: 'Fill 'em up again.'

'Man alive, no,' said Arthur – 'Ah'm not finished yet.'

'Make it one, then – ye'll have to learn to knock 'em back quick'n that, Arthur.'

'Ah'm sorry, Jackie. But it's a big glass – ye could nearly swim in it.'

Fisher laughed: 'Hear that, Dickie? There's one contented customer – here can he have a look at the Long Room?'

185

'Suit yourself,' said the landlord, stooping to a switch below the counter. The dark room was now ablaze with light. Three or four times the length of the bar it had cubicles on either side and a big mirror at the far end.

'See, it's a trick mirror!'

They saw themselves immensely tall, but bent. 'Hold your pint out,' said Fisher, putting an arm around Arthur's shoulders. The curved figures quivered to their laughter, not reflections but visitors looking through a window at another world.

'They've got art as well,' said Fisher, throwing out his arm and slopping ale on the mosaic floor. There were a dozen or so oil paintings, battered survivors of a more spacious age.

Side by side a bag of game endured decay with a dish of fruit; a child warmed its hands beside a dying cottage fire; horses leapt; a monster bull lowered his head in homage to a ram twice his size with enormous, curlicue horns; a stag with pierced haunches sneered from one evil eye.

'Look at this floor!'

The mosaic represented a bevy of naked women pouring wine into the gaping mouth of a hairy man. 'As good as real, eh?' said Fisher, pointing to reality with the toe of his boot.

'It's a queer place,' said Arthur.

'Queer's the word. Ever hear of the underworld? This is where they come, pickpockets, safebreakers, the lot. They're just human, same as us, see?'

'You're kidding!'

'God's honest truth – but don't mention it to Dick,' he cautioned. 'Tell ye something else...come ten tonight ye'll see a marvel...chap walks in an' lays a bet–an' always wins.'

'Wins what?'

'Ten glorious pints – he never fails. Bets anybody he can drink ten while the clock strikes ten; there's always a taker, every night in every pub.'

'That's fast pleasure.'

'You've a long way to go to catch up with him – drink up an' we'll have another.' Arthur succeeded in draining what was left in one swallow, but only just. At the last moment his stomach revolted and what was left ran from the corners of his mouth and over his chin to his shirt.

'Now ye're christened,' said Fisher, taking the glass from his hand.

'It's time Ah was goin'.'

'Have another – keep me company till Norman comes.'

'Well, all right,' he said to his own astonishment. He didn't want another, was determined not to have another, but somehow another person had spoken for him. Sticking his thumbs into his belt he strolled along the room, viewing the pictures, until his reflection in the mirror pulled him up. The long stooped face gazed back at him with melancholy reproach. If only Norman would come! But at seven there was still no sign of the fat man. 'Ah'd better be on me way, Jackie.'

'Ach, man, stay a bit longer . . . but Ah'm forgettin'; it's your night out with the old man.'

'Ah can just make it,' said Arthur.

'OK, Ah'll see ye off . . . tell Norman Ah'll be back, Dickie.'

'If he comes,' said the landlord cynically.

'He'd better, else Ah'll have his guts for garters.'

When they were out he suddenly decided to run Arthur home. 'There's no need,' protested Arthur, secretly glad – he'd be home in half the time.

'Ach, it's no trouble at all,' said Fisher, and the little car shot into the stream of traffic like a pike-pursued minnow, crossing the white line to overtake, skimming betwixt kerb and trolley, scattering pedestrians and always beating the lights by a split second. Then, just as they reached the clear road out, Fisher slammed on the brakes. 'It's Norman!' he yelled and leapt out. Leaning over, Arthur watched the hunter but failed to spot the quarry. Five minutes later a breathless Fisher returned to the wheel: 'Lost him – he must've mickied into some house or other.'

'Ye've sharp eyes,' said Arthur.

'How's that?' said Fisher, sharply.

'Ah didn't get a glimmer of him – fat as he is, he's fast.'

'Not as fast as he was last night when he was on the treat,' remarked Fisher bitterly. 'Pin to a penny Ah'll miss him now . . . he'll get tired of waitin'.'

'He was goin' the wrong way for the Vulcan.'

'That's right – bet he's callin' at the Bluebell to pay his slate . . . mind if we run down to make sure?'

'It's gettin' late, an' ye said he'd wait for ye.'

'OK, then if ye're in a hurry,' said Fisher sulkily.

'Well, it'll only take a minute . . .'

But Norman wasn't in the Bluebell. They couldn't leave without having a drink and when eventually they emerged,

Fisher suggested returning to the Vulcan – it seemed as though he was mortally afraid of being alone. With some uneasiness, and contrary to his wishes, Arthur went with him. Unlike Fisher, he wasn't surprised to find that Norman was still missing – he was beginning to feel that the fat man had never existed; and the look in the melted chocolate eyes of the landlord confirmed his unbelief.

'Have another Scotch ale?'

'Ah've been drinkin' on you all night,' said Arthur with a sinking heart. 'It's time Ah was – was gettin' them in.'

'Oh no you're not,' said Fisher. 'It's on my invitation.' Arthur, hand in pocket, let the pay-packet drop, safe and inviolate. And Fisher came back grinning with a tray loaded with two Scotch ales and two milk stouts: 'Now we're set for a bit,' he exclaimed in high delight. The place was now crowded. They were engulfed in a sea of talk. Darts whizzed perilously close. Laden trays swayed by. A fat lady set a pint on the floor for her poodle and shook enormously when the glass muzzled the creature and it lifted its heavy head in mute misery. As the gaiety increased Fisher grew more morose. 'Too many ould hens in here!' he shouted above the din. 'Let's away into the Long Room.'

To Arthur, swaying like a tethered balloon, the older man seemed like a purposeful bull elephant as he pushed his way through the crowd. But Fisher's weight was useless confronted by a succession of occupied cubicles. Whilst Fisher stalked back again Arthur amused himself with the mirror; he *did* look light enough to take off. Raising himself on his toes – he was off! Not up, down. The crash of the glass seemed to come seconds after he saw it in splinters; miraculously, the other glass was still in his hand. He put the glass to his lips – doubly miraculously, the milk stout was still there too. A hand came into view: 'Here's a hand,' said a girl's voice. His eyes travelled along the slender fingers, beyond the delicate wrist and the tremendous bangle, to a small mask of a face – and a giggle. 'Ye'd make a fortune on the stage,' she declared. 'Come on, get up, there's room in here.'

Safely seated opposite he discovered her hand still in his. He discovered he couldn't meet her eyes, or release the hand which moved with restless little movements, each movement almost a caress.

'Ye'll let me have it back?'

'Beg pardon – what's that?'

'My hand – you funny man. And my name's Joyce.'

'Sorry, Ah've had a bit to drink,' he said, releasing her hand. 'Ah'm called Arthur.' Conscious of her delicious femininity he said hastily: 'Ah've got a pal with me – he's somewhere around lookin' for a seat.' Standing up he called Fisher, then, very suddenly sat down. 'Oh, but you are pickled,' she giggled irrepressibly.

'Everybody has to have a first time – never been on the booze before,' he explained. 'You're no better'n me – you had your first time.'

'That would be goin' back a bit!'

Fisher arrived: 'What's on here?'

'Young woman offered us a seat. Name's Joyce – Joyce, me pal Jackie.' Nodding, Fisher sat down beside Arthur. 'Move over a bit,' he complained. 'Never seen the place so crowded – like a bloody football match.' Suddenly he said to the woman: 'You come here often?'

'Not regular.'

'Thought ye didn't,' he returned triumphantly. 'Ah'm a regular, see. Matter of fact, was here with a pal last night. Fat lad called Norman... ever met him?' She shook her head and Arthur stared, fascinated, as the copper-coloured hair remained in place, and the glass pendants of her earrings swung madly. Placing his two fists on the table Fisher said: 'What would ye call a man that ye treat all night, for a full night, and he promises to come the next night and doesn't come the next night.'

'Ah'd call him a stinker.'

'He said he was broke,' continued Fisher. 'Clean skint. So Ah said: "Norman, kidda – Ah always call him kidda – kidda, Ah says, ye can have a night on me till the ship comes in." An' it was him that told me to come tonight – same place, same time, he says, tomorrow night. Then he doesn't turn up.'

'Now what would you think of a character like that?'

'Ah'd watch him the next time.'

'Ah'll watch him – drunk a barrel, we did, an' he never put his hand in his pocket.'

Uneasily aware of the parallel, Arthur said: 'My turn to treat ... What'll the lady have?'

'Port an' lemon.'

'Move out, Jackie, an' Ah'll get them in.'

'You sit still,' said Fisher firmly. 'Ah was the one that brought ye in.' And he made towards the bar. But Arthur, skidding from his seat, caught him by the shoulder and forced him back. 'Now, Arthur,' protested the older man. 'Ah told ye it was my night – just sit still an' Ah'll get them.'

'It's my turn,' said Arthur.

'Ah wouldn't want ye to break into your pay,' said Fisher in some agitation.

'My business,' said Arthur, pressing him firmly into the cubicle.

'He's determined,' said the lady.

'Once Ah make up me mind Ah'm a bad 'un to shift,' said Arthur, and made for the bar. 'Two Scotch Ales an' a port an' lemon,' he shouted to the landlord, at the same time feeling for the paypacket. But it wasn't there – nor was it in the other pocket of his donkey-jacket. He chased into every possible pocket with rising panic; even the trouser pockets which he knew were holed.

Suddenly his head became a cold and empty space and he distinctly heard his mother's voice – 'Ah wonder what's happened to the lad?' Rushing back to the cubicle he cried, 'Ah've lost me pay, Jackie.'

'Ye must've dropped it,' said Fisher with a stare.

Dropping to his knees Arthur looked under the table. 'No, it's not here,' he exclaimed. 'Stand up a minute, Jackie – it might be on the seat.'

But it wasn't there either and in complete despair he cried: 'Ah've had me pocket picked – that's what it is.'

'Here, go canny,' said Fisher. 'Maybe it's where we were sittin' before?'

'Ah'll have a look,' said Arthur, hopelessly. His feet were very much on the floor now; he walked like a man on stilts for the first time and expecting to crash at any moment.

'Better go with him,' suggested the girl. But Fisher, for some reason, seemed rooted to the seat. 'It couldn't be somebody playin' a joke?' she suggested.

'Poor sort of a joke,' muttered Fisher.

'It's wicked – that poor lad!' said the girl. 'Never mind, there's a couple of plain-clothes men due in – they make the rounds every night: *they'll* soon mend it.'

'By gum, they will an' all,' said Fisher at a tangent, almost as if talking to himself.

'You watch, they'll search everybody.'

'Who says it's been pinched? Might turn up yet.'

'Stands to reason. You're a regular – you should know the company here.'

'Hey, Ah've just remembered!' exclaimed Fisher, starting up. 'It could be in the car.'

'No need to get excited,' said the girl. 'Pay-packets don't jump outa pockets, y'know.' Fisher sat down again.

'What d'ye mean by that?'

'All sorts could happen . . . but those donkey-jacket pockets are pretty deep. Think again.'

'Think of what?'

'Well, ye might be takin' care of it for him,' she said coolly. 'A kid like that needs lookin' after, there's eyesight in it. Or maybe as Ah said, ye're havin' him on with a joke . . .'

'Ah like that – tryin' to put the finger on *me*,' said Fisher in acute alarm.

'Well, if the cap fits,' she said lightly. 'Ah wouldn't know – or care. But them CID men are smart – no flies on them!' Snapping open her handbag, she continued: 'Could be wedged between the end of the seat an' the wall . . . well, time for repairs.' Viewing herself in the mirror, she murmured, 'If it's a joke, now's your chance, kidda – otherwise come mornin' and ye'll be in a place without bars, but with them, if ye see what Ah mean.' Holding up the bag with its interior mirror, she began to make-up her face.

When she had finished the packet lay on the table. 'There! You went and found it after all.' But Fisher didn't answer. Rising, wordless, he buttoned up his jacket. Then Arthur returned – 'It's not there . . .' he began.

'It was here all the time,' said Fisher.

'Wedged at the end of the seat,' added the girl. 'You wouldn't believe it would ye – must a scuffled it along with ye sittin' down an' gettin' up.'

'Well, all's well that ends well,' said Fisher gruffly. 'Ah'm scarpin' off, Arthur. How 'bout you?'

But Arthur was looking at the packet. 'By gum, Ah thought Ah'd never see it again,' he said with a shaky laugh. 'Me mother would've blown her top.' Then, ripping it open. 'The drinks'll be waitin' – t'hell with the old lady – she mightn't have had anything at all. Hang on, Jackie, an' we'll have a last pint.' Then added, with a slap. 'Ah'm insistin' – the drinks on me this time.'

After he had gone Fisher said: 'Ah'm gannin', anyhow. Tell him Ah left.'

'It mightn't be a bad idea,' she said.

'Ah shouldn't have brought him – he's as green as they come – follows me like a dog.'

'Well, he certainly thinks you're next to the Lord God Almighty.'

'There's no need to tell him anything. Ah'm not askin' favours...'

'Haven't ye heard the tale, kidda – dog never eats dog.'

'He's only a kid; chase him,' he said.

'Well, there's an even chance he'll go home to the old folks, providin' you stay.'

'Oh, to hell an' blazes, it's not my worry,' he exclaimed and stumbled out.

He had gone when Arthur returned with the drinks: 'What's happened to Jackie?'

'A sudden engagement,' she said with a wink.

'That's not like Jackie, runnin' out that way,' he said. 'Must be off colour. Notice how he went right down?'

'He was maybe worried about your money, kidda. Never worry, he knows what he's about... and there's more for us that's left.'

'It's not like Jackie,' he muttered.

'He's a big man, an' he can look after himself,' she said impatiently.

'Naturally. Well, cheers.'

'Cheers, kidda.' Putting her glass down she gave him a long look. 'Ye've a nice face, Arthur. Bonny blue eyes: Ah can see meself in them better'n a mirror.'

'Yours isn't so bad either.'

'Well, thanks!' Leaning forward, she touched his hand: 'My, what big hands ye've got.'

'Well, it's a rough job me an' Jackie work on. It's the work develops the hands. Mind, there's a knack to it – Jackie showed me the ropes.'

'You watch pal Jackie.'

'Ach, Jackie's all right.'

'For himself.'

'He's been a good pal to me.'

'Ah can see it's in your nature to be loyal,' she said. 'Ah like ye all the more for that, ye're loyal an' that's a fact.'

'Stand by your pals, that's what the old man says – drummed it into me.' He thought a moment. 'Ah'd forgotten *that*,' he said ruefully. 'There'll be bloody ructions on tonight – first time Ah've ever broken into me pay. But the old man'll understand: ye've got to stand your turn.'

'How about me for a pal?' she asked, putting her head to one side and smiling appealingly.

'Ah'd like that.'

'Oh, the way ye look!' she exclaimed. 'There's devilment in them eyes.'

'Ah've never set eyes on a girl like you,' he murmured. 'Like – like best china... Ah wouldn't dare lay hands on ye.'

'What if Ah dared ye!' she giggled.

'Among all these folk – no fears.'

'Course not here. Where Ah live. It's just around the corner. Come along an' see it.'

'Ach, it's gettin' late,' he said uneasily. 'They'll be worried...'

'Well, if ye've got to get back to your Mam an' Dad...' Drawing on her gloves she became completely aloof, hard as the glass pendants of her earrings, no longer the fragile creature he had discovered but indestructible in her sure feminine pride.

'Ah don't want to offend ye – but Ah'm not used...'

'Silly,' she chided, as suddenly softening, and he stared in delighted amazement. 'Come on, drink up an Ah'll see ye to the trolley... maybe ye'll change your mind on the way.'

'It's a long way out... Maybe Ah can see ye tomorrow night?'

'Or maybe ye can crown this night,' she said softly. 'Might as well be killed for a sheep as a lamb.'

'Ah but they'll be walkin' the floor,' he said, gloomily adding: 'Ah'm the only one, see. Ye've no idea...'

'Might know more about it than you imagine,' she said. 'It's up to you, kidda. Make a night of it! Take a taxi home!'

'Never used a taxi in me life.'

'Well, there's always a first time for everything,' she said with a deliberation that sent his blood racing.

Even with her help he found the steps difficult – they seemed to have a life of their own. But it was a great joke. 'Made it!' she panted when they reached the entrance, and took his hand. Through the chink between leaning buildings he could see the mystery of the sky. 'The nights are drawin' in,' she murmured, shivering. Thinking she was cold he drew her towards him, within the jacket. Deliciously her hands crept to his back. 'Your heart's poundin' like a drum,' she murmured. 'Poor boy...'

Once again a shock cleared his head. *She* was kissing him, but his mind was quiet and quite apart, savouring the slight, exciting movements of her lips. He remembered the girl in the woods; she had given nothing like this. Yet the night was drawing in – he'd been away too long. He was kissing her, but at the same time there was an uneasiness. Something was going, and he was afraid.

He was aware of strange, dancing streets and, high above in the darkening blue, the great round face of the cathedral clock swaying gently. The booming notes shivered through his body like combers. When they were alone he insisted on standing still while he tried to steady the face of the clock. 'What's the matter?' she asked.

'We missed the ten pint trick,' he murmured. For some unutterable reason he felt like crying.

'What trick?'

'The man that drinks ten on the clock.'

'Oh, that old joker! It'll keep. Come on, hinny.'

Then they were passing the sign below which people waited, immobile, yet shifting quickly, like chessmen, on the edge of vision. And like magic, a buttercup bus came sweeping in with a tremendous splash of sparks from the strands above.

'My bus – Ah must go,' he said, pulling away from her.

'Wait for the next – there's no hurry,' she said.

He was looking down at the small, piquant mask. 'No, Ah must get home,' he pleaded. 'Will ye see me tomorrow night – at that place?' He was speaking from the platform while people brushed by.

And her face had changed. 'Not likely. Why should Ah put myself out for you – leavin' me high an' dry like this: ye don't know your own mind.'

'But Ah cannot stay – not tonight...'

'You meet your pal tomorrow night,' she said. 'Meet the pal that picked your pocket, you bloody greenhorn. Ask him what happened...' Her voice, low and deadly at first rose to a higher pitch as the bus moved out. His white face was a target for her fury. 'Ask him!' she screamed. 'Ask him an' watch his face – see what he is – rotten to the core, like all the rest of ye.'

All the way home he clung to the handbar, as if hoping its rigid, unyielding strength would somehow pull together again all the night had pulverised – all that he had lost. Once he touched his pocket, but there was no reassurance in the thought that he still had the money. Hearing him, the conductress winked understandingly at the other passengers, yet wondered at a big lad crying for all the world to see. And how was she to know his grief when he himself, through all the long nights of a drinking life, would never rightly understand?

[1959]

A Pint or Two, *written in 1959, is like a preliminary sketch for the two Newcastle novels,* The Day of the Sardine *and* The Watchers and the Watched. *The apprentice Arthur prefigures the young tearaway Arthur Haggerston in* Sardine *and Tiger Mason in the other book; he faces the same kind of trials and dilemmas.*

Both novels were critically acclaimed and sold well, though not on the scale of other "Northern" books like Stan Barstow's A Kind of Loving *or John Braine's* Room at the Top. *Anthony Burgess called* Watchers *'gloriously comic and moving' and the* Guardian *described Chaplin as a writer who 'reveals the bewilderment, fury and tenderness of human beings'.*

During the productive years of the sixties, Chaplin also wrote two novels – Sam in the Morning *and* The Mines of Alabaster *– with settings outside the North-East. But even though he was writing about London and Tuscany, Newcastle continued to contribute to his work:*

In a sense, the city is my laboratory and workroom. If ever I feel my judgement has gone wrong in a matter of human nature, all I have to do is walk out and look at people again. It doesn't make one iota of difference that the characters may be moving very far from Newcastle; superficial differences apart, the great truths of human nature run alike. Naturally, one must make allowances for upbringing, tradition, tribal custom, etc; this is important, but often a bus ride into the city and back again with a study of faces and bearing is sufficient to put one on the right track again.

By the time The Mines of Alabaster *was published in 1971, Sid Chaplin was beginning to contemplate taking early retirement from his job as the* NCB*'s specialist writer. He wanted to devote more time to his own work; at 55 he felt he still had a few books inside him, the chronicling of his class was not complete. When he did retire in 1972, he set to work compiling a book of essays,* A Tree with Rosy Apples *(a follow-up to* The Smell of Sunday Dinner, *published in 1971) and embarked on a major novel about the Durham coalfield. Then in 1973 he had a heart attack; for two years he was plagued by pain and discomfort until he had a heart bypass operation (during which he nearly died) at Shotley Bridge Hospital. He was the first bypass patient ever to ask for a book in intensive care.*

Heart Case

The bonny blue kingfisher which flashed over the muddy brown waters of the Ouseburn for me on New Year's morning will stay in my heart for ever. Bright as a jewel in winter murk, it is the perfect emblem for the renewal wrought in me by the heart surgeons.

Less than twelve months ago the kind of scramble which made this vision possible would have been out of the question. Life and being was dominated by that Regimental Sergeant Major of pain, Angina Pectoris, which, taking over by default of the coronary arteries, exacts the most instant and stinging obedience.

For the heart patient it is pain – not faith, hope and purpose – which becomes the dominant reality of life. Like Jacob on the way back to Canaan he must first wrestle with the stranger whose name is Death... although, like me, it may take him a long time to admit this. Foremost in every patient's life is this unending battle. Is it any wonder, then, that news of the possibility of liberation comes like the ringing of a victory tocsin?

That was one milestone in my progress. Another was my first meeting with Mr Holden of the cardio-thoracic unit at Shotley Bridge and the surgeon who would head the team which would operate on me, in the office of Dr Dewar, Head of Cardiology at the Royal Victoria Infirmary. Between Dr Dewar and myself a strong bond had already been established. Very little was said that I now remember, but the outcome is unforgettable. An intolerable burden fell away. Now at last I could let myself go.

What marks those days is, in fact, their carefree, almost exhilarating quality, once tests had established that I was a suitable case for treatment and a date had been fixed for the operation. My cares sloughed away; I had never worked better in my life before. Yet oddly enough I never once bothered to seek further information, despite all the sources which were open to me. As a result, warnings that I was about to face an exceptionally heavy operation passed over my head, and I went into hospital virtually unaware what was about to take place, or of the long period of mending which would still face me if the operation proved successful.

Fear, of course, lay behind my attitude. I wasn't going to die, no, not I, I told myself, but all the same deep within me a kind of holy terror told me that I was. I can only describe the experience as a kind of "visual scream", as stark as it was instant – and instantly suppressed.

In the end it was the simple experience of a stroll along the old Derwent Valley Railway line the day before the operation which brought me to the truth about myself. In a lovely little glade I picked a bunch of violets and big yellow primroses, cowslips too, then from a little bridge gazed at far moorland horizons. 'Well, if I do have to die tomorrow,' I remember thinking, 'I couldn't have picked a better place for it than this.' At last it was out in the open – not just a statistic about five in every hundred patients not surviving the operation, but the fact that tomorrow I might be one of them. I won't say that I wasn't fearful, but in the upshot I could say to the good green earth with a certain amount of confidence, 'Well, be seeing you soon,' knowing that even if I did die not all would be sadness, not now or in the total stretch of existence.

Later, in a session crowded with visitors, I felt the need to say something to my wife, and considered writing what might well turn out to be my last letter to her. Now I decided against it. Partly the reason was that the little nosegay of flowers I have given to Rene for my granddaughters also represented a message for her, partly that I felt a farewell letter of this type would represent a betrayal of the life-enhancing experience I had had during my walk.

In many ways this was perhaps the most difficult decision I have ever made in my life, and I remember thinking, 'But what if you have to go tomorrow? How awful for Rene not to have a word or two.' Then I thought, 'But you aren't going to die,' and put pen and paper away.

Leaving the ward is a great experience. You know there is absolutely nothing you can do except perhaps demean your manhood and in that short trip all the robes of pride and prejudice fall away, and you are the naked primordial man again.

There is a lift from the adrenalin as well, I suppose. Everybody says good luck, and Charlie White, another ex-miner, walks beside me as I am pushed out. People are important as well, forming as they do the strands of a glistening pattern of thought and care which runs parallel with the enormously complex life-support system which will sustain you during the critical hours ahead. A pattern of people who care...Mine included not only the Dominican Sisters who prayed for me but the porter who always had a word of cheer and comfort for my wife during the very darkest days at Shotley Bridge.

Vivid in my mind is the pause before I was pushed into the operating theatre. The oddly inwardly opening doors struck me – airlock doors? In their construction they certainly resembled the airlock doors which I saw as a boy of fifteen on my first trip underground with the blacksmiths. Big fine men, a team of thirteen working as one. Craftsmen all, they are still bright in my memory.

More than anything else in the world I honour and respect the skill of men working together in unison. It was one of the cardinal experiences of my boyhood. I reckon it is the highest point of human achievement. Now that it is embodied in me, I can never forget who I am or why I am living. What the life-savers have given me is not only a second chance, but the opportunity to renew my source-springs.

Whatever the problems along the way they fade into insignificance beside the restoration of physical well-being. Recovery for the bypass patient means the rediscovery of an entire range of physical sensations and delights – of being able to walk freely uphill and down dale again, of enjoying (not fearing as baleful) wind, frost, snow and rain, the exultation of striding out and not caring about the consequences, above all the joyous, even content of working fruitfully.

When told I was writing this account a friend tentatively expressed the opinion that it would only be complete if I included my own first-hand account of the operation which saved me. I must disagree. This is my own case-history, and the triumph of the account is that I am able to write it. To have been a slave and to have been set free – that is the story. To try to say any more would be to try to express the inexpressible.

[1976]

Chop-Sticks

Enoch Taylor, a craneman in Sampson & Maloch's Slipway, and Tommy Marling, who ran the big drawing-office but knew the ratio of plate steel to buoyancy better even than Enoch, were making their way to the Ferryman's Rest, which lies immediately above the shipyard. Normally at shift's end both men would have been smoking – the one dragging at his small thin fag damp as a rag, while the other drew at his curved pipe; but not so tonight. Somehow it seemed too solemn a moment – besides which, a nor'-easter bustling up the narrow valley had made lighting up impossible. Not until they were seated in the pub did Marling speak.

'Same as usual, Enoch? Pompey. A brown and bitter.' As if by rote the pair marched to the corner by the fireplace, each carefully placing his glass on a mat. Moodily they sat. They seemed to hesitate even over their drinking; the one waiting on the other. Marling lifted his glass first. 'Here's to Cyril,' he toasted. 'To Bennet, God bless him – Ah wish he was suppin' with us,' grunted the normally reticent Enoch. 'It was his only bit pleasure.'

'Gettin' away badly, is he?' asked the landlord.

'Badly,' said Marling briefly. 'The missus saw him yesterday. Fadin' away, she says – all legs and beak, like a moll heron. Chronic bronchitis they reckon, but Ah call it heart failure. What with th' lass that was his pride and joy runnin' away, and one thing and another, he just gave up.'

'Her and her clartin' and fartin',' said Enoch savagely. 'There's no rest for him. If yer drop a bit ash from your fag, she's out with the dust-pan and hand-brush. Ah'd sooner live in a morgue.'

'He deserved better,' said the landlord. 'He's the best Johnny Fortnight in these parts. Always welcome, was Cyril; and many a book he's kept right.'

'Johnny Fortnight?' asked Marling. 'Ah never heard him called that before.'

'Gerraway!' cried the landlord. 'You of all folk! Why, man, he's the insurance agent. That's the trouble wi' all you fellers that move up in the world – yer forget all yer were brought up to.'

'Ah mind now,' said Marling, meekly accepting the reprimand. 'Many a time Ah've seen me mother lock the door against ours, because she hadn't the coppers. It was a sin and a shame not to pay in them days, when times were hard.'

'It costs as much today,' said the landlord. 'Price of a good second-hand car. Ah, well, we all have to come to it,' he sighed poignantly. 'Even your Johnny Fortnight.'

'There's more than what'll bury him,' said Marling significantly. 'That's what irks me – he works hard to provide for himself, and she has the enjoyment of it, hard-faced bitch that she is. Sup up, Enoch – we've a tidy walk in front of us.'

'So you're off to see him, are you?' asked the landlord. Marling nodded. 'With a little bit of good cheer,' he said, jingling the money in his pocket. 'Ah'll take one of your bottles of stout, landlord.'

'Why, man, you'll have us shot!' cried Enoch. 'What if it kills him?'

'Blessing or curse, if it's the last drink he has, he shall have it,' answered Marling. 'Thanks landlord,' tucking the bottle into his raincoat pocket. 'You've forgotten your change,' called Pompey as they departed.

'Keep it landlord – and spare a thought for Bennet,' returned Marling.

'Are ye out of yer head!' Enoch demanded, as the door closed behind them. 'First tipping landlords and the next thing you know you're smuggling drink into invalids. If she catches us, she'll have our guts for garters.'

'What the eye doesn't see, the heart doesn't grieve over,' said Marling slowly.

'Aye, but what if she asks you to take your raincoat off?' demanded Enoch. 'You know what an old fuss-pot she is.'

'You leave me to worry about that,' said Marling. 'Ah can be a bit of an old fuss-pot myself.'

Reaching the top of the bank, the two turned right along the winding riverside roadway and then sharply left again, into the arched tunnel called 'The Gob' which led to the back of the terrace. Dark, dank and cobbly it brought into view the solitary old house, perched on an eminence, which the locals named 'The Gob-House' in flat contradiction to the polished oak panel which swung in the doorway, bearing the legend 'Balmoral'. Looking up from the tunnel mouth they saw the landing light gleam yellow as a vague figure descended the stairs. Then the light went out.

'Front door?' whispered Enoch.

'Front be damned,' exclaimed Marling. 'That's for the vicar and such-like. It's the back for such as us.' They stumbled round in the dark.

'Dam' an' blast it!' muttered Enoch when a dustbin lid went clattering. It cost half a box of matches to replace it. Ships hooted eerily. In the dry-dock below there was the stutter of a rivet-gun.

'Ho, so it's you two, is it,' said Mrs Bennet. 'Ah thought the back wall had fell down!'

'No more than half of it, Dora,' returned Marling. 'We've come to ask about Cyril.'

'See how he is, like,' mumbled Enoch.

'Better come in,' said she, adjusting her head-scarf. 'Mind, you'll get a shock when you see him.' She led the way in.

'New hair-do, Dora?' asked Marling.

'The first, the very first perm, Ah've had myself in months,' she returned, nervously patting it. 'Our Katie came and looked after him. You remember our Katie, don't you?'

'He'd have a short memory if he didn't,' simpered that lady, emerging from the parlour. 'Shared the same desk at school, we did.'

'And a right bonny lass you were,' said Marling, regarding straightfaced the tall gaunt figure before him. 'Mind, that is a nice perm you've got yourself, Dora,' he said to his hostess.

'Funny how fashions come back,' said Enoch. 'Me Great-Aunt Jane did her hair like that – fringed along the front and what-not. Not that it doesn't become you,' he added, viewing her critically with his head askew.

'It's no use letting things slide,' said the lady, absently straightening a vase containing a selection of dried flowers. 'If the worst comes to the worst Ah'll be ready.'

'Don't you be pushed and rushed, Ah told her,' said the sister. 'There'll be no time for perms, I told her, if he goes off sudd –'

'If you take your coat off, Mr Marling, Ah'll take you up to see him,' interposed Dora Bennet.

'No, thanks missus; we're not staying long,' said Marling firmly.

'You'll not feel the benefit of it when you go out,' she warned, still hesitating at the foot of the stairs.

'Nor will your chair,' he returned emphatically. 'It's me trousers, they're saturated through with oil.' With a sombre look the lady regarded Taylor. 'Nay, missus, Ah'm all right,' protested the latter. 'Ah change out of me overalls at work. This you might say is my evening attire. Good enough for me.'

'Well, it wouldn't do for me,' said the lady, surveying him from head to foot, and with a latent sharpness in her tone. Then she led the way upstairs. The sick man lay wan and still. They noticed the sharpness of his nose as he turned. 'You've got visitors, Cyril. Look who it is,' said the wife, fussily adjusting the counterpane. 'God bless you lads,' whispered the sick man. Exhausted, he momentarily closed his eyes. Briskly the woman replaced his head in its former position. 'Now now, old lad,' said Enoch cheerfully, seating himself on the bed.

'Better sit here,' said the wife hastily, dusting the chair thus designated. 'That counterpane's clean on.'

'Aye,' said Enoch, with a wealth of meaning.

'Well, Ah'll leave him with you,' said the woman. 'And no smoking, *please*,' she added, noting certain involuntary movements. 'Not with him in his condition,' and with a last searching glance she departed.

The sick man was suddenly and violently alert. 'For God's sake light up, Tommy,' he said. 'Ah'm dyin' for the smell of it. Light up, Ah tell you, and do me a favour.' The two men looked at each other. 'Just a bit whiff,' pleaded the patient. 'Now that Ah'm banned from smokin' myself.' As Marling lit up a smile stole over his face. 'Puff away, Tommy lad,' he murmured, 'and open the window Enoch; she's got a nose like a bloodhound. My sangs – it's as good as havin' a pipeful myself.' Ecstatically he sniffed then suddenly was racked by spasm after spasm of coughing. 'Hey, lad,' cried Marling, hastily putting his pipe away. 'Tha's choked.' Tenderly he saw to his friend. 'We shouldn't 'a done it. There now, that's better,' as the sick man rid himself of the sputum.

'Fust time Ah've cleared me tubes for a week,' croaked his friend, smiling wanly. 'Ah tell you lads, Ah'm a gonner; they'll sharp be layin' me out.'

'Is he all right there?' came a voice from the foot of the stairs.

'Waft that smoke away!' hissed Marling to Enoch. 'Waft it with your cap.' Then, rushing on to the landing. 'Trouble with his pipes, that's all; he's all right now,' he called. The situation was desperate. The horse-faced sister, holding a glass, had joined her, and he could see that Mrs Bennet was in half a mind to investigate further. He went down to meet them. 'Now there's nowt to worry about,' he reassured them. 'Only he needs shaving. If you'll just give us his electric shaver we'll tidy him up before we go.'

'Bit of a waste of time, isn't it,' said the sister, visibly swaying. 'Isn't that a job for the underta –'

'That's very thoughtful of you, Mr Marling,' said Mrs Bennet hastily; and so the day was saved. Shortly Marling, having replaced the bedside light with the plug, handed over the shaver to Enoch. 'Now what?' asked the patient.

'Just a bit of a shave, lad,' said Marling. 'But fust a treat – something to clear your pipes,' producing the bottle of stout. 'Switch it on, Enoch.' To the patient. 'Now heave up, canny lad,' embracing him with the one arm while holding the bottle at the ready.

'Ah hope you know what you're doin',' whispered his companion, above the bee-like swarming of the shaver. 'Shave yourself,' ordered the draughtsman, 'and stop yammerin' on. If we can't help a pal on his road, we cannit help nobody.' Feebly the sick man gulped. 'What's this?' he croaked. The liquor spilled from his mouth and clung in shining little globules to the stubble of his whiskers. 'Call it milk, lad – the milk of human kindness,' Marling murmured.

The sick man looked at him. 'Ah've done well with me friends, if nowt else,' he croaked, and gulped eagerly again at the bottle until at last, sinking back, he whispered: 'That's my finish – Ah'm sorry, lads.' 'Finish! It's not the finish,' cried Marling sturdily. 'There's many a bright year in you yet. Let's drink on't'; and solemnly the two finished the bottle between them, raising it each in turn before drinking. Then quickly but gently they shaved him. When the job was completed he sank back exhausted. They made him comfortable. Gradually the wan face relaxed in sleep. Looking at his companion Marling slowly nodded at the door, and cautiously the pair tiptoed towards it.

'Ah thank you, lads; you've been true pals to me,' murmured the patient again. 'Ye've done me good.' For once even the voluble Marling was silenced, too moved to speak. 'It's no more than you'd have done for us; no more and no less,' said the reticent Enoch. 'Oh, no; Ah wouldn't have dared to,' Bennet whispered, painfully shaking his head; and in a rare gesture of affection Marling, walking back to the bed, leaned over and rested his hand on the patient's. 'You'd have dared all right – through hell and high water,' he said. The sick man's eyes filled. Briefly he murmured. 'What's that?' asked Marling, bending over him.

'No more Friday nights, he says,' said Enoch, who had sharper ears. 'Plenty more to come, ould lad – plenty more, Ah'm sure,' said Marling sorrowfully; and the sick man smiled. 'Rev your engine tonight, Tommy – rev it in the Gob. It'll give me comfort.'

'Now what's he on about?'

'You want us to call tonight, ould lad? It shall be done,' promised Marling. Turning to Enoch he elucidated: 'He wants us to back into the Gob tonight, same as we always used to...' Returning to the patient, 'Same time and place Cyril. Don't you fret ould lad, we'll be there.'

'Grand!' The sick man sunk back. 'One last happy time...' To the watchers it seemed as if he had already in spirit taken his accustomed place at the club, bright-eyed and embracing his glass two-handed. Silently they crept out. To them it seemed that their friend was sleeping peacefully. And so it seemed to the two women when later that evening they paid him a visit. But with keener vision than the menfolk they quickly detected the telltale flush; and from this a sharper more laboured note in his breathing. Little they knew of the difference between excitement and crisis.

'He's goin',' announced the wife to the sister, after the brief examination, little knowing that the husband remote and happy in his first peaceful doze for weeks, was eavesdropping. 'But he looks that peaceful,' muttered Kate, who at least had had the grace to clap her hand to her mouth at the verdict. 'They always are, at the turn,' said Mrs Bennet somewhat begrudgingly. Deftly she twitched the counterpane so that its folds outlined more tildily the wasted body.

'Shouldn't we send for the doctor?' ventured the sister, timidly moving closer.

'Too soon for that,' said the wife. 'Much too soon. But he'll go before midnight.' And with a knowing little smile she started clearing away an assortment of pills and expectorants. The younger woman shivered. 'You mean you know – just by looking at him? How awful...'

'Ah've lived with him too long not to know,' said the wife, thoughtfully chewing her bottom lip. 'No, it isn't that Ah'm worried about but who to get...'

'There's Robinson's,' murmured Katie. 'Big flash cars they have. They've carried Royalty, you know.'

'That's flyin' high. No, Ah'm not havin' a lot of swank and palaver,' declared Mrs Bennet. 'Robinson puts a good show on, but Benson's cheap – and shoves in a tiptop funeral tea as well. No, it's the last thing he'd want – something flashy.'

'Ah suppose there's enough and plenty,' ventured the sister.

'He's well covered, that's one thing Ah'll say for him; he's left me well provided for,' said Mrs Bennet with dignity, and turned quickly as her sister gave an exclamation. 'Now what, for goodness sake!' expostulated the elder. 'He – he smiled,' shuddered Katie. Ashen-faced, she retreated doorwards. Mrs Bennet leaned over her man. 'Imagination,' she declared, 'it must've been a spasm. Look at his lips; blue as the deep blue sea.'

Timidly the sister returned. 'It's hard to believe he's goin',' she murmured. 'And him such a regular man; Church Institute on Mondays and Wednesdays; his club on Friday and Saturdays. And always before he went out he'd fill the scuttle and chop the sticks ready for laying the fire. Regular as clockwork, he was.'

'Aye; that's one labour he saved me,' said Mrs Bennet, not without a trace of bitterness. 'Ah'll have to depend on somebody else now. Either that or chew on myself.'

'What about Mr Marling or Mr Taylor? Ah'm sure they'd help you out,' suggested the sister, unaware of the sensitive nature of the subject. 'If there's one thing Ah'm grateful for,' declared Mrs Bennet passionately, 'it's that Ah'll see no more of them two; sly, sneaking snakes in the grass that they are.' Momentarily the sick man's eyelids flickered open. Feebly he tried to lift his hand, then as she continued, dropped it again. 'Sarky the pair of them; sarky and impitant. Many and many's the time Ah've caught them at it. That, and the way they battened on Cyril... frittering our good money away on beer. As good as kept them, he did.'

'Kept them – you mean it was that bad?' asked the horrified

Katie.

'They drank like draught-horses, the pair of them, and he paid for it,' said Mrs Bennet, passionately. Soberly she considered. 'Ah think we'll make it Simpson's,' she mused. 'There'd be no sense in spending a lot.' The sick man sighed.

'He uttered – did you hear him!' said the timid sister, and leaning over him the wife intently searched his face. 'He's going all right,' she pronounced. 'Better get on with that list. We've a lot to sort out.' She switched off the light. 'But you're not goin' to leave him in the dark,' cried the sister. 'He's no need of the light now,' said Mrs Bennet pathetically. 'It's all over for him, but Ah'm left to fend for myself...'

Unbeknown to them the patient beyond the door sighed deeply again. His eyes were open now, fixed on the narrow chink of light from the lamp that illuminated the way up from 'The Gob'. In his mind's eye he imagined the cobbled paving in the tunnel, and the whitewashed stones which picked out the pathway beyond. For a long time he considered – long enough to thread through forty years of courtship and marriage, parenthood ending in painful severance, stolen evenings of snooker and fellowship. Then at last he murmured 'Pot black' in the darkness, and cautiously edged his way to the edge of the bed, until at last he dropped with a thump to the floor. Well it was for him then that the wind was rising, storming with ever increasing violence about the chimney-pots and moaning through the window-sashes. It took him an eternity to reach the door and close it; then raise himself by the glass doorknob. There he hung, gasping, until he had strength enough to raise himself to his full height; pausing again before he reached up for the switch. Even then he was in a quandary, wondering first where she had hidden his clothes and then where he would find the strength to dress himself. In the end he contented himself with simply pulling his trousers over his pyjamas, making a rough bundle of all he was unable to manage, including shirt, underclothing and socks. It was while wrestling with his shoes that disaster struck. 'Dam' them laces!' he muttered, mistaking their elusiveness for his own ponderous swaying to and fro; then as he lurched, the chair fell over and he pitched forward.

'By, but it's wild tonight,' said Dora Bennet; and for some reason she shivered. 'You'd think it knew.'

And upstairs the sick man was tugging at the bed-clothes;

clawing his way to the softness and security that lay there. At last he slumped crossways over it. Here he could rest, for ever, if need be.

Downstairs the women sat uneasily. 'Listen to it moaning and groaning out there! Ah'm sure it'll blow the house away any minute,' said Mrs Bennet. 'Here, your glass is empty. Let me fill it up for you.' As the wind shook the house, the sister jumped, spilling her sherry. 'Nerves,' she laughed shakily. 'Ah'm sure Ah don't know what's up with me tonight.' In spite of themselves they listened. 'Only a car revving,' murmured Mrs Bennet reassuringly. 'They often back into the Gob to turn.'

'Then what's that?' Ashen-faced the sister clutched her. 'There's something on the move . . .' Eyes dilated Dora Bennet was incapable of answering. White-faced she stared. Haltingly something moved; then was gone. 'Ah tell you he's walkin'; he's comin' to get us!' screeched the younger sister.

'Stuff and nonsense,' said Dora Bennet. But she made no effort to investigate. 'It's only the wind.' Somewhere a door opened. Then followed the unmistakable sound of someone chopping firewood; first the heavy thumping as the log was split then the rapidly clicking action of someone methodically chopping. 'Oh, my God,' said the wife, and "keeled" over, as local parlance has it.

It was quite half an hour before they were able to pluck up sufficient courage to venture into the scullery. The two coal scuttles were full to brimming; the pile of sticks laid neatly beside them – the back door swinging. It was only then that they discovered the empty bedroom . . . a scene that beggars description.

Parked outside the Boilermakers' Club, the three men drained their bottles. 'That's better,' said Cyril Bennet. 'Where now, lad?' asked Marling. He switched on the engine. 'You name it; we'll take you.'

'You'll have us shot,' said the reticent Enoch. Somehow he said it proudly. 'Take me to my daughter,' said Bennet. 'Any way, any road, so long as it's as far away as can be from that hell-hole.' 'You're the boss,' said Marling. 'Aye,' said Bennet. 'Ah reckon Ah chopped her sticks for her this time. Well and truly.' And for the first time in months he smiled.

[c. 1968]

Sid Chaplin at Newfield. In his later years, the writer returned to the short story form, using his heartland – the Durham of the 1920s and 1930s – as the setting for most of them.

Once he'd recovered from the operation, Sid Chaplin went back to work on that big novel. But the words would not come. He started another novel, but couldn't get past the second chapter. It was no good: something had happened during his long illness and lay-off. It wasn't that he couldn't write at all – he did after all tackle a new medium, television, in this period, with scripts for When the Boat Comes In. But it did seem that the immense physical and mental effort required by a sprawling novel was beyond him. This made the man miserable and wretched, but eventually he set to and returned to first principles – and his first love as a writer. He began to write short stories again. Two volumes – On Christmas Day in the Morning (1978) and The Bachelor Uncle (1980) appeared. Most of this new batch of stories were set in his heartland – the Durham of his boyhood. He continued to chronicle the people and places of a world that had fallen apart.

A Letter from Pancake Tuesday celebrates the memory of William Slater, a strange, wonderful man who Sid got to know through Rene Chaplin. Mr Slater was a pitman at Mainsforth Colliery in Ferryhill; he was what would now be called a primitive artist, decorating Bibles, making mobiles, covering the stairway of his small terraced house in Wolseley Street with a watercoloured jungle of plants, ferns and bushes, with a huge aspidistra on a stand as the centrepiece. Mr Slater was a gently devout man who never trimmed his white hair or beard because he wanted to look like Jesus. When his 16-year-old son Edward was killed underground, he kept vigil alone and wrote a letter to God on the coffin, thanking Him for the loan of his son and commending him to His care. The letter was later read out in Chapel, at the boy's funeral.

Like the other stories of this period, A Letter from Pancake Tuesday and Swallows Will Build (based on Grandfather Charlton) have a lyrical, almost mythical quality. But there's something else: behind the gentleness, there's an urgent, angry, uncompromising note. That distinctive voice rang out still, demanding to be heard.

A Letter from Pancake Tuesday

'Never mind, pet,' said my mother. 'It's Pancake Tuesday a week today – at least you've got that to look forward to. Tid, Mid, Misera,' she bent over her fingers as she counted, 'Carling, Palm, Pace-egg Day. What did I tell you? I'll order a few extra eggs next Friday.' Shoving bait-tin into one coat pocket and tea-bottle into the other, she saw me off to the pit. Five o'clock of a dark Tuesday morning, with a mad March hare of a wind racing down the street, and almost drowning out the thump of the compressor and the pit's ventilation fan. 'Now are you sure you'll be all right?' she asked. 'Why, aye,' I said, terrified in case somebody should overhear her words. 'Stop pestering me – I'll be fine.' Little knowing what awaited me.

By daylight the pit was a three-masted clipper bereft of her canvas which easily rode black billowing waves of pit-muck and slurry – a picture I'd often admired; forgetting the figures that crept homewards, the muffled threatening roar of the engines and the great black gobs that littered the pavement. Now all was different. The pit was vast and shadowy, a beast crouched ready to spring. Her firehole eyes, her mouth, her form spat menace. The moment I saw her I knew I was for it. Not the pit but the law that the pit had made saw to that. On deck and amidships she was a pirate. Thus I found out.

There first as an innocent new starter I planted myself right beside the bait-cabin fire. 'I wouldn't sit there if I was you,' said Tan Ridley, the first arrival.

'What for?' I asked. 'It's a good seat, isn't it? You can have it when I'm finished with it.'

'Not for a thousand quid,' he said. 'You watch if you don't catch it.'

'Who's this, like?' asked another arrival. He'd a baby face with eyes like chips of muddy grey ice, and was maybe a couple of years older than the rest of us. Quietly while he spoke he rearranged all the tea-bottles ranged around the fireplace so that his was in the most favourable place.

Tanny started to tell him. 'You shut up,' said the boss-lad, and turned to me. 'You can bloody speak for yourself, can't you?' he said to me. 'Chris Lee, is it? he asked, scratching himself under his armpits. 'Well, my name's Bill Robinson and that's my seat, so you'd better get out of it.'

'Neither for you, nor a dozen like you,' I told him – the business of scratching had lulled me; and the next thing I knew he'd picked me up and I was sprawled out full-length with the full weight of his pit-boot on my chest and the tip of his iron toe-plate cold on my chin. 'Next time I'll throttle you,' he said.

Then the buzzer blew and like rats we all scurried down to the picking belts. There were six of them all rising from a common pit below tipplers and shakers, their iron-plated muzzles each rising gently so that the pay-load could rush helter-skelter over the clashing loading booms to the rail wag-gons below. 'Who's this, then?' said Danny Lancaster, the chargehand.

'A cheeky young bugger, if you ask me,' said Tan Ridley. 'He's bin in a fight with Scratcher Robinson.'

'Bit of a tartar, are yer?' said Danny.

'I believe in me rights,' I said.

'He took his bloody seat,' said Tanny Ridley.

'Baloney to him,' I said. 'You see if I don't get my own back.'

'Did you hear that!' said Tan Ridley. 'He'll not say that to his face.'

'I will and all,' I said.

'You're talking daft,' said Danny. 'Never pick a fight with a chap two stone heavier, and a better reach. Smile at him, and bide your time till you're ready to belt him.'

'I'll get him when I'm ready,' I said.

'You're talking like a book with all the pages out,' said Tanny, and walked away.

'You stick in and maybe I'll teach you how to handle your-self,' said Danny.

'Gerraway!' I said. Everybody knew he'd been a champion heavyweight and had won a belt once.

'I will, though,' he said. 'If you've got savvy enough.' Then the engineer turned the power on and everything we said was swept away by a typhoon of noise which raged all around us.

It must have been an amazing sight to see – loaded tubs

converging from all quarters down the tracks to the six tipplers all ranged out in line (one tippler per coal seam), with the goliath shakers down below going like merry hell and the furiously picking lads spread out along the endless steel-plate conveyors which emerged from beneath them, each carrying its own pall of dust as well as its load of paydirt; but personally I can never remember taking time to enjoy it. We were too much geared to the endlessly returning machinery ever to have time to pause. When visitors did – directors, shareholders etc – we hated them with a hate that was deeply felt and abiding but which had nothing to do with our misery.

We worked two-handed, you see, and were as clever as jugglers with it, the brasses and grey shale mounting up in dust-covered hillocks behind us... clever as a cageful of monkeys, and that's just how they regarded us. The belt was only stopped when a particularly dirty tub came along, and it was then that the meaning of our slavery stood revealed. We picked furiously into stout wooden boxes which were conveyed in our arms up the steep wooden ramp to a kind of immense wall-frame into one of whose innumerable recesses the muck would be tipped, there to be held as evidence against some recalcitrant coal-hewer, who was probably half-blind any way. Many a pitman had his wages for the day nearly wiped out by this system. So a lad working for less than two bob a day would sweat his guts out to penalise his own father – the crowning irony. That is why we hated the visitors. They had seen our shame. Our one consolation was to hurl the most deadly hair-trigger insults in our sign-language at their retreating backs. In that language was a sign for virtually everything. Many a time hatred and despair flashed across the dust-laden atmosphere. But there were no symbols for joy or delight.

But the odd thing was that in all this time I never harked back to my old job in the bakery, when everything had been so pleasant and promising. I look back on it now, of course. Now I can see both the pleasure and the pain. The period when I thought back to it as paradise is stuck somewhere in the middle – roughly about the period when I went down the pit – which is only another way of saying that I still had to learn to suffer. Where the screens failed the thin seams and stinking tunnels did for me. It was then that I remembered the bakery – crickets singing, the smell of dough and cake mixture mingled with the scent of white-coated girls who moved like goddesses as we all worked together on a rush order for a wedding, and the concerted 'Whoo!' as the topmost cake of the three-tier centre-piece was placed into position: the cosy evenings when Mr Ransome and I, having stayed behind to clean out the flues of the bakehouse fire, leafed through back copies of the *Baker and Confectioner*, planning sensational new lines – my overtime pay a whopping big bag of fancy cakes, my favourite vanilla slices predominating.

Now all this was erased – vanished with every other past happiness. Too much was happening – there wasn't room for anything else. The steel-plated conveyors, each twenty to twenty-five yards long and each perpetually returning back upon itself, so that the stream of coal and debris while always in motion seemed always eternally fixed, dominated my life. And while the juggernaut was tenderness itself to the pay-load – preserving every size from the most minute particle to the big black roundies which shone like fresh-picked blackberries, we ourselves, it seemed, were the real object of its vengeance, continuously being ground away, so that at the end of each day all we were, or had been, was funnelled back into ourselves like graphite, fine and free-flowing as mercury. In short, we were reduced back upon ourselves. And always the only relief from our slavery was the fetching and carrying of the heaped-up laid-out boxes, armoured and framed in sharp-edged steel, slipping and sliding down the iron-ridged floor and painfully up the Golgotha-ramp to the tippler-deck, there to be bullied and stormed at by Scratcher, who was the boss-lad.

Day after day he'd watch me while I was sparring with Danny – big and slow-moving, but as fast as a cat when he struck, and would be waiting for me the very next box that I took. 'Go on kidder,' he'd whisper as he took the box from my hands. 'You get stuck in and learn to handle yourself. Then just you start and I'll flay the living daylights out of you.' It was all mouthed but I knew what he was saying.

He was a small-boned lad, light-footed and lish as a whippet, and one day – I don't why – when we got to arguing in the bait-cabin I got round to asking him. 'Why,' I asked him. 'What good will it do you?' His blue eyes went blank at first. Then his face cleared. 'Why shouldn't I?' he asked. 'You're askin' for it, aren't you?' He was dead-right, of course. The pit made the law, and the pit placed him above me. And I wasn't content with my place in the hierarchy. In all my will and pride I considered myself a cut above him. It was as clear-cut as a diamond. He had to get me down. When all's considered, what else has a working man got than the place he has won amongst his peers and over and above all the others? But this dawned on me much later. All I knew then was that I feared and hated him.

Night and day his face haunted me – that face thrust into mine as he promised to kill me – and, to be honest, I wasn't making much progress with my boxing. 'Come on, get me, right in the solar plexus,' Danny would invite me. 'I'll not hurt you' – and then when I landed him one he'd forget himself and belt me as only an ex-champion can. And to be honest I didn't want to kill anybody. I just didn't want to be hit, providing I hadn't to buckle in. If that was the price then I couldn't pay it. Not because I was brave, but because my pride wouldn't allow me. So I knew there was no way out of it. I was going to be slaughtered.

That week was a nightmare. In the afternoons, after a bath and a sleep, I used to walk miles, but always in the opposite direction to the pit, and always on the same circular route, but no matter where I went the smooth brutal face of Scratcher went with me, obliterating every sight, sound and sensation. I could walk all the way blindfold to this day – down the bank and round past the lime-kilns, then working away through the woods back to Green Lane and the old row of pantiled cottages they called Woodbine Terrace, which in those days were reserved for ancient pitmen whose families had left them, and almost always without speaking a word to a soul. Those I passed must have thought I was half-crazy the way I used to lope along, head down and more often than not muttering to myself as I rehearsed a conversation with my enemy.

It's funny, too, how the mind in that condition picks up each individual sight and sound, each smell and flavour, with a kind of dryness, never lingering over a single particle but at the same time tucking it all away for future reference, so that later I knew exactly where to look for the odd primrose and walked like a tracker-dog, from the big clump of hawthorn under which the cuckoo-pint grew, to the tree where the thrush poured her heart out.

Well, for five days running I took that very same walk, and

every morning that God sent I came home with my mind clouded; then on the sixth day, which was a Saturday, I had a vision in the wood and came out transfigured. I looked up a woodland road, and saw it as the ramp – wooden cross-bars placed there so as to keep us from slipping, the hand-rails with their inch-thick layer of coal-dust – and, in a flash, I saw what I must do to defend myself. Only let him pester me again and I'd be ready. Suddenly, I was at peace with myself. I came out of the woods with a primrose in my buttonhole, whistling like a laverock. Once again I was master of my destiny.

And I found myself walking along the pavement by Woodbine Terrace, with the gardens stretching up to the doorsteps and roses climbing up every dormer window. In every one of those gardens the old pitmen – mainly shifters on permanent nightshift – were busy digging; fine old men, broad in the shoulder, methodically working, the brown earth sliding from the bright silver of their spades. And just the same as every other day, the womenfolk were calling their men in, arms akimbo.

'Howay Buller yer bugger, yer dinner's ready,' or 'Dick, I've told you before and I'll tell you no more – your plates on the table and your tea's poured out.' Betsy Maggs didn't shout – she'd be too busy feeding her face. I could just imagine her. 'Howay, pet, let's tuck in and enjoy ourselves while he wears hissel' out,' she'd be urging her spinster daughter.

Only one man had more than a minute for me, and that was old Joe Craig. 'Now lad,' he said, leaning on his spade, 'I'm glad to see thous in better fettle th' morn – I hope thou hasn't been in trouble?'

'Not now, Mr Craig,' I answered.

'Another lad, is it?' he asked.

'Another big bully,' I retorted. 'But I know how to deal with him now.'

'As one human being to another?' The question hung in the air.

He shook his head. 'Eeh, man, but tha's wrong tha' knows. Best to make friends with him.'

'You don't know him,' I answered.

'Oh, but I think I do,' he countered. 'The world's full of them – I've lived a long time longer than thou, and I know it. For every one of them tha' brays down, there's another dozen waiting to take his place.' A big feller came down from the house. He was carrying a basin in a crimson white-spotted handkerchief knotted at the top to make a handle. Setting this down on the wall he gently took hold of the spade. 'Sit down and get your bait, da,' he said, 'and I'll give you a spell.'

'Like a machine, isn't he?' said the old man proudly. 'That's Edward, my baa-lamb, the youngest of my five lads.' Neatly, with the crimson hankie tucked in under his chin, he was eating his taties and dumplings. Turning to Eddie he said, 'This is young Chris Lee, Eddie, and he's spoiling for a fight.'

'Well, you know what my views are,' said his son. 'Let them get behind the pit-heap, the two of them, and fight it out of them.'

'There's a lot better things than fighting in this world,' said the old man. He turned to me. 'Come on, lad, and I'll show you what I mean.'

The son stuck into the ground with a mighty thump of his right boot to establish it. 'Will you get your dinner, da,' he said. 'Now just you get it, or there's goin' to be trouble.'

'Just you hark at him, bully-ragging,' said the old man, but all the same he sat down on the low garden wall and resumed his dinner again.

'You get a bit of good grub into you,' said the son, 'and build yourself up. There's five of us and only one of you, but you're the nonpareil.'

'What's a nonpareil?' I asked.

'You tell me when you come back,' said Edward, grinning, as the old man led me up the path to the house. And what a house it was!

'Well?' asked Edward, when we'd returned.

'I've never seen owt like it in all my life before,' I said, and meant it. In that little colliery cottage were all the treasures of the world – paper towers that turned like magic, first one way and then another, a set of chess-men carved from Weardale bog oak, sticks with snakes twined around them and sticks with the loveliest of leaping salmon handles; and on top of the cabinet full of pace eggs glittering with life and colour, an illuminated Bible, which was the greatest wonder of all.

'But what do you think of him,' pressed Edward.

'Why, man, he's the daddy of them all,' I exclaimed in rapture. 'There's nobody to touch him. He's in a class by himself.'

'Now you know what a nonpareil is,' said Edward. 'And what did you think of the Bible?'

'The Bible!' I cried. 'Man, you should have seen the little foxes he did for the Song of Solomon. And the Leviathan! You never saw such a monster.'

'He did one for all of us,' said Edward. 'If you sweetheart him proper he might do one for you.'

'By golly, I wish I was as good,' I said. 'Only I haven't the talent.'

'Everybody has a talent,' said Mr Craig. 'Only you've got to look for it.'

'I've got nothing, Mr Craig,' I told him. His face lit up. 'Everybody's got something, lad. Lose yourself in delight, son, and you'll find it, sure as life you will.' It was as if his eyes had bored right through me. In a flash I saw what he had seen, and the crust which was part pain and part despair fell away. I walked home on air. Now at last I'd discovered who I was and where I was bound for. My enemy had power over me no longer.

Going up the street who should I bump into but Scratcher Robinson. 'Can't you watch where you're going, you dreamy bugger,' he rapped – and for the first time I was able to laugh in his face. 'Well, at least I've got something to dream about,' I told him – it was something as daft as that; and his eyes nearly popped out of his head. Not at the claim – it was the laugh that stung him. When I looked back he was stood there where I'd left him, staring at me, and I knew then I was for it. But do you know what? I didn't care a damn. As long as I had old Mr Craig and Edward behind me I knew I could master him.

Only it wasn't to be. On the Monday before Pancake Tuesday young Eddie Craig was killed, and his death caught me out as a traitor. In those days, you see, we often had three to four fatalities a year at our pit, and if a man died on the coalface or on his way out to daylight the death-buzzer would blow, and the entire workforce of 2500 men and boys would be laid idle – as a mark of respect, so to speak. Except that we never heard the buzzer. The power would be turned off and then as the machinery came to a halt, the tippler lads would run along the gangway with a hand curved round their mouths in silent mime of the dreaded death-buzzer – symbol of liberation for us.

Only this time it didn't happen that way. Since the buzzer started blowing as I left the house, my first reaction was to start running under the impression that the clock was wrong and I'd slept in and was listening to the five o'clock buzzer. Then the buzzer went on and on, its deep grave note, sounding above the clatter of my own running footsteps and heart-beat, began to tell me what I was listening to. But I still kept on running, only now – I'm telling no lies – I was running lightly in the gladness of my heart. All I could think about was one day of freedom – one blessed day away from the gaol. Then I ran right smack into a bunch of pitmen. All I could see was the whites of their eyes and the shine of their teeth: for the rest they were all tattered and torn. 'It's no use running, kidder. There's been a man killed.' The words hit me like a thunderbolt, because that's just what I'd been thinking. I remember that morning. Black and raw, with a dirty drizzle sweeping down from the coast and not a star in the sky. It was like walking into the maw of hell. They reckon that it's in the early morning that your resistance is at its lowest, and the dirty thoughts come sneaking in by the back-door; but I'm making no excuse for myself. And it's no use telling me that my thought could have no earthly influence on the happening, especially when what's happened occurred before I'd had it. I feel rotten about it still.

'A man killed,' I echoed. 'Who – who is it, like?'

'Young Eddie Craig,' said the man. 'The old feller came out with him. He was dead-felled. What's the matter, like? Did you know him?'

I walked on without answering. Oh, you needn't fret, I wasn't doing any weeping – you don't when the bottom's been knocked out of your life, at least not immediately. I was sorry for nobody in the world but me. Then doubling back into the cross-entry at the top of the street I stood and shivered. For the first time in my life I knew what it was like to die. The blood froze in my veins, I lost the feel of my arms and legs and the world grew black about me. Any moment now the hand of a living man would spread itself over my face and close my sightless eyes.

'Is that you Chris?' somebody asked. It was Tan Ridley, walking back home from the pit, I realised. 'Go away,' I said, but instead he came up closer. 'Well, I'll be buggered,' he said. 'I think he's cryin''; and in that moment I struck. It was only when he'd gone that I knew what to say. No Tanny, I keep telling him, there isn't a tear in my eye – I'm only hiding here in this corner because I know that I'm going to die. Only I didn't have the words to tell him then, and even if I had, they hadn't a chance. Rigor mortis had set in and my vocal cords were frozen.

That evening it was all round the village that the old man – sitting in the very room where Edward was coffined – had written a letter of thanks to God for his son. The arguments raged back and forth. Some said what a marvellous old man he was while others called him a silly old fool, but for some unaccountable reason the letter affronted me. The big leaf of coal tumbled over him so smoothly, they said, that there wasn't a mark on his body when they found him. His skin was like a new-born bairn's. Once again I felt the spread of fingers over my eyelids, shutting out the living daylight. What thanks were due to God for that – especially when they'd never open again? The fish imprinted on shale would swim again before that happened; and it made no odds to me that old Craig had consoled himself by writing down on notepaper his thanks for the twenty-six years that he'd had his own ewe-lamb beside him.

'I'll never make pancakes again,' vowed my mother, when I pushed my plate aside. 'Mind I mean it!' Even if I'd told her I was in mourning for my own vanished childhood I daresay she wouldn't have known what I was talking about. Anyway, if all hell had been behind me I couldn't have told her. The time when I'd poured out all my troubles to her was a million years away behind me. Silence is the curse of the poor, and I wasn't only dead and coffined. They'd screwed the lid down on top of me. All I was was a living zombie, waiting to be triggered off to kill.

And sure enough when I staggered up the ramp the following morning, weighed down by the box and with a jagged piece of metal digging into the palm of my hand, my enemy was there to meet me. Untipping the debris into one of the shelved recesses I turned to face him. 'Yer grit soft Dick, yer bloody grit cry-babby,' he mouthed silently, and wiped away an imaginary tear – then roughly shoved a dum-tit into my mouth. I spat it out. All I could see was the sneer. His eyes were vaguely the same colour as Edward's. The eyes did it, and I came up with the box under his chin. The blue eyes were wide with surprise, like a child's. Maybe he expected a smile, I don't know. Instead I punched him right bang in the middle, just as Danny had taught me. Only maybe I got a bit too low. He went back doubled and I followed him. Only at the top of the ramp did he straighten up. By then I'd snatched the pulley-belt adjuster from its place. 'Why, you little snot,' he mouthed, 'I'll skin you alive in a minute'; but by then I was too fighting mad to be frightened of him. 'Will you?' I mocked – and advanced upon him. Then he tripped – I'm not sure that I didn't push him – and down he toppled. Head over heels he went. Like Satan falling from heaven.

I can still see Danny bending over him, the colour returning to his face as he looked up and said 'I think he's going to be all right,' – pausing a moment before he added 'Only I wish you hadn't done it.' By now the power was off, the machinery silent, and the boss had arrived. 'How did it happen?' he asked. 'I'm sorry, gaffer,' said Scratcher, 'but I must have missed my footing.' It was the immutable law of the pit that he should say so. But all the same he was done for. And so was I. Nobody talked to me much after that. I was an outsider.

Within a year or two we were all separated and going our different ways – either left or scattered around the pit, too bone-tired to look up from our work, let alone hold a grudge. So all ended happily, you might say – even for old Mr Craig, who settled down to a long old age. Each spring that came would find him in his garden, supervising the digging which his four remaining sons took in turn. Only he never talked about Edward, his youngest, and somehow I always had the feeling that he never quite trusted me. More than Blake's *Virgil* or the Kelmscott *Morte d'Arthur* he knew that I coveted one of his illuminated Bibles; but he always held back. Night after night I'd look at the lilies and the foxes, the Leviathan sounding deep; but he always put the book away with a smile. Oh, yes, he knew all right. But while he'd allow me to look he never yet gave me one. Then he died, and I never saw that Bible again – but by then it didn't matter anyway: the book had become part of my being. Or perhaps it went deeper still. All I know is that the inflexible old man was right. The love which had brimmed over on to those pages would have been wasted on me. My destiny was to live out the book of my own life, until my every last Genesis and Exodus had been re-enacted, and my view from Sinai had shown me the Promised Land – an old man, happy in his garden and the gift of his five strong sons. As long as the old man was alive – as long as I am breathing – Edward is living.

For all men are not born equal. Some are born to run as fleet as racehorses, while others crawl, no matter how famous or clever or wealthy they may be, and some are born to remembrance. So, dear Mr Craig, this is a letter addressed to you – wherever you are, from Pancake Tuesday nearly fifty years ago, the day the roof fell in, just to say that I'm beginning to understand: but only now – after I've written my own Book of Psalms not only with my blood but the blood of my own dear friends. I grew up in the pit and by some miracle was preserved from the acilular waters my roots sucked on to flourish like the green bay tree. There is fire underground, rivers of blood, subterranean oceans of bitterness and grief – and where the winds appear like mighty rushing torrents from nowhere it is no surprise to find a pillar of cloud to guide you by day, and by night a pillar of fire, to give you light; to go by day and night. Do you remember, Mr Craig, the square by your little chapel – the one in which the home-coming men wore a footpath in the clay for the houses that were never built? It was there one night after a party, drunk on rice wine bottled before ever I was born, that I saw ten streets majestically upend themselves and dance before the altar of the Lord. Is it any wonder then that he cleared a highway for me through the rubbish of Times Square and all through the airways to the bull-pens of Detroit, Chicago, and Knoxville; or that the hate-filled South opened all the way before me to New Orleans and beyond? Folk everywhere are common clay. Even the Kirghiz are people. All we need are Kremlins of the human spirit. Folk everywhere are dying and everywhere folk never stop building. Only theirs are not houses made with hands.

But you and you alone are the master where our own folk are concerned; and only you can stand up and look into the face of God while you address Him. It's our own dead that trouble me – not Edward but Danny Lancaster, gone and unremembered in the stinking ward of geriatrics; Tan Ridley who coughed a lifetime of Busty dust away; and Scratcher, the all-time loser, still playing the part of the boss-lad in the dormitory asylum where a line of beds represent tipplers and the space down the middle a ramp. Who'll speak for them, Mr Craig, but you? So tear out the pages of your book, Mr Craig, and light such a fire that it will be seen in heaven. Then stand up and speak for us.

[1980]

Lament for the Little Hills

Aye, Brusselton, is the
Lone larch
Still on your stark brow?
Pink nipples and resin
In the spring?

Many a fine time
We had of it
Among the raspberry cane,
On hands and lips
The scarlet stain.

Aye, Redworth, how many
Hares have pranced
Since we two sat up there?
Watching the sun go down
And the moon come up.
Where now it's side by side,
And a creaking rocking chair.

[1943]

Swallows Will Build

Twenty-six was the year of doom for our town. The strike was the great black stallion that ran the year's course and never got to the finishing post; the black stallion that trampled Grandad's savings into the mud and broke the lives of thousands. Grandad shook his head at the whole business and held back, but inwardly hoped that the workers would win. But the race was lost, the black stallion never romped home, and things were never the same again.

To start with, trade was bad. Then came rationalisation, plus new machines. Men laid off, pits closing. Brockenback first, Brockenback that seemed eternally fixed, where Timothy Hackworth's winding-engine had run a century and over – and where for years the cages had dropped on fresh-cut whinny bushes to obviate the jar which had given the pit its name. It was unthinkable, but it happened.

And through Brockenback closing there came a flood of water. It found its way through old workings and natural channels. It made a way for itself, a trickle at first, and then a flood that poured through a network of dark passages into Dabble Duck. And the Duck pit pumps were too small, couldn't stem the flood. The owners were small capitalists and couldn't afford new pumps. So the Dabble Duck pit closed. And the water flowed in a torrent into Datton colliery workings. Slyly at first, almost secretly, the water gathered itself, then impetuously broke through; a dark treacly, chemical-smelling slow-moving mass that lashed itself into a fury the nearer it got to the shaft, like some caged beast seeking release. I spoke to one of the six men it pursued that Sunday afternoon. 'Man it stank, and it licked at our heels like a live thing,' he told me. As the cage lifted they heard it follow with a snarl, and a blow that collapsed the shaft entry. Rationalisation had already doomed Datton, and this was a good excuse for closing down. The swelling torrent was the last powerful argument for death.

The blow fell at last. Twelve hundred notices. The manager,

Tom, Dick and Harry. The overman, engineer and lampman along with every common manjack. Gaffer and workman, it made no odds. All finished and done, sacked and scrapped.

Grandad took to his garden and greenhouse for consolation, but failed. For there, in full view, were the silent pulley wheels, the rusting engines and decayed buildings. The blacksmith's shop, where he had ruled for thirty years, lay silent. No thrashing of steam-hammer, no double-drumming on anvil of companion hammers or outburst of cheerful singing. The sidings lay empty. No craft, no men, no harvest; just decay and an old man in a garden tending roses or sweet peas, whose fragrance seemed offensive.

Only the swallows worked, building nests on the cliff-like sides of the heapstead and the vertical winding-house. They at least were allowed to work. No iron law of economics forbade them to nest.

Of course, materially speaking, the situation wasn't so bad for Grandad. He had a small pension from the firm and retained his colliery house at a small rent. But still he worried. About his men, about his family. One by one his six sons left home, and letters came instead, letters from all over England and one at least from abroad. It didn't seem right to him that they should go like that. To get married, yes. But not to leave the home to rough it any old where. Especially when below the ground and locked in by swirling water lay 20 million tons of the finest coking coal in the world.

He also worried about our town. There was a time when our town was so wealthy that it built up the embankments of the first passenger railway in the world of coal, or coke breeze; and out of the wealth below our feet Pease and the other ironmasters had built an empire with ramifications stretching from Moscow to the Pacific. From a mere hamlet Datton became a thriving metropolis, with its own merchants, musicians, judges and philosophers. Today, all this was ended. People drifted about like ghosts. Women looked at shop windows, sighed, and walked on. Men stood at street corner-ends and couldn't even afford a thrippenny bet.

It hurt him to see young lads hunting like wolves in the gutters for fag-ends to smoke. When the council needed a roadman, two hundred applied. Old families emigrated to other counties and far countries. Only the girls found work, in domestic "service", and their small pittances eased life a little.

Work was scarce, winters were cold and clothes were thin. The Government appointed commissioners and invented names. At first it was Distressed Area. But that was too coldly true, so they changed it to Special Area. Blessed are the poor...

The slow years went by. There were political changes, but nothing happened in the town excepting that things seemed to get more threadbare. Someone got work, planting fir trees on the pit-heap. Grandad had been convinced that one day the pit would reopen, but this killed the last spark of hope. Often he'd shake his head. 'They'll need the coal under there some day, but oh no! it's all waterlogged now.'

One day he went over to the pit and looked down No. 1 shaft. Two hundred fathoms deep, and just thirty feet down the water was swirling. A man was unloading bricks from a lorry. They were going to brick up the shafts. This made him fret a long time. The pit meant more to him than it did to all the shareholders. It *was* his; I see that now.

National Government, Hitler, Fascism, Spain, Rearmament, all these meant nothing to him. He just went on pottering around his garden, being delighted with roses and potatoes. When war broke out he shook his head and said, 'Again?' and went up to get a bunch of roses for Grandma. He always watched for the swallows, though. He liked to see them weaving about in the air.

One morning a red and blue monster was crawling at the base of the heap, a tractor. It dug up the red slag where the heap had been burning and emptied each mouthful into a lorry. The slag was for the new factory a mile or so away. All the miners were working there now.

The factory brought new life to the town. People began to look prosperous again. There were big wages for the people. But it was different from the old pit town. The miner's wife no longer laid out his duds or pit clothes and filled up his bait-tin ready. Instead she went to work with him.

It was a grim prosperity, but better than being part of something depressed or distressed. And his prophecy came true. There was an outcry for the waterlogged coal, and everywhere pits were being reopened and worked full blast. But not his pit. They couldn't cope with the water there. But he never said, 'I told you.' He was very quiet.

I think he was watching the tractor. Having devoured into the heap, it was now biting into the stout old walls where the swallows nested. While he lay ill he often looked out of the bedroom window. What would they do when they returned and found their homes demolished?

On the day of his funeral they returned. They swooped down from the skies above the levelled heapstead, then flew on until we could no longer see them. When we buried him I felt sorry about the swallows; and I felt we were burying the old pit for ever. But waste you cannot bury, not even under piles of concrete. Not even rock and earth and millions of tons of water can hide it. There are bones among the waste. One day that waste will rear up like an apparition over a nation naked and starving. I tell you there will be no redress till men build happily – like the swallows on the heapstead. These were my thoughts the day they buried my Grandad. These – and a vision of blood and chaos. But next day I was glad to see the swallows build again – under the eaves of the new garage they were putting up on the site of the old colliery. Then I knew that men like my Grandad who wrought in darkness never die. The life he gave to me lives on and will be my son's in turn. The million pitmen will break through to daylight – they and their sons and grandsons. Swallows build instinctively. They will build – or know the reason why.

[1984]

The Last Hour

Each hour has nailed me to a cross,
Each ticking minute's been a flail;
Slow time has whipped me to the bone,
My heart's pumped acid, not red blood...

Here Time's a bastard;
Bastard born of Man,
And borne by me
In silent misery

Remind me of swifts that pierce the air,
Dandelions that, red-yellion dare –
Remind of time's most natural pair
Swifts have no part down here;
Flowers?
Such things don't rhyme with leaden hours.

One hour to freedom, note the time;
One hour from harebell's distant chime:
One hour from the grasshopper's leap –
Sixty minutes from Heaven.

NOTE: *The last hour before 'lowse' or 'kenna' (shift's end)
is traditionally the longest of a miner's shift.*

[Written underground at Dean and Chapter Colliery, Ferryhill, 20 July 1941;
read at Sid Chaplin's funeral on 17 January 1986.]

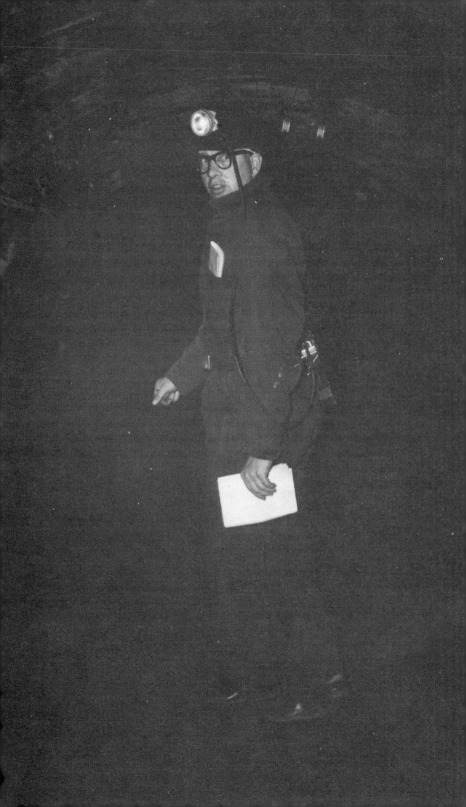

Glossary

bank, surface; alternatively, daylight.

boody-teeth, false teeth, after **boody** (pottery).

booler, ring of steel used, with hook, as children's toy.

brake, horsedrawn vehicle.

cage, the lift-type container which carries men and equipment up and down the shaft of the pit.

duds, clothes.

dum-tit, baby's dummy.

eldritch, weird, hideous, uncanny.

glass-alley, glass-marble.

grey hen, a stone jar used for storing jam, fat, mincemeat, etc.

heapstead, the elevated frame of wood or iron which stands over the shaft entrance, usually carrying the cage winding-wheels.

hettled, planned, rostered.

kist, a chest used underground to store tools, etc; also, underground deputies' meeting place.

laverock, lark.

lish, lean, fit.

outbye, towards the shaft [**inbye,** away from the shaft towards the coal-face].

penker, ball-bearing used as children's toy.

press, a cabinet, usually with drawers and cupboards above.

proddy-mat, a mat made at home on a frame out of old coats, socks, etc.

screens, large building at heapstead where stone was sorted from coal emerging from underground (now done mechanically in coal preparation plant).

seam, a bed of coal which runs horizontally through the rock strata.

shakers, a type of conveyor, consisting of a series of steel pans, the coal being shaken from one pan to the next.

shifter, man who prepares a face for the gang about to work it – timbering, setting doors, building stoppings, etc.

slops, police.

tipplers, mechanical device used to tip the tubs over at the top of the screens emptying the coal onto the conveyors.

tub, open-topped box of wood or iron on wheels used to carry coal from the face to the surface and materials underground.

Sid Chaplin: The Books

1946 **The Leaping Lad** (Phoenix House). A collection of stories
set in the mining villages of Co. Durham. This first book
was acclaimed by the critics, one noting 'its raising of
ordinary folk to almost legendary significance, so that
we seem almost on the edge of myth'. The book won an
Atlantic Award for Literature and Sid Chaplin used the
£300 prize money to take a year off from the pit and write.
He went back, the next novel completed, when there
was precisely one shilling left. Reprinted by Longmans
in 1970; still in print.

1949 **My Fate Cries Out** (Phoenix House). A good old-fashioned adventure story in which the lead-miners of Weardale struggle against a tyrannical Prince-Bishop of
Durham in the 18th century. Reprinted by Cedric
Chivers in 1973.

1950 **The Thin Seam** (Phoenix House). A powerful and uncompromising novel which describes a series of episodes
occurring during one single night shift underground,
as seen by the narrator, a young miner called Christopher
Jack. Almost 20 years later Alan Plater used **The Thin
Seam** and other Chaplin stories in his script for the
legendary play with music **Close the Coalhouse Door**.
Reprinted by Pergamon Press in 1968.

1951 **The Lakes to Tyneside** (Collins). One of the *About Britain*
series of guidebooks published to coincide with the
Festival of Britain; edited by Geoffrey Grigson. With
general description, illustrations, gazetteer and touring
routes.

1960 **The Big Room** (Eyre and Spottiswoode). In a large house
on the fells, the impoverished Clitheroe family con-
gregate in the one big room they can afford to heat. Here
they argue and bicker, their fights settled by the crippled
patriarch Grandpa Noah, their needs serviced by the
young girl of the family, who watches as she grows up.

1961 **The Day of the Sardine** (Eyre and Spottiswoode). The first of the Newcastle novels follows the progress of the young school-leaver Arthur Haggerston as he struggles to make his way in the world while all around him, in the redeveloping slums of Newcastle's East End, the old working-class communities are being broken up. Reprinted by Panther in paperback; by Eyre Methuen in 1973 and by Amethyst Press in 1983.

1962 **The Watchers and the Watched** (Eyre and Spottiswoode). The setting this time is Newcastle's West End, the Scotswood Road, where the newly-wed Tiger Mason reaches maturity and a full understanding of himself and his people, overcoming the pressures caused by the break-up of family and street life. Reprinted by Panther in paperback; and by Eyre Methuen in 1973.

1965 **Sam in the Morning** (Eyre and Spottiswoode). A book about an ambitious young man, Sam Rowlands, who moves to London to pursue a career in business with a huge multinational who make money from waste. Reprinted by Panther.

1971 **The Mines of Alabaster** (Eyre and Spottiswoode). The first (and last) Chaplin book with a (largely) foreign setting, stemming from the man's love of Tuscany. The book follows a young actor, Harry John Brown, from Greenwich to Pisa, as he searches for his lost love. A story of the road, and of a restless, rootless travelling man.
The Smell of Sunday Dinner (Frank Graham). A collection of essays, mostly about the North-East, largely culled from Chaplin's three-year output as *Guardian* columnist during the sixties.

1972 **A Tree with Rosy Apples** (Frank Graham). A sequel to **Sunday Dinner**.

1978 **On Christmas Day in the Morning** (MidNAG/Carcanet). Chaplin returns to the North-East and the short story form to produce eight pieces on the theme of Christmas.

1980 **The Bachelor Uncle and Other Stories** (MidNAG/Carcanet). Familiar Chaplin territory – Durham in the twenties – is explored in this collection of stories, stories 'that stick in the mind like burrs'. Includes a number of stories with a contemporary setting, darker and more disturbing.